JESSICA SORENSEN

SCATTERED ASHES

A SHATTERED PROMISES NOVEL

For information:
jessicasorensen.com

Cover Design and Photography:
Mae I Design
www.maeidesign.com

Interior Design and Formatting:
Christine Borgford, Perfectly Publishable
www.perfectlypublishable.com

Shattered Ashes *(Shattered Promises, Book 4)*
ISBN: 978-1507680728

CHAPTER
ONE

Gemma

T HE SKY IS dark like a rainstorm; only, no rain is falling from the clouds. The air is cold and crisp, and I can smell death, taste it, feel it through the humidity seeping into my skin.

I'm standing alone in a forest just at the edge of a field. Through the thick tree branches, I can see where three human figures are leaning over something with their heads bowed.

I slowly walk toward them, my bare feet burning against the snow with each step. Tree branches scratch at my face, my arms, my legs, trying to hold me back, a warning not to go any farther. Still, I press on, shoving them out of my way, until I finally trip into a flat opening where the trees part.

"Hello!" I call out, but they don't turn around.

Snowflakes float from the sky and melt against my flesh as I inch closer. Who are they, and what are they looking at?

"I can't believe she's gone," one of them sobs.

Wait. I know that voice.

Aislin.

She's standing between two people who I recognize are Laylen and Alex. My heart leaps in my chest as fear pulsates through me.

Something's wrong.

I race for them, but a flock of crows swoop from the trees and dive for me. I hunker down, shielding my head with my arms as they circle me, pecking at my skin. Finally, I let out a scream, and they scurry away. But one remains, flying above Aislin, Laylen, and Alex.

I straighten an inch closer, my heart knocking in my chest as I approach them.

Aislin slips her fingers through Laylen's, and they turn from whatever they were looking at. Their eyes glisten with tears as they look through me and walk toward the forest.

I twist back to look at Alex. His head is still tipped down, his body still.

"Alex," I utter softly.

He rakes his fingers through his hair. "Forem," he whispers the words of our Forever Blood Promise then turns to leave. His shoulders are hunched, his eyes are red from tears, and he looks so heartbroken, so in pain.

And I want nothing more than to make it all go away. Forever.

"Wait." I reach for him, but he vanishes in a heartbeat.

"No!" I cry out, my voice echoing around the forest.

Turning back to where the three of them were standing, I finally see what they were looking at. On the ground is a black coffin with the lid open. Inside, a girl lies with eyes shut, her skin as pale as snow, and her hands are overlapped across her heart.

"No." *My voice trembles as I trip back.* "No, this can't be happening. I'm not dead."

"Oh, but you are," *someone says from directly behind me.*

My back bumps into something solid and cold, and I don't have to turn around to know who it is.

I shake my head. "No, I'm not. I'm not dead. You're lying . . . this . . . This isn't real."

Suddenly, the half faerie, half Foreseer, and one-hundred percent dead Nicholas emerges in front of me.

An evil grin spreads across his face. "Yes, you are. And denial isn't going to get you anywhere." *He gestures over my shoulder at the coffin.* "Look again, Gemma. And I mean* really *look this time."*

My eyes burn as I lean forward and look into the coffin.

"It's not me," *I stammer, shaking my head.*

"Look closer," *Nicholas purrs,* "and you'll see it."

Suddenly, the girl's eyelids lift open, and I find my own violet eyes staring back at me.

"No!" *I scream, stumbling back.*

Nicholas chortles. "Welcome to the Afterlife, Gemma, where only the soul survives."

He shoves me forward, and I fall into the coffin.

"No!" *I cry out again, scrambling to get up, but an invisible force holds me down.*

Nicholas peers down at me with a crow perched on his shoulder. I start to get to my feet, but the coffin lid slams shut, sealing me inside with nothing but myself.

Forever.

CHAPTER TWO

Gemma

I OPEN MY eyes and breathe easy again when I realize I'm not inside a coffin, but in the safety of my room. The nightmare of my funeral has constantly haunted my sleep for the last few weeks now. It's always the same, never changing no matter how much I want it to. I know it has more meaning to it than just showing me my death, that it might be my inner conscious showing me what I fear the most—my approaching, unavoidable death.

I try to settle back to sleep, but now that I'm awake, I'm hyperaware of everything going on around me. My boarded up window may block the outside world from me visually, but it can't conceal the horrible sounds of the crackling fires and screams that plague the air like a toxin. They're always there, painfully reminding me of the damage I've caused by messing around with visions.

Ever since I shifted the vision back to what it originally was before my father tampered with it, the Mark of Malefiscus has taken over the streets of the human world.

Fey, vampires, witches, and even a few Foreseers run wild, tormenting and killing innocent people. And nobody can seem to stop them.

After tossing and turning for a half an hour, I flip on the lamp, climb out of bed, and then pad over to the mirror hanging on my door. My reflection stares back at me; only, I look more tired than I remember, more worn out. My skin is even paler than normal, almost sickly; my violet eyes have shadows under them; and my brown hair is a tangled mess.

Shaking my head at my appearance, I sweep my hair to the side and catch sight of the circle enclosing an "S" tattooed on the back of my neck—the Foreseer's mark. Just beneath it, a circle traced by fiery gold flames brands my skin—the Keeper's mark.

"Admiring your own reflection," Nicholas says. "How very vain of you."

I scowl at the ghost faerie that suddenly materializes behind me. "Go away. I see enough of you in my dreams."

He presses his hand over his heart, his golden eyes twinkling mischievously. "Wow, Gemma, I'm honored that you think of me so often. But what I'd really like to know is what exactly happens in these dreams?" An impish grin curls his lips. "Are they naughty dreams, Gemma?" He reaches for me. "I bet they are. I bet you let me touch you because, secretly, that's what you want."

"I think those are *your* dreams." I dodge out of his reach and spin around to face him. "And I don't dream of you, Nicholas. I have nightmares of you." I back away from him and onto the bed. "Always nightmares."

"So you say." He smirks, stepping toward me. "But deep down, we both know your words don't match your thoughts, that really, you want me just as bad as I want you." His eyes scroll across my body, lingering on my chest before dropping to my hand. "Otherwise, you'd take the ring off."

I glance down at the ring on my finger. My father told me it holds the answers to saving the world, but all the damn thing has done is given me the gift—the curse of seeing one very obnoxious ghost.

"You know what? You actually have a point." I start to slip the ring off.

"Gemma," Nicholas warns, his body tensing, "I wouldn't if I were you."

I inch the ring toward my fingertip. "Why? So you can keep driving me insane, make your perverted remarks when you shouldn't?" I wrap my arm around my stomach to emphasize my point, even though it really does make me feel ill.

I haven't told anyone yet about the heartbeat I heard that night or how Nicholas implied that I might be pregnant. Saying it aloud means dealing with the fact that I might be carrying around another person inside me, which is terrifying in itself. However, there's a whole lot more to it than that, like the fact that if I have to die in order to save the world, so does it.

Nicholas shakes his head, brushing strands of his sandy blonde hair out of his golden eyes, then glares at my stomach with disgust, as if suddenly remembering I might be pregnant. "I'm not just here to drive you insane." He looks up at me. "And if you take the ring off, you'll never learn the real reason I came back."

He could easily be lying or telling the truth. It's hard to say. Right now, however, I'm tired, and whether he can help me save the world or not, I really need a break from him.

"I think I'll take my chances." I take off the ring and drop it onto my bed, and just like that, he's gone.

I blow out a breath of relief as a tiny bit of my stress alleviates. From now on, I'll only put the ring on when I need Nicholas's help.

I check the time on the clock. Even though it's early, I'm too wired to fall back asleep. Climbing off the bed, I tug on a grey Henley and a pair of jeans then tiptoe downstairs. The house is so quiet I figure I'm the only one up until I walk into the kitchen and see Laylen stretched out on the floor. His blonde hair is damp, and his tattooed arms flex as he twists a wrench around a pipe underneath the sink.

Laylen is utterly gorgeous and dangerously sexy, and we get a long fantastically. There are rare occurrences when I look at him and wonder what it'd be like to be with him. But I know it's mostly my hormones and newfound emotions possessing me. That I sometimes might be attracted to him, but there's only one person who can make me feel . . . Well, I haven't completely accepted what I feel for Alex. Deep down, I think I know where my emotions are headed, though.

"What are you doing?" I ask Laylen through a yawn.

Laylen dips his head and smiles up at me. "Hey, Sleeping Beauty. You're up early."

"So are you." I sink down into a chair at the table. "Fixing the sink, I see."

"Yep." He taps the wrench against the pipe. "That stupid drip has been driving me fucking nuts."

"God, I wish every problem was that easy to fix." I picture picking up the wrench and banging Nicholas on the head with it over and over again until he finally spills whatever secrets he's keeping from me.

Laylen's brows knit. "Are you okay? You seem really depressed lately." He frowns as if realizing something terrible. "It makes me worry that I'm not doing a very good job when I promised Alex I'd make sure you're okay."

"It's not that." I shake my head, loathing that I've been so down lately and hating even more that Laylen is concerned. "I swear I'm fine." I force a smile. "I'm just stressed out"—I wave at the boarded window—"with the apocalypse happening and everything."

His expression softens. "Gemma, you need to stop worrying so much. We're going to fix this"—he pauses—"without sacrificing you and Alex."

"I hope so."

He sternly points the wrench at me. "Well, I know so, so cheer up."

"Okay." I force another stiff smile.

"Are you sure that's all that's bugging you?" he asks, growing concerned again. "You know you can talk to me about anything."

I absentmindedly splay my fingers across my stomach. "Can I?" I whisper. Just thinking about telling him everything makes me want to vomit. "Laylen, I swear to God I'm fine. I just don't feel very good. That's all."

He gives me a skeptical look before leaning back and reaching for the pipe again. After he fiddles around for another minute or so, he tosses the wrench onto the tiled floor and sits up.

"That's it. I give up," he surrenders, throwing his hands into the air. "Clearly, I suck at the plumbing thing." He stands up, stretching his arms above his head, giving me a glimpse of his rock hard abs that I try not to gawk at too obviously. "I guess we're just going to have to deal with the dripping." Lowering his hands, he pulls up a chair and joins me at the table. "You never said why you're up so early. Is it your nightmares? Or is Nicholas bothering you? Because if he is"—he cracks his knuckles as a smile plays at his lips—"I can totally take care of him for you."

I contemplate on where to start. "It's that stupid nightmare again that woke me up. I can't stop dreaming about my death, no matter what I do."

His expression plummets. "Is it the one with you in the coffin?"

I nod. "Yep and everything happens exactly the same, no matter how much I tell myself I'm going to try to manipulate my dream."

He drapes an arm around my shoulder and pulls me close to him, stroking my shoulder with his fingers. "You know I won't let that happen. You're not going to die until you're super old and have lived a full, happy life."

I rest my head on his shoulder, hoping somehow he's right. "I wish it were that easy—that you could just want something to happen and it would—but nobody can control the future." I gesture at the back door that has five deadbolts and three chains securing it. "Otherwise, stuff like what's going on outside happens."

A scream comes from outside, adding an emphasis to my point.

"We're going to fix what's happening," Laylen promises, giving my shoulder a squeeze. "But without anyone dying. There's been too much death already."

My heart hurts as I think about all the deaths that are happening. People are dead because I changed the world's future, and people are still dying and will continue to die unless I fix what I did.

Laylen leans back in his chair, nibbling at his lip ring with a contemplative look on his face.

Desperate for a subject change, I ask, "So have you heard anything?" I nervously fiddle with the ceramic cow in the center of the table, avoiding his gaze as the thought of Alex consumes my mind and soul. I haven't felt the electricity in weeks, ever since he left, but sometimes, when I think of him, I can almost feel the tingling sensation kissing every inch of my skin. "I mean, from Alex?"

Pity fills Laylen's eyes as he reluctantly shakes his head. "I'm sure he's fine, though. And Alex, he can take care of himself."

"Yeah, I know he can."

Sometimes I think about going to find Alex by using my extraordinary power to track him down and Foresee to wherever he is. If I close my eyes and picture his face, I could pull it off. But in the aching part of my heart, I know he left for a reason: we can't be together; otherwise, we'll die. I've seen it happen with my own eyes.

A bang on the back door interrupts my thoughts. I jolt, standing up with Laylen, my chair tipping back and toppling to the floor. Laylen hastily retrieves a knife from a drawer while I hurry to the back door and peek out through a crack in the board across the window.

"It looks like they might be witches," I hiss to Laylen. "But I'm not one hundred percent sure. It's still too dark outside for me to see their marks."

"God fucking dammit." Laylen cautiously approaches the door, holding the knife. He peers through another crack in the board and curses again. "I wonder if they're here just because or if it is something else."

By something else, I know he means me.

I look through the crack again, peering at the bottom of the porch at a tall woman with wavy black hair and green eyes. If she is a witch, then we're in deep shit because their magic gives them the upper hand.

She glances back at a few people standing behind her, and then her hand erupts with a glittery, purple glow.

"Go get Aislin. It's definitely witches," I hiss, a ripple of tension waving through my body.

"Don't do anything until I get back," Laylen says then races off toward the stairway.

The witch says something to her group, and then they all cackle. Panic flares through me as I ransack the drawers for another knife. I end up choosing a smaller one with a razor-sharp edge.

"This is all your fault," I whisper to myself as I move back for the door.

Before I can look out, Laylen and Aislin come barreling into the kitchen, out of breath and panting heavily. Aislin's golden hair is disheveled, and she's blinking her green eyes, looking a little groggy.

"How many are there?" she asks me, cracking her knuckles.

I peek through the boards again. "Five, maybe six."

She nods, flexing her fingers. "Which one's going to open the door?"

Laylen opens his mouth, but I cut him off because this is my mistake, mine and mine alone.

"I got it." I wrap my fingers around the doorknob, my pulse erratic and my hands a little unsteady as I count down. "On the count of three. One . . . two . . . three." I swing the door open.

The witch closest to me jumps back in surprise, but her hands are already aimed at me, and she starts chanting a spell underneath her breath.

Wasting no time, I charge out the door and shove her back. She trips down the stairs, and I start to step back when she seizes ahold of my ankle and pulls me with her into the snow. My arm instinctively cradles my stomach as fear slams through my body. Thankfully, my Keeper instincts kick in, and I'm able to catch myself from landing too hard.

A cold chill seeps into my bones as reality crashes over me. If Nicholas is right—if I am pregnant—I have to stop taking so many risks.

I fight to get away from the witch, plowing my elbow against her head, and she laughs as I roll on top of her. Then I smile and clock her in the face.

She chortles, her mouth bloody from my punch. "Nice try, princess." She grabs my necklace and snaps the chain from my neck. The glittery purple glow ignites in her hand again as she shouts. "Animam tuam!" The light levitates from her hand and slams into my stomach.

"Oh, my God. Oh, my God!" I've never felt so ill in my entire life as I collapse back, my stomach radiating with so much light I can hardly see.

Through the brightness, I spot Laylen and Aislin working quickly to remove the Mark of Malefiscus from a witch's wrist while the others close in on them. I blink crazily, waiting for the spell to do something—hurt me, kill me, turn me into a bunny or something else equally as crazy. The thought makes me violently sick and overwhelmed with guilt.

I should've just stayed inside. If not for myself, for it.

I stare down at my belly, feeling the smallest bit of relief when nothing seems to happen.

The witch's expression drops before she grabs hold of my arm, whispering words I don't understand.

I dig my fingers into her hands, stabbing my nails into her skin. "Let me go." I jerk back, but she tightens her grip.

"You're the one," she whispers, her eyes widening in awe. "It's you."

She has to mean the star. Shit. This is so bad since she's marked. What if word gets back to Stephan that she saw me here?

No. I can't let that happen.

I crane back my arm before slamming my fist into her face, my knuckles cracking against her nose, the sound enough to make me sick. Her eyes roll back and her lips part as she slips into unconsciousness and slumps against the ground.

I jump to my feet, only breathing freely again when I see Aislin and Laylen are safe, and the other witches are wandering around, free of the Mark of Evil, confused over how they got here.

I dust the snow off my clothes. "This one knows who I am," I tell Aislin, picking up my locket the witch ripped from my neck.

"Okay, I'll make sure to erase her memory before I take the mark off," Aislin says, walking over.

I nod, feeling guilty over erasing someone's mind. Even if it's to protect, having my own mind wiped clean makes me have a soft spot for anyone else who has to endure the loss of their memories. Then I look down at my stomach and remember that drastic measures have to be taken to protect everyone.

I retreat to the house, not wanting to watch Aislin as she slips her fingers into the witch's head to extract her memories.

Laylen races after me, snagging my hand as we enter the kitchen. "It has to be done, Gemma. No one can know where you are."

I bob my head up and down, but tears prickle at my eyes. If I had never messed around with visions to begin with, this mess wouldn't exist. I keep the thought to myself, though, because Laylen would only try to convince me none of this is my fault. That's just who he is—a kind, caring person who feels bad for everything and who's always worrying about me. I don't want that. I want the same thing for him as he wants for me—for him to live a happy life.

I rub my stomach, which isn't glowing anymore yet burns like I'm hungry. I hold my breath until I hear the steady beat of a second heart. I'm surprised by how relieved I am to still hear it, and then I feel the softest tap of a prickle prodding at the back of my neck.

"The witch, she threw a spell at me," I tell Laylen with my hand still pressed against my stomach.

"What kind of spell?" Aislin asks as she walks inside. She shuts the back door, locking the dead bolts before collapsing against the door, looking exhausted.

I rack my mind for the words the witch uttered when she threw the spell at me. "Animam tuam."

Aislin's eyes pop wide, and her back straightens as she stands upright. "Oh, fuck."

Panic knocks the breath out of me. "What'd she do to me?"

"I don't . . . It's just that . . ." Aislin stares at the floor, avoiding my gaze.

"Just spit it out," Laylen and I shout at the same time.

Aislin gulps, meeting my gaze. "She took your life."

"No . . . No . . . No . . ." I shake my head as my knees give out on me. I listen for the heartbeat, hoping to hear it again, but everything seems so quiet—too quiet.

"We'll fix it." Aislin rushes to me. "Gemma, I can fix it.

You're going to be okay."

"It's not me I'm worried about!" I cry, tears streaming down my face as I rock back and forth.

"Gemma . . . I don't . . ." Aislin's brows knit as she stares down at me. Then her confusion shifts to total and utter horror when she notes how protectively I'm hugging my stomach. "Oh, my God."

"What's wrong?" Laylen's expression bounces between worried and puzzlement as he looks back and forth between Aislin and me.

Aislin crouches down in front of me and leans in, keeping her voice low. "Gemma, are you . . . Are you pregnant?"

I swallow the lump in my throat and force myself to deal with the reality I've kept trapped inside for weeks now. "I don't know . . . Maybe. Sometimes I swear I can hear this heartbeat, and Nicholas said . . ." I give a shrug then shake my head, fighting back a sob.

A moment or two ticks by where Aislin simply gapes at me in shock. Then, in the snap of a finger, she collects herself and stands to her feet. Her fingers fold around my arm before she gently pulls me up and steers me toward the doorway.

"Where are we going?" I let her guide me out of the kitchen with a very baffled Laylen tailing behind.

"I'm going to help you first," she says with determination in her eyes.

"And then what?" I ask.

She pauses, her gaze dropping to my stomach. "And then we're going to find out for sure what's going on with you."

I nod, feeling the slightest bit of relief that I'm no longer completely alone in this. But what I really want is Alex here with me to help me go through whatever lies ahead.

Maybe that's why when Aislin lays me down and orders me to rest while Laylen keeps an eye on me. I fall asleep, finally dreaming of Alex and not my death. Maybe it's the stress, but whatever the reason, I welcome the break and let myself tumble into dreamland.

"What's going on?" Alex asks, appearing in front of me. He glances around at the flat, grassy field around us that seems to lead to nowhere.

Seeing him here, standing in front of me, even if it's just a dream, sends my body into a mad frenzy. There's no spark or electricity flowing between us, yet somehow the need to be close to him is more potent than it has ever been.

"I have no idea," I say then crash my lips to his.

He groans, grips my waist, and pulls me close. Our legs, hips, chests align perfectly as he slides his tongue deep into my mouth.

"I've missed you," he says between kisses, his hands wandering all over my body. "God, I can't believe we're here."

"Me, either," I whisper against his lips, my fingers trailing down his chest to the bottom of his shirt. Gripping the fabric, I lean back and tug it over his head.

His lips pull into a lopsided grin as his hands travel to the bottom of my tank top. With his eyes trained on me, he slowly lifts the shirt over my head and discards it on the ground. His palms are searing hot as he glides them up my spine then unhooks the clasp of my bra. He throws that on the ground, too, and then presses me closer, kissing me slowly, deliberately, as he lowers me to the ground.

The grass brushes my back as his warm body covers

mine. Beneath him, I feel safer than I have in weeks.

We kiss for what feels like hours, only breaking apart to strip off the rest of our clothes. With a thrust of his hips, he then slips deep inside me as I grip onto him for dear life

"I just want to stay here," I whisper as I struggle to catch my breath.

"Then let's stay here forever," he says then kisses me passionately, rocking his hips against mine.

I groan, my nails clawing into his shoulder blades as I drift farther and farther from reality.

"Harder," I beg. "Please."

He gives me what I want while I try to hold on to him for as long as I can, but I suddenly feel him slipping away from me.

"No . . ." I plead, but it's too late. He's already gone . . .

My eyes snap open, and I jolt upright in bed.

"What's wrong?" Laylen asks, quickly getting to his feet and hurrying over to my bed.

I swiftly shake my head, trying to catch my breath. "Nothing. I was just . . ." Just what? Having a dream?

But if felt so real.

"You look flushed," Laylen notes, reaching for my forehead. "And you feel a little warm."

As I think about the hot, sweaty sex Alex and I had in my dream, my skin warms. "I think I'm just a little overwhelmed with . . . everything."

He glances down at my stomach then fidgets with a leather band on his wrists. "Yeah . . . That's understandable."

An awkward silence stretches between us, one I don't like at all.

"Are you hungry?" he asks, breaking the quietness

between us. "Because I can go make you something to eat if you are." His eyes beg me to be hungry, as if he's in desperate need to get away from the awkwardness already building between us again.

I nod, even though I'm not. "Yeah, food would be great."

Looking relieved, he dashes out of the room.

I lie down on the bed again, letting the loneliness sink in, desperately wishing Alex was here.

CHAPTER
THREE

Alex

I FUCKING HATE the smell of these kinds of places. Every single goddamn person reeks like they just rolled out of a gutter.

"You seem down, sweetie," a woman wearing a long, grey dress says as I pass by her. Her blonde hair is way too thin for her round face, and her yellowish-brown teeth are cracked. She extends her hand toward me, her sharp nails skating down my chest to the top of my jeans. "Maybe I can help you with that?"

I push her back with intolerance. "I'm looking for a man named Draven. Ever heard of him?"

From the look on her face, I can tell she has, but she has no intention of telling me. At least that's what she thinks. I'll get her to tell me, though, no matter what I have to do.

She smashes her lips together. "Never heard of him." She spreads her fingers across my shoulder. "Why don't I help you forget about this Draven?" She leans in and puts her lips next to my ear. "Let me make you forget about him. I can make you forget about everything if you'll let me." Her hand starts traveling toward the top of my jeans again.

I snag her wandering hand, clutching it tightly as I lean toward her. "I know what you are, so cut the fucking act and take me to Draven."

She steps back, smiling her Banshee smile. "I don't know what you're talking about."

Banshees are the worst of the faeries. I know this, just like I know the ragged state of this woman in front of me is only armor. Beneath her façade, she's probably less worn out, even pretty, and also alluring. Her seductive attempts work well on humans and can even put them in a trance, but since I'm a Keeper and know she's really a sign of death, her attempts to seduce me don't work.

"If you know what I am," she purrs, "then you know your future is coming to an end."

"I'm not asking you about my death." I jerk on her arm. "I'm asking you to take me to Draven."

She traces her pinky nail under my chin, scratching the skin. "What makes you think I know him?"

"My patience is wearing thin," I warn through clenched teeth. "Either you'll willingly take me to Draven, or I'll fucking make you take me to him. It's your choice."

She keeps grinning, but I detect the slightest wince as I grasp her hand more tightly. "How much is seeing this Draven worth to you?" Her brow arches. "Your wealth? Your strength? Your life? Tell me, would you give me your life and soul to see this man?"

"My soul already belongs to someone else," I say, calm and in control, trying not to think of Gemma or how much I miss her. I want to be with her, kiss her, touch her, feel her like I did in that dream this morning.

It was so strange. Usually, my dreams aren't very vivid, but last night, I dreamt I was with her, kissing her while slipping deep inside her, and it felt so real.

"And that's fine. I'm not asking for your soul now," the Banshee says. "If you want me to take you to Draven, all I ask is that you let me be the one to collect your soul— your life—when you die." Her grin widens as her lips curl. "Vow to me that, when you die, I can be the one to carry your soul to the Afterlife, and I shall take you to Draven."

I consider what she asks, but not for very long, because in the end, it doesn't matter. Only one thing does— saving Gemma.

"Fine. Just take me to him."

She grins in pleasure, completely oblivious to the fact that she can't have my soul even when I die. Like I already told her, I already promised my soul to someone else. Literally. And a Blood Promise is much stronger than any other vow.

She turns toward the alley that runs between two lofty, steel buildings, and I follow her. As she walks, her blonde hair thickens, her rough skin turns smooth, and her teeth whiten to a shade so bright the moonlight reflects against them.

"This way," she instructs then ducks behind a large dumpster.

I reluctantly follow and discover a door is hidden back there. She unhooks a chain that's around her neck, and on it is metallic key. She puts the key in the lock and then pushes the door open, and we step inside a small room.

The murky air reeks like pond scum, and I have a hard time keeping track of her movements as her silhouette blends in and out of focus. I squint my eyes, refusing to look away from her, worried if I do, she'll vanish.

We hike down a narrow tunnel until we reach the end where there's another, much larger room with walls the color of blood. In the center is an oval table surrounded by eight chairs. In the corner, a Black Angel is sleeping in an iron cage, such a sad creature that I pity sometimes, being trapped until someone frees them. I remember when Gemma almost released one. Thankfully, I got to her in time; otherwise, she would've turned into one and been imprisoned.

"Have a seat," the Banshee says then exits the room through a door at the back of the room.

I sit down and mentally prepare what I'm going to say. I know if I'm wrong about all of this, then I've wasted a lot of precious time. Although, part of me doesn't want to be right. Part of me doesn't want *her* to be one of *them*.

When the door opens again, the blonde Banshee returns with a man beside her. He has dark hair and eyes and the palest skin. Many would probably mistake him for a vampire, but I know better. He's more dangerous than a vampire, and even the knife I have tucked in my jacket might not do any good against him.

He takes a seat across from me, taps a cigarette against the table, and then puts it in his mouth. The Banshee moves up beside him and lights the cigarette for him before shuffling back.

After he exhales, his eyes narrow on me. "I was told you want to talk to me about something?"

I carry his gaze, refusing to be a coward or feel fear, remaining calm, just like I was taught. "I need to know the location of a particular woman."

Draven remains quiet for a maddening amount of

time, thrumming his fingers against the table and puffing on his cigarette. "The Lord of the Afterlife doesn't associate with mortal women, so I'm not sure how I can help you."

"I don't believe this woman is mortal," I say with my hands resting steadily in front of me on the table, showing I don't fear him. "I think she might be one of them." Without looking away from Draven, I nod in the direction of the Banshee.

He deliberates what I said while flicking ash from his cigarette. "This woman you seek, does this she have a name?" he finally asks, taking another drag.

I take a deep breath before speaking so my voice will come out steady. "Alana." Just hearing her name makes me feel as though I'm being strangled.

Draven waves his hand in front of him impatiently. "Alana . . . ?"

A lump rises in my throat, exactly like it did when I read her name on the pages of the journal. I swallow hard, forcing the lump back down, right along with my pain.

"Her name is Alana . . . Alana Avery."

CHAPTER
FOUR

Gemma

"**I** KNOW YOU'RE there," I say aloud as I stare up at my bedroom ceiling. "I can feel you watching me."

Nicholas chuckles. "How can you tell I'm here without the ring on? Or are you just mentally picturing me like we both know you've done a thousand times?"

"No, I can hear you breathing." I roll my eyes, playing it cool, even though I'm a nervous wreck on the inside over what's going on with my body. I push up on my elbows and rest against the headboard. "How can you even breathe if you're dead? It doesn't make any sense."

"How can you see me if I'm dead?" he quips. "That doesn't really make any sense, either."

"It kind of does, though. I mean, I am kind of a freak of nature." I lie back down and turn to the side, resting my head on the pillow. My thoughts drift to my stomach, to what might be inside it. I wonder if it'll be normal. Or strange like me. Or what if it isn't anything at all? Never was. Or worse, what if the witch's spell hurt it? I quickly shake the thought from my head. No. I'm not ready to go there just yet.

"Would you please go away?" I ask Nicholas. "I'm trying to sleep, and your heavy breathing is making that really hard."

"Oh, my hell. You are so dramatic sometimes. Now, would you please stop feeling sorry for yourself? The witch didn't take your life or your little bun growing in your oven."

I crinkle my nose at his word choice then realize something else, snapping my eyes open. "Wait, how'd you know about the witch thing?"

"Because I was listening," he answers. "God, what did you think? That just because you couldn't see me, I'm not there?"

I sit up, scanning my room as a cold chill slithers up my spine. "How often do you do that? Just hang around listening like a creeper?"

A low chuckle reverberates through the room. "Maybe you should start leaving the ring on; otherwise, you'll never know when I am or when I'm not. Or what I see." Another chuckle fills the room, making me shiver. "Nice place for a Keeper's mark by the way."

I touch my shoulder blade, cringing as I think of all the times he had the chance to see the mark. "You're such an asshole."

The idea of him watching me without me knowing is too much, though. I scoop up the ring from my nightstand and slip it on.

The blonde faerie appears before me with a huge-ass smile on his face, which means I've done exactly what he wanted.

"I knew that would get to you," he says, winking at me.

Shaking him off, I climb out of bed. "You said the witch didn't take my life. How do you know that?"

He rolls his eyes, his head bobbing back as he groans with irritation. "You know what? I'm kind of getting sick and tired of answering your questions. I'm still really upset with you for taking the ring off and leaving me in the dark by myself." He juts out his lip, faking a pout. "I get lonely."

"Sorry," I mutter a half-ass apology. "Now, can you please just answer my question without complicating things even more?"

His frowns, looking dejected. "Okay, I will, but no more taking the ring off."

The sadness and loneliness in his voice makes me feel a tad bit sorry for him, which makes me feel guilty when I lie to him, but not enough to stop myself

"All right," I say. "I'll keep the ring on. Now fess up. What do you know?"

"The witch can't take your life," he says, moving in front of me. "Because your life isn't yours to take."

A pucker forms at my brow. "I'm not sure I'm following you."

When he sits down on the bed and pats the mattress, I hesitantly take a seat next to him.

"No one can just take your life," he explains, "not without taking someone else's along with it."

"You mean Alex's?" Saying his name aloud causes a deep longing to form in the pit of my stomach. I miss him so much. His touch. The sound of his voice. The way he makes me feel safe. His kisses. The way he makes me feel . . .

"You two both have to die together," he says then grins. "Which, if I'm remembering correctly, you eventually will."

I remember all the times either Alex or I have almost died, but death never completely happened, either because we woke up or one of us did something crazy like changed a vision to bring the other back. So many times, we should've been dead, yet as far as I know, we're both still breathing.

"Is it because of the star?" I ask. "Is that why we have to die together?"

"That, and the Blood Promise you two made," he says with a shrug. "You two are linked together so wholly you're practically one person." His expression hardens as if he just realized the truth of his own words. "The witch might have stolen some of your life, but you'll be fine." He shrugs again, like there you go.

"What about . . . ?" I trail off, looking down at my stomach.

He plays dumb. "What about what?"

I sigh, already getting a headache. "You know what."

He taps his finger against his lips, shaking his head. "I do?"

I press my fingers to the brim of my nose, knowing it's a lost cause. "So, what happens if one of us actually dies?" I change the subject, hoping Aislin returns soon so we can figure out what's going on inside me, and so maybe, just maybe I can relax. "And I mean, really dies, like forever."

"You won't." He rests back on his hands, his gaze fastened on the boarded window. "You both have to go down together; otherwise, you'll come right back to life."

Hope rises in me that maybe there's a chance Alex and I can make it out of this alive.

"Don't get too excited. You're both going to die soon. Remember the lake?" he says, being his typical killjoy self.

I scowl at him. "Does Alex know about this death thing?"

Nicholas gives a nonchalant shrug. "Who the fuck knows what kind of stuff he's got locked away inside that messed up mind of his? Just think of all the lies he's told you."

"You calling Alex a liar is like the pot calling the kettle black."

He smirks. "I guess it kind of is."

Normally, I'd be upset with him, but I just found out Alex is alive. I was worried something might have happened to him, but if what Nicholas is saying is true, he has to be alive since I am.

Then another thought cross my mind, and my elation plummets. If we're alive, then Stephan can open the portal. It's only through our deaths that the world can be saved.

So, why do my nightmares contradict all of this? Why do I keep dreaming of my funeral that Alex attends while he's alive?

I get out of bed and head for the door.

"Where are you going?" Nicholas calls out after me.

Ignoring him, I go downstairs to the kitchen to find Laylen.

"I'm going to be okay," I announce, startling him from his endeavor at making grilled cheese sandwiches.

His gaze drops to my stomach. "You mean, you're not . . ." He trails off, shifting uncomfortably then focusing on flipping over the sandwiches on the griddle.

I hate that this has created awkwardness between us. I don't even completely understand why it's happening.

Or maybe, deep down, I do get it. Perhaps part of me has always wondered if I should be with Laylen. Perhaps it's the same way for him, and now he knows the answer.

"No, it's not that. I still don't know what's going on with me and . . . that . . ." I place my hand on my stomach. "I just know that everything is going to be fine with the whole witch-taking-my-life thing. I'm not going to die yet. I can't."

He turns to me with a furrow in his brows and the spatula in his hand. "What? Huh?"

I sigh and open my mouth to explain to him what Nicholas just told me, but I'm cut off when Aislin materializes in the middle of the kitchen. She has a brown paper bag in her hand, and her eyes are wide, as if she just escaped something horrifying.

"Are you okay?" Laylen asks her worriedly.

She nods, setting the bag down on the table. "It's just crazy out there." She slips off her jacket and drapes it over the back of the chair before taking a deep whiff of the air. "Wait, are you cooking?"

Laylen glances at the sandwiches on the griddle. "Attempting to."

"Yummy." She wags a finger sternly at me. "I thought I told you to lie down and rest."

"I was," I tell her, "but I just learned something that might help everything relax a little."

She lowers into a chair, her face twisted in confusion. "Okay . . . ? What is it?"

I explain to them everything Nicholas told me while I was upstairs. By the time I'm finished, Laylen has finished cooking, and we're diving into out grilled cheese sandwiches

"So, Alex is okay, then?" Aislin asks, looking more

relaxed than she has for the last couple of weeks.

I nod, taking a bite of my gooey sandwich, which tastes freaking amazing. "He is, if what faerie boy said is true."

Her mouth sinks to a frown. "How do we know he's not just being . . . well, you know, himself? He might be feeding you bullshit."

I shrug, picking the crust off the bread. "We don't know for sure, but I don't know; it kind of makes sense. I mean, how many times have we both almost died, yet we miraculously came back to life?"

"She makes a good point." Laylen rips his sandwich in half. "Still, whether Nicholas is being truthful or not, I think you should take the ring off and take a break from him. It's not healthy to be around his constant, twenty-four seven mind-fucking."

"It doesn't do any good just to take the ring off," I explain, internally cringing. "He can still talk to me. And his voice is the most annoying part of him. Plus, I don't feel comfortable not being able to see him when he can still see me. All the time," I press.

Aislin's face contorts in disgust. "Oh, my God, that's so disgusting," she mutters, pushing her plate away. "I think I just lost my appetite."

Laylen balls his hands into fists. "If you want, I can take care of him," he offers. "We don't really need him around, do we?"

"We actually might." I graze my finger across the purple stone on the ring. "So far, he's the only ghost I've seen. Somehow, he's got to play a part in fixing the apocalyptic mess. Besides, you can't actually touch him since his body is nothing but air."

He reaches over and taps the ring on my finger.

"Maybe I should put this on and see if I can see him." He pops his knuckles, acting as my protector, which makes me smile. "We could have a nice, long chat about how he needs to back the fuck off."

I pat his arm. "Thanks for the offer, but chatting with him will only make him act like more of a creeper probably."

"I agree with Gemma, and I think we need to stop focusing on Nicholas so much. We have so many other problems," Aislin says with excitement sparkling in her eyes. "Speaking of which; I almost perfected the Scutum Distillans spell."

"Is that the shield lowering spell thing? The one that will help us be able to . . . well, you know, kill Stephan despite his immortality?" I stuff the rest of the sandwich into my mouth and wipe my fingers on a napkin.

She nods, picking up her previously discarded sandwich and taking a bite of it. "I only need one more ingredient before I should be able to pull off the spell. Then we can drop the Shield Spell from my father and attack him."

I rub my hands up and down my arms, trying to erase the goose bumps. The idea of simply attacking Stephan and his army of Death Walkers seems scary, even if he's killable, because it means risking my life and the lives of the people I care for greatly . . . who mean everything to me . . . who I . . .

Who you what, Gemma? Do I feel it yet? That emotion burning on the tip of my tongue?

"What's the last ingredient you need?" I scoot my empty plate out of the way.

She sulks as she stares down at the half-eaten grilled cheese. "More power."

"I know where you could get some of that." Laylen

elbows me and winks, trying to lighten the mood.

Abruptly, Aislin stands from the table, puts her plate in the sink, and then picks up the brown paper bag. "You need to come with me," she says, motioning me to follow her as she whisks out of the room.

I glance at Laylen who shrugs. "I have no idea what she's up to," he says.

"She seemed kind of upset. She's not still mad about the . . . incident between us, is she? Because it really meant nothing."

"If she is, she'll get over it eventually."

"You should be more sympathetic." I pinch his arm and scowl.

"Ow." He laughs, rubbing his arm. "I don't even get what the big deal is. We just fell asleep together, and it was completely accidental."

"You should make it up to her," I suggest. "Do something nice."

"And you should go see what she wants before she gets even more upset." He smiles at me, but it doesn't quite reach his eyes

Getting up from the table, I leave the kitchen to go find Aislin and spot her waiting for me near the downstairs bathroom of all places.

"Look, if this is about the other night, you should know we didn't mean to fall asleep," I tell her.

She appears briefly puzzled, but then it clicks. "You two need to stop stressing about that," she says, waving me off. "We've talked enough that I know you and Laylen are just friends." With a small smile on her face, she hands over the brown bag. "Even though you can't admit it yet, I know your heart belongs to my brother."

My heart misses a beat, and my chest swells with a

feeling I don't think I've ever experienced. How can she know that when I don't even know for sure?

"What's in here?" I change the subject, staring down at the bag in my hand.

"That's going to help us solve the mystery of"—she gives a pressing glance at my stomach—"what the hell is going on inside your cute, little belly."

I open the bag and peer inside. "What the . . . ?" My head whips up at her. "A pregnancy test?"

"What'd you think it was going to be?"

"I don't know. Some kind of witchy thing, maybe."

Her brows arch. "Like a witchy pregnancy device?"

I shrug, feeling stupid and naïve. "I have no idea . . ." I clutch the bag. "I've never had to deal with this before."

"I know. And I know it's scary." She pats my shoulder, trying to be encouraging. "But no matter what, everything will be okay. You're not in this alone."

"Thanks." Sucking in an extremely large amount of oxygen, I step into the bathroom and lock the door behind me.

Since I've never done a pregnancy test before, I have to read the instructions, which seem pretty simple, yet doing the test itself just about does a number on my nerves. I nearly start bawling as I wait to see if either one or two lines appear. It takes several minutes longer than the instructions say, and I grow worried that perhaps the energy of the star inside me is causing the test not to work properly. Then I begin to wonder if I've lost my damn mind thinking such ridiculous thoughts. I'm still human, at least mostly, so of course the test is going to work the same.

But in the end, I end up holding a test with an extremely faded pink blur as I walk out of the bathroom.

Aislin is leaning against the wall, waiting nervously for me. When she sees me, she stiffens. "So . . . ?" She glances down at the test in my hand. "What'd it say?"

I shrug then hand her the stick. "It might be a dud. Either that or it doesn't work on me."

"It could be faulty. That does happen sometimes," she mumbles, studying the stick.

I wonder if she knows all about this stuff because she's had to deal with it before.

"Well, I guess I'll just have to get another one, and then we'll find out." She gives me back the stick then heads for the kitchen. "Come on. Let's go tell Laylen. I know he's probably stressing out."

"Over this?" I ask. "Why?"

"Because it's a lot to deal with."

"It is," I say, swallowing hard. "When I first heard the heartbeat, I thought . . . Well, it scared the shit out of me."

"Oh, Gemma." She turns around and hugs me, throwing me completely off guard. "You're going to get through this, no matter what the next test says."

"Thanks." I awkwardly hug her back. "And I mean that. Thanks for everything."

"You, too." She pulls away, smiling. "Now, come on. Let's get this figured out." She grabs my hand and tows me into the kitchen, but then releases her hold on me. "Where'd he go?"

I look around the empty room. "Maybe upstairs?"

She backs for the doorway. "You sit down and rest, and I'll go find him. When I get back, I'll make another trip to the store."

Before I can say anything else, she hurries out of the room, leaving me with nothing but the quiet. At first, I enjoy the silence until I detect the quietest beat of a heart.

The longer I listen to it, the more I just know the test had to be faulty. There's definitely something inside me, and for some crazy, unexplainable reason, I have the strongest urge to protect it.

This isn't just about Alex and me living anymore. It's about Alex, me, and our unborn child. That's what I want. If only I could figure out how to make it happen.

It isn't like I haven't tried. I've tried repeatedly, but every path I take seems to have a loophole or a severe, more damaging consequence. Change a vision and I mess up the world more. Kill Stephan and Demetrius can still survive and go through the plan. I could kill all of them, including every last Death Walker, but the only way that would be possible is to create my own army that doesn't include Alex, Laylen, Aislin, and the human being I somehow know is growing inside me.

A cool breeze appears out of nowhere, and a moment later, I hear heavy breathing from right behind me.

"Go away, Nicholas," I say, slumping back in the chair with a heavy sigh. "That is, unless you're ready to tell me what the ring's for."

Silence is my only answer.

I glance around at the kitchen, the locked back door, and the boarded windows. No one seems to be around, but the stillness makes me restless. I get up and peek in the living room with the strangest feeling someone's watching me, but I can't see anyone anywhere.

Scratching my head, I turn back, and my body instantly smacks into something. I quickly scoot away, blinking.

My hands fall to my side as my jaw smacks the floor at the sight of the ghost in front of me, a ghost that has brown hair, blue eyes, and features similar to mine.

"No . . . no . . . no . . ." No matter how many times I try

to deny what's in front of me, the truth remains standing there, raw and brutal like a punch to the jaw. "Mom?"

A sad smile touches her face. "Gemma, I'm so sorry"

CHAPTER
FIVE

Gemma

I SHAKE MY head in denial, blinking my eyes, doing everything in my power to make this horrible nightmare end.

"You're not dead. You can't be."

"Gemma, sweetie," my mom says, still standing in front of me. "There's no point wasting time trying to deny what's right in front you. We don't have time for that."

I want to cry. Scream. Yell.

"But you can't be dead. I-I barely had time to get to know you."

"I have to be dead," she says solemnly. "Otherwise, he would've used me to get to you."

I don't need to ask who he is.

"Stephan," I bite his name out like it's poison to my tongue. "He did this to you?"

She shakes her head, sighing exhaustedly. "I did it to myself." She traces her finger along the inside of her wrist where the Mark of Malefiscus used to be. "I had to, or I'd have led Stephan straight to you." Her hand falls to her side. "It was supposed to be this way. I don't belong here, never have. I was always supposed to be part of death, whether it was in The Underworld or in the Afterlife as a ghost."

The pain is so unbearable, so lung crushing, so breath stopping, so heart dying. Everyone is gone. My dad is locked up in his own mind, maybe forever. Alex is gone to who knows where. And now my mom is dead.

My hands tremble as my stomach winds into knots. "How did . . . how did you . . . die?"

She presses her lips together, and without saying anything, she wanders into the kitchen and takes a seat at the table. "That doesn't matter. What does is that I'm here to help you."

Tears sting my eyes. I want to hug her, but it's not possible. The loneliness that possessed me for most of my life is resurfacing, and I don't know what to do with it. I don't know how to breathe, don't know how to keep going when everything around me seems to be ending.

With wobbly legs, I join her at the table, taking a seat in the chair across from her. "Help me with what? Saving the world?"

"I'm here to help you figure out what you're supposed to do." Her gaze zeroes in on the ring on my finger. "I'm here to help you use that."

I cover the ring with my hand. "I don't want you to help me with that." Hot tears spill down my cheeks, even though I try to fight them back. "What I want is for you to return to your body and keep living."

"That's not a possibility," she says, reaching for my hand, but then pulls back, realizing she can't touch me. "At least not for me."

A few more tears fall from my eyes before what she's saying really sinks in "Wait a minute. Are you saying it can be done? That someone can die then return to their body and come back to life?"

She wavers. "Perhaps. If done correctly and by someone who knows what they're really doing."

My thoughts drift back to my nightmare, to the crows, the coffin, and how I lay awake inside it, yet everyone thought I was dead.

"Am I . . . Am I going to do it?"

She nods with the faintest smile. "You are, but it's not going to be easy."

"But what about Alex? Is he going to die, too, and come back?"

She shakes her head and clasps onto my hand. "No, sweetie. He's the one who's going to bring you back."

CHAPTER
SIX

Alex

I TUCK THE address into my pocket then step out from behind the dumpster and into the moonlight. I'm still uncertain how I feel about what just happened with Draven, whether I like the answer he gave me about my mother or what I offered to get it—a year of my life to the Lord of the Afterlife, which means doing whatever he wants me to do.

What the idiot doesn't realize is that my life is probably going to be over soon, so really, none of this matters. Only one thing does, at least to me, and that's saving the girl I might just be in love with.

Love. Am I really there?

The idea is mind-blowing. All those years I spent being beaten by my father and being forced to ignore my emotions, I thought he broke me. I thought was broken beyond being replaced, and now here I am, contemplating love, even though it could kill me.

Shaking my thoughts away, I head out to the street lined with burning buildings and mad chaos. Ignoring the feeding vampires that seem to be accumulating everywhere, I make a left and stride toward the corner of the sidewalk. Each vampire, witch, and fey glance at me, hunger gleaming in their eyes as I hurry by them. They can sense what I am, know I'm not an easy target, so instead, they focus right back on tormenting humans.

I should stop them, but I'm in too much of a fucking hurry to find a witch so I can get where I need to go and make all of this right. I never considered what a huge pain in the ass it would be to not have a witch on hand or a very talented Foreseer to make traveling easier.

Just thinking of Gemma makes my fingers ache to touch her again, to return to the dream. It makes me desperate to get back to her, to hold her, kiss her, lose myself inside her.

Growing uncomfortable with where my emotions are heading, I force the thought of Gemma out of my head, despite it feeling like it's going to kill me. If I don't, then I know I'll cave and return to her. And I can't do that yet, not until I find a way to save her. She deserves to live the life that was stolen from her, and I'm not going to give up. I'll keep searching for a way to make this right. Forever, just like I promised.

As I'm about to veer right, I spot a woman across the street with a crescent moon and star mark on her neck. Perfect, just what I was looking for.

I stride across the street with a purpose, sidestepping around an injured faerie sprawled on the asphalt, begging me to help him.

Humans aren't the only ones in danger. The faeries, vampires, and witches who don't bear the Mark of

Malefiscus are also targets, which pretty much adds more insanity to the madness.

Although the witch sees me coming and grins, she is fidgety and on edge as she peers around. "Can I help you with something?" she asks, but her voice carries a threat

I raise my shirt to show her my Keeper's mark on my ribcage. "Still want to use that tone on me, witch?" Honestly, I'm not sure how she is going to react to my cocky attitude. If she has the Mark of Malefiscus, she might try to kill me. But I need a witch. Like fucking now. If she goes crazy on me, then I simply take her out.

"What do you want?" Her tone is icy, her gaze narrowing on me.

I lower my shirt. "I need you to perform a spell for me."

Her pale blue eyes are locked on me, but she seems nervous, which has me wondering if she's just a normal witch, not under the possession of evil.

Good, then I won't have to kill her.

"What kind of a spell?" She glances up and down the street as a brick building suddenly erupts in flames.

"A transporting one." I step onto the curb. "I need to get somewhere quick, and transportation right now is really fucking limited."

The corners of her mouth quirk. "I could do that for you, but I need something from you in return."

I shake my head in annoyance. This journey is really starting to test my patience. "What the fuck do you want?"

"Your help." Her grin broadens. "With removing a mark."

I pretend to have no clue what the hell she's talking about, but I'm tense inside, worried she might know more about me than I want her to.

"I can't help you with that."

"I know you can't," she says, "but you know someone who can." Without explaining further, she grabs my arm and steers me into another alley. The noise quiets as we step farther into the shadows and away from the street.

"I heard a rumor there's a Keeper who possesses Wicca powers," she whispers when we're out of earshot from anyone. "And she's created a spell that can remove the Mark of Evil."

Aislin?

"Look"—I pry her fingers from my arm, trying to keep my cool—"even if that's true, if there is a witch who can do that, it doesn't mean I know her."

"Fine, if that's how you feel, then I guess I can't help you." She turns to leave.

"Fuck," I curse under my breath then grab ahold of her arm and pull her back. "You get me to where I need to go first, and then I'll help you find this witch."

She nods before a warm smile comes over her face as she slips from my hold and sticks out her hand. "I'm Amelia, by the way," she says, and I shake her hand. Then she waits for me to give her my name, but I don't, so she starts back down the alley, signaling for me to follow her.

She leads me out to the street and to the nearest building that isn't on fire. It's a small space, covered with shelves that carry headless dolls, odd-shaped cat statues, and lots of strange incense. She locks the door behind us then rushes for an armoire in the far back corner. Then she unlocks the main drawer with a key she fishes from her bag then removes a black candle and purple amethyst before setting them down on a small, oval table.

A scream comes from somewhere as she lights the candle, and my hand instinctively moves for my knife.

"That's my daughter," she explains. "That's why I need your help. She's cursed with the mark that haunts the streets and possesses the mind with madness."

I keep my hand close to my pocket. "Where is she?"

"Chained to the wall upstairs." She pulls a red pill out of her pocket, sets it down on the table, and smiles up at me. "Whenever you're ready.

I roll my eyes. "You seriously think I'm going to take a mortem pilula?"

"You are if you want me to help you." She slides the pill toward me. "This way assures me you'll hold your end of the deal. No offense, but a Keeper's word means nothing to me."

Growling with frustration, I snatch the pill from the table, realizing screwing her over isn't possible, because if I do, I'll drop dead.

I pop the pill into my mouth and force it down my throat. "There. Are you happy now?"

She smiles, satisfied, and then gestures for me to take a seat. Once I'm sitting, she asks, "So, where am I taking you exactly?" She starts to dip the amethyst toward the flame.

"To Niveo Mountain," I tell her, feeling nervous the moment I say it.

She jerks the amethyst away from the flame. "To the Keeper's Castle?"

"Yeah, but that's not where we're going." I push the candle toward her, growing impatient. "We're going to the graveyard nearby it."

CHAPTER
SEVEN

Gemma

"WELL DON'T I feel honored," Nicholas says as I barge into my room, fuming mad. He's sitting in the windowsill, looking as unbothered as ever. "A visit from two Lucas's. What's the occasion?"

"Shut the hell up." I stride toward him, battling back the overwhelming compulsion to wring his neck. "You're already on the shit list."

"I'm always on the shit list." He yawns as if I'm boring him to death. "In fact, I think I might even hold the top slot on it."

I march for the faerie, wishing to God that I could actually get my hands on him. "You knew all along what I had to do, and yet you wasted weeks of my time, of everyone's time. You let people die, and now there's hardly any time left until December twenty-first."

He jumps to his feet, grinning with his hands out in front of him "That's because you kept asking the wrong questions."

I clench my hands into fists, stopping just short of him. "God, I wish I could just . . ." I growl in frustration.

"Just what?" he asks curiously. "Hurt me? Kill me? Because deep down, I really think all that aggression can only be taken care of by letting me fuck it out of you."

I elevate my fist, ready to strike, even though I'll only hit air.

"Gemma," my mom says softly, appearing at my side. "You need to move past your anger with him. You have more important things to focus on."

Although it takes a lot of effort, I manage to keep my rage under control. "How do I get to the Afterlife?" I ask Nicholas as calmly as I can.

Of course, he decides to test my patience even more. "The what?"

"You know, the land of the lost souls, the Afterlife where the queen reigns." I glare at him. "How about that? Is that the right question?"

He claps his hands, laughing. "Bravo, but I might add how slow you are at getting there."

"Fuck you," I grit out through my teeth, but when my mom says my name again, I force the fakest smile I can muster. "How do I get there?"

His gaze flicks to my mother. "Why doesn't she just tell you? She's a ghost. She should know."

Tears sting at my eyes from the reminder that my mom is dead. "She doesn't know how to get there. For some reason, she can't cross over. But you're a faerie—and a dead one at that—which gives you direct contact to the queen since she's fey."

"Didn't I explain to you once that I'm only half-fey?" he asks. "And that makes other fey, dead or not, not very fond of me."

"Are you sure that's the real reason?" I snap. "Because I'm sure your amazing personality helps, too."

He shoots me a dirty look, but then he grins wickedly. "You know what? I really don't feel like talking to you, not with that kind of attitude." He stuffs his hands into his pockets and backs toward the window. But then he stops and reaches forward, letting his hand slip through my body, painfully reminding me that I can't do anything to him, at least physically. "Perhaps if you are really, really nice to me, I might be more willing." His gaze deliberately scrolls up and down my body, making my skin crawl.

"You're such a—"

A gust of wind flows around me as my mother zooms straight into Nicholas. She grabs him, her hands circling his neck.

"You can't make me say anything," he says with a choked laugh as she slams his body into the wall.

My mom looks in my direction, looking wildly out of her mind, like she's lost touch with her humanity. "I'll be back in a while," she says. "Don't go anywhere."

My jaw drops as the two ghosts dissipate, and the room grows empty again. My legs immediately give out on me, and I flop down on my bed and let the tears out.

My mom's gone.

She's gone, and I'm never getting to know her.

I'm alone.

Always alone.

My hand drops to my stomach.

Thump. Thump. Thump.

Well, not completely alone.

I allow myself five minutes to lose my shit before I suck it up then go find Laylen and Aislin to tell them what is going on. But when I enter the hall, the house is eerily silent. Fear courses through my body as I step back into my room to get the knife Alex gave me from my dresser drawer. With a weapon in hand, I pad down the hall toward Laylen's room. My hand is steady, my Keeper blood manifesting, but every time I face danger, my heart still pounds insanely.

When I reach Laylen's room, I hesitantly press my ear to the door to listen, but I can't hear anything, so I gently push it open. The room is empty and soundless. I start to turn around to check downstairs, but my shoulder bumps into something solid.

I jumped back, startled, but then relax when I see Laylen standing in the doorway, his blonde hair ruffled, his lips oddly a little swollen.

I press my hand to my heart. "Shit, you scared me."

He eyeballs my knife then cocks a brow. "What are you doing with that?"

I shrug, lowering the knife to my side. "It seemed too quiet, and I thought maybe something was going on."

He takes the knife out of my hand and tosses in on the dresser. "You're going to hurt yourself."

"Hey," I say, "give me some credit. I'm not as klutzy as I used to be."

He doesn't smile, only steps toward me and backs me into the room. Then he closes the door and locks it, sending red flags popping up everywhere.

"What's wrong?" I ask, gripping the foot of the bed.

He shakes his head, his gaze never wavering from me. "I don't think I've ever told you how thankful I am for you never judging me." He picks up the knife and drags the blade across his palm. "You accepted me, even when I was at my worst, even when I was pure fucking evil."

"Laylen, just because you're a vampire, it doesn't mean you're evil." I want to touch him, to try to comfort him, but the dark look in his eyes stops me. "You're good. You just don't realize it."

"Still . . . you trust me. It's never made any sense."

"Of course I trust you," I say, but right now, I'm not so sure. "Sometimes I trust you more than anyone."

His lips curl into a grin. "I know." He moves in front of me and traces his fingers down my arm, causing me to shiver. He smiles as he notices. "You have the softest skin."

I try to remain calm. This is just Laylen. There's nothing to worry about.

"Is something wrong?"

"You know, I never thanked you for that day in the alley," he says, his hand traveling up to my shoulder. "When you saved my life, letting me bite you like that, it was really fucking amazing . . . You tasted really fucking amazing"

I shift uncomfortably, remembering the bite and all the feelings that came with it. He's right; it was amazing, way, way too amazing. Just thinking about it causes my body to tremble and my pulse to quicken.

He smiles like he can sense what I'm feeling.

"I couldn't let you die," I whisper.

"But you could have." His fingers press against my neck, right where my pulse is throbbing. "You didn't have to let me bite you, yet you did."

"No, I had to." My voice cracks as lust fills his eyes. "I couldn't let you die."

He wets his lips with his tongue. "God, you smell so good."

"Are you okay? You seem kind of . . ." I start to inch away from him, but he grabs my wrist.

"Kind of what?"

"Off."

The hunger in his expression causes me to jerk back, but his fingers constrict around my wrist, securing me in place.

"Off how?" He cups the base of my throat and strokes my skin. "You're so beautiful right now, all flushed and turned on, even though you won't admit it."

Something's definitely wrong. This isn't the Laylen I know.

I grip his hand, trying to lift it from my neck. "I don't think—"

He slaps his hand across my mouth. "Stop talking," he hisses, and then fangs slide out from his lips, murderous blood seekers ready to devour me.

I yank away, but he snatches ahold of both my wrists and jerks me against him. His body is cold like ice, but his breath is hot against my neck.

"You smell so good . . . I just can't . . . can't . . ." He growls before his fangs sink into my neck, and he pushes me onto the bed.

I scream, but his fangs only dig deeper.

CHAPTER EIGHT

Alex

DRAVEN WASN'T LYING. I had my doubts about the Lord of the Afterlife telling the truth, but here it is, my mother's gravestone, exactly like he said.

I left Amelia back at the iron-barred entrance, wanting to visit my mom's grave alone. Her headstone is plain, only the initials A. A. marking it. There's no mention of her being a mother, no date of her death. If I was just been passing through, I never would've given the stone a second glance. To most, she's probably no one. To me, she's the only link to my past that doesn't cause agonizing pain.

In her journal, she wrote that she worried my father was going to kill her because she knew things she wasn't supposed to. She worried he'd find out her secret. But if all else failed, she'd give her soul to the Afterlife so she could one day reunite with Aislin and me and put a stop to my father's evil plan.

She knew everything. Then she died, and almost

everyone forgot about her.

I place my palm to the headstone, wondering how she died, where she was when she breathed her last breath. Was she in pain? Most of all, I wonder where she is now, because if what Draven told me is right, this is just where her body is, not her spirit.

As I glance up at the hill a ways away, the one that hides the Keepers castle, anger blasts through me, a deadly storm. Before I can even comprehend what I'm doing, I storm across the graveyard. The wind howls as I bash my fist into a tree trunk repeatedly until my knuckles bleed, and the emotional pain inside me is overridden with physical pain.

"Fuck!" I kick the shit out of the tree until I can't breathe, and then I rest my head against the bark, trying to calm the fuck down "Come on. Get you shit together."

Counting to ten, I push away from the tree and finish the walk back to the gate.

"Did you find what you were looking for?" Amelia asks as I stride up to her.

I stop in front of her and cross my arms. "I need you to take me somewhere else."

She narrows her eyes and shakes her head. "No way. Not until you take me to the witch who can remove the mark."

"Look," I say with zero tolerance, "I get that you need to remove your daughter's mark, but I need to make a stop first. It's important."

She jabs a finger against my chest. "Maybe you need to be reminded of our bargain?"

I smack her hand away. "Watch it, witch," I warn. "You're crossing a dangerous line putting your hands on me like that."

"You're the one who needs to watch it," she says, a slow grin creeping up her face. "Remember what happens if you back out on our little bargain."

Fuck. I want to punch the grin right off her face. I don't have time for this shit.

"Fine," I grit through my teeth, popping my neck while telling myself to chill the fuck out. "I'll take you to the witch who can help you."

WHEN WE LAND in the living room of Gemma's house, I become too aware of how close I am to her. I can sense her nearness, feel her in my veins, feel her fueling my body with energy, longing, and desire that needs to be filled.

I take a deep inhale to cool myself down and focus on why I'm here.

Everything looks normal: all the chairs are upright, the TV is off, and the photos are still on the wall. They've boarded up the windows, which was smart of them. I remember hearing the news about when the world was first taken over by the Mark of Malefiscus. The letter arrived via Aislin's witch powers, which meant a small, flaming ball of paper landed on my head and singed some of my hair. I read the letter but never replied, just in case the letter fell into the wrong hands.

I knew I needed to protect Gemma in every way possible, and that meant keeping her away from me, no matter how shitty I felt about it. I deserve to feel that way after the hell I've put her through.

But now I'm back in her house, about to blow everything if she discovers I'm here.

"Where is everyone?" Amelia asks, warily glancing around.

The place is quiet, making my Keeper instincts go on high alert. I draw a knife from my pocket.

"I'm not sure."

"What are you doing?" she asks, eyeballing the knife in my hand. "And where's the witch? This better not be a trap."

"It's not." At least, I hope it's not. "Stay here a minute, and I'll go find her."

Amelia takes a seat on the sofa. "Oh, don't worry your pretty little head. I'm not going anywhere." She crosses her legs and sits back.

My fingers itch to shut her up, but I turn my back on her and head for the stairs. With every step I make, I cringe, worried Gemma might hear me. If I play this right, I can get in and out without her ever realizing I was here.

At the top of the stairway, I notice her bedroom door is cracked open, and suddenly my plan goes right out the window. Emotions possess my body like the fucking devil himself, and I can't control my own actions. It is like my legs don't belong to me; they belong to her, only her. Every part of me does.

By the time I reach her door, my heart is about to explode inside my chest. My body scorches with need as I open the door and look inside. I used to be more cautious about mistakes, think things through first, but with Gemma, I have no control over anything. She owns my mind, my body, my soul, and part of me wouldn't have it any other way.

When I see her lying in her bed, I just about lose it. My hands actually fucking shake as I cross the room toward her bed.

She's resting on her side with a blanket pulled over her, her hair a halo across the pillow, and her eyes are shut. I should leave. I'd be a better person if I did, but I'm a selfish fucking asshole who can't walk away.

I reach for her and brush strands of her hair away from her face, and all the emotions I felt in the dream crash through me at once. It takes every ounce of strength I possess not to wake her up and rip her clothes off. I want to kiss her, crash my lips against hers, wake her up by spreading her legs and licking every inch of her. But I can't. I have to stay in control of myself.

She doesn't move as I stroke her cheek, which seems crazy since the electricity is so damn hot I can barely breathe. Then she lets out a long sigh and nuzzles against my hand.

Shit. It's time to go. Now, Alex. Just walk away.

I start to back away but freeze as she rolls over onto her back. What I see makes me so sick, so angry, so possessed by rage I can't see past the anger.

Ropes are cutting into her wrists, binding her hands. Blood covers her neck and stains her shirt.

I sweep her hair back, and my jaw clamps down. There are bite marks on the base of her neck.

I collapse to my knees and cup her face between my hands. Our skin torches as heat flows through my body.

"Gemma, open your eyes," I beg. "Gemma, can you hear me?"

Her eyelids flutter, but she struggles to wake. I press my palm to her forehead and feel how ice-cold her skin is. I shake my head. If he turned her, I'm going to fucking kill him.

"Alex," she mumbles, her eyelids lifting open. She blinks up at me, and then her violet eyes widen.

"You're okay," I say quietly, but with how pale she looks and with how fast the electricity is fading, I'm really not so sure she is.

CHAPTER
NINE

Gemma

AT FIRST, I think I am dead, that Laylen drained all my blood and left me to rot away in my bed, that Alex is a ghost, that somehow he died and joined me in death. Or maybe I'm dreaming again.

Then I feel the dizziness mixed with the sparkle of electricity, and my body ignites with fire, waking me right up.

"You're here," I mutter, moving to sit up.

As the room spins, vomit burns at my throat.

He places his hands on my shoulders, steadying me as I sway. "Don't move too quickly, okay?" he says gently.

I lift my bound wrists and touch a finger to my neck. "Ow." I wince.

"What happened?" he asks, seeming even more urgent and eager than he normally is.

I don't want to tell him. If I do, he might end up doing something stupid. What Laylen did to me wasn't his fault. Right now, he's under the control of pure and utter evil.

"I can't remember." I mash my lips together when he glares at me, reading right through my bullshit.

"Gemma, don't lie to me." With the knife in his hand, he cuts the ropes and frees me.

"I'm not lying." I rub my wrists, trying not to think about how the ropes got there, but it's all I can think about. "And if I did tell you, you'd just freak out."

"Gemma." He fights to keep calm. "Just tell me what happened, and I swear I'll try to keep my cool."

I think about lying again, wanting to protect Laylen, but then I realize we're probably in danger and need to get the hell out of the house. I jump to my feet, surprising him and my head. The room twirls with bright colors and blurry shapes like a merry-go-round on crack.

"Whoa . . . head rush." I clutch my head, stumbling from side to side.

He wraps his arm around my back then lifts me into his arms. God, it feels so good to be here with him touching me, looking at me with desire in his eyes, just like he did in the dream.

"Did Laylen do this to you?" he asks, his voice cracking as he stares into my eyes.

I nod, unable to look away from him. Want and desire blazes inside my body to the point that I actually start to sweat.

"He couldn't help it, though. He's marked."

He turns pale. "By the Mark of Malefiscus, I'm guessing," he says and I nod. "How did he get marked?" Then, without warning, he sets me down on the bed and reels for the door, his knuckles tightening as he raises his knife. "Wait. Is he still here? And where the hell are Aislin and Aleesa?"

I sigh heavily as I lower my feet to the floor, wanting

to go to him, to hug him, run my fingers through his messy brown hair, kiss his soft lips, do all sorts of things to his lean, muscular body that I haven't done in weeks except in my dreams.

"They all have the mark."

He shakes his head, a deep growl rumbling in his chest. "How the hell did that happen? I thought Stephan had to put the mark on them. And if he was here, I'm sure you wouldn't be."

"I really don't know." I offer him an apologetic look. "One minute, the house was totally quiet, and the next"—I flick my wrist, gesturing at my neck—"Laylen freaked out and bit me."

His jaw tautens as he stares at the bite marks on my neck. "So, you don't know if he's still here?"

I shake my head. "The last thing I remember is that they tied me up."

A loud crash from downstairs sends me leaping toward him and desperately grabbing his arm. He looks down at my fingers delving into his skin, and desire flashes in his eyes again, sending a spiral of heat coiling in my stomach.

My stomach.

Suddenly, I remember there's so much more I need to tell him.

Before I can get the words out, Alex takes my hand, and holding the knife out in front of him, he heads for the stairs, keeping me close.

"Stay here," he whispers when we reach the top of the stairway.

"No way," I hiss. "You don't just get to show up and take over. I'm going down with you." I march past him and down the stairs, cupping my hand over my neck, hyperaware of the heartbeat inside me.

Alex chases after me, taking the stairs by two. He beats me to the bottom and flashes me a cocky grin, so I stick my tongue out at him, making him chuckle.

For a moment, it feels like we're just two normal people playing around and flirting. Then I hear the other heart beat as another bang rips from the house. We tense and Alex spins around, positioning me behind him.

"Stay behind me," he says. "I'm being serious, Gemma. I *need* you safe."

There are a thousand things I want to say to him, yet it doesn't seem like the right time for any of it. So instead, I settle on a, "Yes, boss," which causes him to look over his shoulder, his green eyes darkening as he quickly drinks me in from head to toe. Then he tears his gaze off me, and we tiptoe for the living room, the floor creaking under from our footsteps.

As we head farther into the darkness of the house, I find myself wishing we hadn't put praesidium everywhere. Sure, it keeps the Foreseers out, but it also traps me in.

As we step through the doorway, I stop when I see a woman lounging on the sofa, eating one of the leftover grilled cheese sandwiches.

"Who the hell are you?" I ask then stop when I notice the crescent moon mark and realize it's not just a woman, but a witch.

Instinctively, I shift my weight and lift my leg, ready to fight, but Alex's arm shoots out, holding me back.

"Easy, tiger." He bites back a smile. "I brought her here with me."

My eyebrows knit as I gape at Alex. "You brought a witch into the house?"

"Amelia's helping me with something," he says, being

evasive.

"Is she the witch?" Amelia asks, gawking at my eyes. I shake my head and cross my arms. "No."

"Then what are you?" Her eyes light up as she wolfs the rest of the sandwich down. "You have so much power flowing off you." Her gaze dances between Alex and me. "Both of you do."

"We just stuck our fingers in a socket," Alex replies expressionlessly. "Hurt like a bitch."

"Don't try to be cute, little boy." Amelia narrows her eyes as she strides forward and jabs a finger against Alex's chest. "You promised me the witch who could remove the mark of evil? Where is she?"

"Alex," I hiss, shocked. "Why would you do that?"

Alex brushes me off with a shrug. "She just needs Aislin's help taking the mark off her daughter. It's no big deal."

Amelia laughs sharply. "That's all? Really? Do I need to remind you of what's at stake for you if you don't bring me the witch?"

I cross my arms and wait for Alex to explain, but he simply shakes his head and gives a half-shrug.

"Look," he says to Amelia with mild tolerance, "we ran into a problem."

The witch folds her arms and stares him down. "Not we. *You.*"

Alex sighs. "It's out of my hands. Aislin . . . She's gone over to the Malefiscus side. Even if we find her, she's not going to take the mark off your daughter unless we can get her to take it off herself, which doesn't seem very likely."

Rage flares in Amelia's eyes as she raises her hands above her head and wiggles her fingers until they glisten a golden orange. "Well then I guess it's time for you to die."

I do a double-take at Amelia. "What? You can't kill him just for not bringing you Aislin. It's not even his fault."

"We can try to find her and see how it goes. Maybe you could use a Tracker Spell on her." Nervousness creeps into Alex's voice, which puts me on edge since he rarely shows signs of being nervous.

Amelia shakes her head. "If that was possible, I'd have found her already. But she's off the grid. No one can find her with magic." Without warning, her fingers sizzle and shoot sparks.

I lunge for her, but she dodges to the side, and then the sparks shoot from her hand and hit Alex.

His eyes widen, and he buckles to the floor.

"You killed him!" I shout, trembling from head to toe.

No, he can't be dead.

Nicholas said so.

But the longer he lays there on the floor, the more I fear Nicholas has once again fed me lies.

The witch scurries around to the coffee table where a black candle is glowing. She picks up a piece of amethyst and chants something under her breath as I hurry for her, ready to kick some witch ass.

"You're not going anywhere until you bring him back," I demand, reaching out to grab her.

She plunges the amethyst into the flame right as I catch hold of her sleeve. My body erupts with heat, and I wrench back, wincing and bumping my knee on the corner of the table. By the time I regain my balance, she's gone.

"Dammit." I rush back to Alex and slide down on my knees next to him. "Please don't be dead. Please don't be dead." I place my hands on his cheeks and watch his chest, but he isn't breathing. And the electricity feels dull, lifeless. I suck back tears and move my fingers to his wrist, feeling for a pulse. "You aren't dead." Tears spill from my eyes. "Nicholas said you couldn't . . . not without me. And I'm here so . . . Please, Alex, just wake up."

The only response I get is the sound of my tears and the heartbeat echoing inside me.

CHAPTER
TEN

Alex

"KISS ME," SHE *whispers, looking down at me, her brown hair a veil around her face. "Kiss me until we both take our last breaths."*

"Then what?" I ask, staring up at her. She's so fucking beautiful I can't stand it.

"Then we die together," she says simply.

"Is that what you want?"

She nods. "It's all I've ever wanted."

Leaning up, I press my lips to hers, and she somehow breathes life back into me. I can feel myself returning, my heart beating, the electricity igniting as I come alive again . . .

Through the darkness, I can hear Gemma freaking out as she searches for my pulse. She keeps taking sharp breathes, and every time her skin brushes mine, my body hums. Part of me wishes I was dead, that it was all over, and I could die happy knowing she was still alive. She could live her life, happy and free. Of course, even if I was dead, my father would still be alive, and as long as he's breathing, Gemma's life will be in danger.

I force my eyelids open, and my gaze collides with her beautiful and wildly insane violet eyes. Without even thinking, I cup the back of her head and pull her lips to mine, which is stupid. Reckless. Dangerous. But she drives me crazy in the best, most dangerous way possible.

"I kept having dreams about this," I whisper against her lips.

She breathes raggedly against my mouth, looking dazed. "About what?"

"About kissing you." I plant a soft kiss on the corner of her mouth. "About striping you bare and slipping inside you." When her breathing quickens, I continue, despite knowing I should stop. "You begged me to give it to you harder."

Her breath catches in her throat as she pushes away from me. At first, I think I spooked her, that maybe she's the one who has the self-control and knows we need to end this moment. But then she says, "You had a dream about that?"

I nod, brushing my fingers across her cheekbone. "It was one of the best dreams I've ever had."

Her eyes are massive as she stares down at me in bafflement. "I had the same dream . . . How is that possible?" Her brows dip. "You don't think I somehow used my Foreseer power to bring you into my dream, do you?"

"I'm not sure, but I wouldn't be surprised." I sit up, and she leans back to give me room. "At this point, I'm starting to believe almost anything is possible."

"Anything, huh?" Her skin pales as she touches her stomach.

"Are you okay?" I ask, scooting toward her.

She swallows hard. "I should be asking you that."

"I'm fine," I assure her, more worried about how sick she suddenly looks than what happened to me just moments ago.

"Alex, you just about died."

"I know, but I didn't." I want to touch her again, but the electricity is already scorching, so I fight the compulsion by clenching my fists. "Although, I'm not sure why I'm not dead. I should be."

She shakes her head, her eyes still wide. "You can't die . . . not without me."

"You think that's how we're supposed to go? Together? Is that how you see it?"

"Yes, but that's not why I think you can't die without me. Nicholas told me something about us."

My face twists in disgust at the mention of that faerie. I fucking hate Nicholas. Not just because he's a pain in the ass, but because of the way he looks at Gemma and all the inappropriate stuff he's always saying to her.

"Wait . . ." I scratch my head in confusion, realizing something. "I thought Nicholas is dead?"

"He is." She sighs, lifting her hand and showing me the ring her father gave her. "I can see ghosts now. Well, just two ghosts—Nicholas and my mom."

My puzzlement deepens. "Wait, your mom . . . but that would mean . . ."

"She died." She blows out an uneven breath as her hands start to shake.

I stab my nails into my flesh until I draw blood. "My father killed her, didn't he?"

She rapidly shakes her head, scooting toward me. "No, she did it to herself to protect me."

"Are you okay?"

She shrugs. "I'm still trying to decide how I feel. I mean, I hardly knew her, and what I did know about her, I didn't like, but . . ."

"But she's your mom, and you care about her a lot." I reach for her, wanting to comfort her, but then draw back, worried I'll end up killing her. "It's going to be okay. I know it doesn't sound that way right now, but her death eventually won't feel as heavy."

"But it'll always feel a little heavy?" she asks.

I shrug. "Losing someone is always hard."

"I thought I lost you a ton of times," she says quietly, staring down at her lap.

"Hey." I cup her face and force her to look at me. "I'm not going anywhere."

She chews on her bottom lip, searching my eyes. "So you're not leaving me again?"

I was planning on it, but with Aislin and Laylen gone, I can't just abandon her. "We need to find Aislin and Laylen."

"Why did you promise that witch you'd bring her to Aislin, anyway?"

"Because I needed a witch to travel around, so I made a bargain with her. I told her I'd bring her to Aislin if she took me where I needed to go."

"A bargain where you had to die if you didn't follow though? Because that was pretty stupid."

"Yeah, it was, but I wasn't planning on breaking the bargain. At least, not after she made me promise with my life." My brows furrow. "But apparently I can't die."

"According to Faerie boy, we're a packaged deal. If one goes, the other goes, too." Her gaze drops to my mouth, and then she mashes her lips together.

I can feel the desire flowing off her, and God, I can feel it in myself, too.

Unable to stop myself, I lean in. *Just one kiss,* I tell myself. *That's it.*

Our lips brush. Sparks burst. I damn near lose it. Then something crashes against the front door so hard the entire house rocks, and I'm on my feet in a matter of seconds, pulling Gemma with me.

"We need to go," I say. "Too many people know you're here."

"What about Laylen?" she asks in a panic. "And Aislin and Aleesa?"

"We'll find them, but we need to get you out of here first." I pull her toward the back door, but she digs her heels into the floor, refusing to budge.

Back in the day, she used to be a lot weaker, but now that she's a Keeper, she's a hell of a lot stronger. And I'd be fucking lying if I denied it kind of turns me on.

"We need to find them now," she demands, holding my gaze steadily. "Before they harm someone. You know as well as I do that neither of them can handle the guilt of hurting someone." Sadness consumes her face. "Laylen's already going to have a hard time forgiving himself for what he did to me."

"Good," I say as my anger simmers. "He should."

"Alex, he didn't know what he was doing. He couldn't help himself. I saw it in his eyes."

"I get it. Trust me, I feel the same way every time I look at you." The words slip out of my mouth, but I don't even try taking them back. "But I also can't control my anger when it comes to someone hurting you. Laylen hurt you, and yeah, I'm pretty fucking pissed off about it."

She points a finger at me. "You won't hurt him.

Promise me you won't."

"I'll try." It's the best I can do. "Now, come on."

She still doesn't budge. "We need to find them, Alex. Seriously. We can't wait."

"I know we do, but it's going to take some time. And I don't even know what the hell we're going to do when we find them. Right now, the only person who can remove the mark is Aislin, and if she's one of them, I don't think she's going to be very willing to perform the spell on herself."

"We'll figure something out," she says determinedly. "And we need to stay here until we do. My mom and Nicholas are going to be looking for me here."

"Gemma," I say, struggling to be patient. "They'll have to find us. We can't stay here, not after that witch now knows where we are. For all we know, she could be tracking my father down right now and making a bargain with him. Besides, he could already know where we are if he's got Aislin or Laylen on his side."

She reluctantly surrenders. "But we have to find a way to save them before they end up doing something they'll regret."

They probably already have, but I don't share that with her, not wanting to worry her even more. She already looks completely tired and fragile, completely breakable.

After a little bit of deliberating, we head outside into the fires and the moonlight.

"Is this far enough away for you?" I ask as we approach the end of the frost bitten driveway.

"I think so." She closes her eyes. "Where should I take us?"

"Somewhere safe." I wrap one arm around her waist and pull her close to me.

She cracks an eyelid to look at me. "You don't want to

say where?"

I shake my head. "No, I'm going to let you decide." Since I seem to be an idiot when it comes to making good decisions. If I wasn't, then I wouldn't be standing here, holding her in such a forbidden way.

Nervously nodding, she leans into me while snow flurries fall around us, and then she takes us away.

CHAPTER
ELEVEN

Gemma

I DON'T KNOW what the hell went wrong. Maybe seeing Alex threw me off my game, or maybe it's what he said about going someplace safe. Whatever it was, somehow I end up thinking of my dad living in his own mind, all alone, and when I open my eyes, we're there.

Alex glances around, his forehead creasing. "Where are we?"

I pull a "whoops" face. "Um, yeah, so I think I accidently took us into my dad's mind."

Alex blinks down at me, his arm still lingering on my waist, making me feel safe. "You took us into your dad's mind?"

I nod, glancing around the area, which has changed since my last visit. The ocean still remains in the distance, but the beach is rockier and the air chiller, as if winter is approaching. The sky is cloudy and grumbles with thunder. Ocean waves crash into the shore, bringing the storm in.

"Yep, I'm pretty sure that's where we are." I look up at him. "It's kind of weird, right? I mean, it's the first time you're going to meet my dad, and we're inside his head."

Alex snorts a laugh. "You're cute."

"What'd I say?" I ask, lost.

He shrugs, tracing his finger down the brim of my nose. "It's nothing. You're just cute. That's all."

Feeling a little squirmy and exposed, I change the subject. "I wonder where he is." I start up the beach as thunder booms above and waves roll over our shoes.

Alex's gaze remains trained on the ocean as he follows right behind me. "So out of all the places to go that could be safe, this is the first place you thought of?"

I shrug. "I don't do very well under pressure, and FYI, you usually don't give me a choice of where we're going, so it threw me off."

"Sorry." He cups my cheek, staring at me with the strangest look on his face. Ever since he showed up at the house, he's been looking at me more intensely than when he left, as if he's fighting his emotions a little more, which makes me feel both afraid and excited.

Clearing his throat, he pulls his hand away. "So where would he be?"

"My dad?" I shrug. "I'm not sure. He usually just shows up."

The corners of his mouth quirk. "Well, we're in his head, so he's got to be around."

I roll my eyes, but a soft laugh eases from my lips, startling us both since I barely laugh. Shaking the weird feeling of elation off, I hike farther down the beach, and he moves with me.

"Where did you go?" I ask, kicking at the sand. "When you left?"

"To figure stuff out." He stares up at the sky.

"But you're staying now, right? You won't leave me again." I sound so needy, but I don't care. Now that he's here, the thought of leaving again is brutally painful, especially with the secret I'm carrying inside me. I know I need to tell him, but I have no idea what to say or how he'll take the news.

"I don't know . . ." He shuts his eyes, inhaling deeply. " I think I should." He opens his eyes. "But I don't want to."

I carry his gaze, my heart beating deafeningly inside my chest. "Then don't."

We stare each other down, our hearts pounding faster, electricity radiating more powerfully than the lightning. Time drifts away, and I start to feel so tired.

He breaks the trance, stepping back then shucking off his jacket. He slips it on me then zips it up. "Your dad might get really worried with all the blood on your neck and shirt."

I tuck my hands into the sleeves and pull the fabric over my nose, breathing in the scent of his cologne. "Did you find out anything helpful why you were gone?" I ask, more to distract my thoughts from his scent, from him.

We head farther down the beach. "Not much. What about you? Did you find out anything that might help our situation?"

"Maybe," I say, and he stares at me in astonishment. "What do you know about the Afterlife?"

He slams to an abrupt stop. "Why would you ask that?"

"Because that's where my mom said I had to go to stop us from dying." The wind gusts through my hair. "She said that I need to visit a woman named Helena."

He promptly shakes his head. "There's no way you're going there. It's the Afterlife, as in the place where lost souls go after they pass from an unnecessary death, which means you'd have to die that way to go there."

"But if it can fix everything, then it's worth it, right?"

His features harden as he glowers at me. "So you're okay with dying? And me, too, since we're supposed to be a package deal?"

I set my hands on his shoulders and look him dead in the eye. "You're not going to die. You're going to bring me back. That's how my mom said it happens."

"No." His shoulders shake under my touch as he inches his face closer to mine. "I'll die and go there if one of us needs to go."

"Alex, she said it has to be me." My voice is even and firm and so is my heart rate. The other heartbeat, though, races inside me, pouring fear through my veins.

"I don't give a shit what your mom said. I'm not letting you . . ." He trails off, a pucker forming at his brow. "What is that?"

I glance from left to right. "What's what?"

"That noise . . . It sounds like it's coming from you . . ." He leans back, studying me. " I swear I can hear your heart beating right now. It's beating really fast. Are you okay?" He lines his palm against my chest, and his perplexity increases. "The sound . . . It doesn't match your heart."

I press my hand to my stomach. I have no clue how the hell he can hear it other than maybe it's the connection of the star. Perhaps it's linked the three of us. I struggle to stay composed, to hide my secret. Now is definitely not the right time to tell him.

But then he looks down and notices where my hand is. Just like with Aislin, I see it click in his eyes the moment he figures out what's going on.

"Holy shit," he breathes, his eyes as round as golf balls as he steps back.

"It's not what you think," I sputter. "It's...I...Fuck..." I stumble over my words until frustration gets the best of me, and hot tears slip from my eyes.

The tears seem to calm him down a little, and his expression softens as he steps back toward me. "Gemma, it's okay. We'll—"

"Gemma, what are you doing here?"

Alex and I blink, and then, tearing my eyes off him, I turn to my dad.

He doesn't look happy to see me. His violet eyes are unwelcoming as he stands there, glaring at me, his silver robe flapping with the breeze.

"You need to go, now!" he shouts, panic flashing in his eyes.

I trip back, slamming into Alex. "Dad, what's—"

Ice crackles as the ocean rapidly glazes over, the waves frozen in place. Figures appear around us, stirring up a cloud of sand. When the sand settles, my jaw hits the ground.

Death Walkers. And they're everywhere.

CHAPTER TWELVE

Alex

NO ONE CAN make me feels as angry, as happy, as terrified as Gemma can. As she stands there, trying to explain to me that she's going to die so she can go to the Afterlife, I want to tie her up to my bed and never let her go. Her casual attitude toward her own life drives me so insane. I wish she could see how important she is, and not just because of the star.

I remember when I saw her at her school the day I went to break the spell Sophia put on her. Gemma looked so innocent, confused, and absolutely beautiful. When I met her again, I was such an ass to her, yet she forgave me. Well, eventually . . . kind of, anyway. I'm still a little confused over how she feels about me.

Sometimes I want her to hate me. It would make things easier if she refused to let me touch her and kiss her all the time, if one of us had control.

I start telling her there's no fucking way I'll ever let

her go Afterlife when I hear something odd. Initially, I think it's a drum, but then I realize the noise is coming from Gemma. It sounds like another heartbeat, and when she places a hand on her stomach, I just about pass out.

She never actually says the words, yet somehow I know.

She's pregnant with my child.

Before I can even wrap my head around that fact, her dad shows up out of nowhere, screaming at her like lunatic. Then comes the biggest pain in my ass—the Death Walkers.

With one swift movement, I slide my hand into Gemma's and sprint down the beach, running faster than I ever have. It's not just about saving her anymore. It's about saving both of them.

As I'm searching for a somewhere to hide her, she slips on the ice and lands on her back, cracking her head against the ice.

Panic strangles me, worried she hurt herself, and I end up tripping over her, which is strange. I never fall, but then again, my head's usually not so crammed in a cluster-fuck of emotions.

I start to land on top of her, but my arms shoot out to catch my weight.

She blinks over at the ice and then up at me.

"Are you okay?" I whisper, examining her face and head for any visible injuries.

She bobs her head up and down. "I think so."

"What about . . . ?" I swallow hard as I set a hand on her stomach.

Her breath falters. "I think so. I mean, I can still hear its heart beating."

"Yeah, me, too."

While we stare at each other, unsaid words hanging in the air, I'm terrified. I've never imagined myself as a father, mostly because I never had time. There's a small part of me that worries I'll suck at it, that somehow, I'll end up like my father, and I never, ever want that to happen.

"Hold on," Gemma whispers, looping her arms around my neck. "I'm going to get us out of here."

Electricity pours through our bodies and melts the ice below us. She shuts her eyes and whispers something under her breath, holding onto to me. She looks so beautiful, and all I can think is *take me now,* because it really seems like the perfect time to die.

Then there's a flash of bright light, and the next thing I know, we're tumbling into nothingness.

After what feels like an eternity, we finally stop falling. I push back and glance around at where she took us, and shock instantly sets in.

We're in the middle of the snowy mountains, surrounded by trees, in the exact spot the piece of the star crashed.

I never wanted to see this place again. It reminds me of everything bad that's happened, everything we still need to fix.

"Okay, we really need to get you a list of safe places." I say, pushing off her.

"I'm sorry," she says as I offer her my hand and lift her to her feet. "But it's kind of a good place to live." She brushes dirt off the back of her jeans. "I mean, who the hell would think of looking for us here? I'm betting no one."

"Yeah, maybe, but we're going to end up freezing to death." I dust some snow out of her hair, and she shivers from my touch. "And I thought you hated the snow."

"I'm getting used to it, but if you're cold . . ." She steps back and reaches for the zipper of my jacket to take it off.

I capture her hand in mine, stopping her. "I'm fine, Gemma. I'm more worried about you and . . ." I trail off, looking down at her stomach while yanking my fingers through her hair.

God, I wish I could say all the right things, but I don't even know what the right thing is for this kind of moment.

She turns away to stare at the tress with her arms wrapped around herself. "I'm still not one hundred percent sure I am. I mean, I can hear the heartbeat and everything, which is super weird and, from what I read online, totally not normal. And Nicholas somehow knew without me telling him." She kicks the tip of her sneaker against the snow. "But I still don't have any real proof other than I can feel something growing inside me. Aislin even had me take this little test thing, and the results are all messed up. I don't know why. If the test was a dud or if it's me or"—She looks down at her stomach—"it."

"It?" I have no idea why that's what I say other than everything else seems really complicated.

She lifts her shoulders. "I don't know what it is, so saying 'it' for now. I mean, for all we know, it might not even be human."

"I'm sure it's as human as you and me," I say, trying to be reassuring and calm when really I'm freaking the fuck out.

She's pregnant.

Holy shit.

"That's what I'm worried about." Her shoulders start to shake, and I realize she's crying.

I suddenly don't give a shit about anything except making her feel better, so I wrap my arms around her and pull her against my chest. "It's going to be okay."

She grips at my shirt, her tears soaking through the fabric. "You don't know that for sure."

"Yes, I do." I smooth my hand up and down her back. "You want to know how?"

She nods her head, sniffling.

"Because I'm not going to let anything happen to you." I pause, tightening my hold on her. "To the both of you."

She nods again, which surprises me. Usually, she's so stubborn. I let her cry in my arms, holding her tightly, even when I start to feel the energy draining from my body. It feels like I'm breaking into pieces, and all of those pieces belong to her. I don't know how to fix it, how to get the all the pieces back, and I kind of don't want to.

Finally, she pulls away, gasping for air.

After she composes herself, she asks, "Do you think . . . ? Do you think he'll be okay?"

I look at her stomach and find myself smiling for some insane reason. "I thought it was an it. Now it's a he?"

She covers her belly with her arm. "No, not that . . . I was talking about my dad."

"Oh, yeah, I'm sure he'll be fine."

A beat or two goes by where she simply stares at me, as if trying to read my thoughts. Horrified she might somehow be able to, I keep talking.

"He's in his own head," I explain, "which means his real body is somewhere else, so I think he's safe." I stare down at the snow. "We need a plan, though. I don't think it's a good idea to just keep going to random places."

"I have two great plans." She leans back against a tree, yawning. "We can either go find Laylen, Aislin, and Aleesa and try to convince Aislin to get the mark off herself. Or we can go track down my mom, find out how the hell I get to the Afterlife, and end all of this." She pauses, assessing me closely. "Unless you know how to get there."

"Why would I know how to get there?" I lie casually. There is no way I am going to offer up information that would get her and the baby killed.

The baby.

Every time I think about it, I feel like I'm going to faint.

She frowns, reading my bullshit lie. "Fine, don't tell me, then. Make this harder than it needs to be."

"Gemma, I'm not lying this time. I have no clue how to get there."

She shakes her head, frustrated. "Then I need to find my mom."

"Not if it involves going back to the house.

The electricity scorches up a notch as she grows angry with me. "You're not the boss of me, Alex."

I bust up laughing, only making her angrier. "I'm sorry," I quickly say, working to pull myself together. "It's just that you used to say that all the time to me when we were kids."

She mashes her lips together, stifling a laugh and trying to remain angry.

"You also used to get this right here"—I smooth away the line between her brows with my thumb—"whenever you were trying to stay mad at me."

She shakes her head, huffing. "I am mad at you."

"No, you're not."

To prove it, I brush my lips across hers, and she groans against my mouth as her fingers slide through my hair, pulling me closer. I kiss her until she's breathless, until my heart nearly gives out, until I'm on the verge of dying.

"We should stop," she whispers, pulling back.

"Just a little bit longer," I beg, needing more.

So, so much more.

She doesn't budge as I lean in, giving her a long, savoring kiss. Then she whimpers as I pull away, biting her lip, and the sound only makes me crave more of her. God, I want all of her, whenever I want, without always worrying over whether I'm going to break either her or myself.

"How did you find me?" she suddenly says, jerking back and staring over my shoulder.

I reel around, ready to fight, but no one's there.

CHAPTER
THIRTEEN

Gemma

H E PROBABLY THINKS I'm nuts standing here, talking to myself. I'm not, though part of me kind of wishes that was the case

"How'd you find me?" I ask the annoying-as-hell faerie. When Alex tenses beside me, I touch the ring on my finger and explain. "It's Nicholas."

His expression plummets. "Great. Just what we need." He pauses. "What about your mom?"

I shake my head, and then my attention zones in on Nicholas. "Where is she? Because the last time I saw her, you two disappeared somewhere."

"She's been detained." His golden eyes sparkle against the fading sunlight. "But don't worry; I'm here to help you."

I roll my eyes. "Yeah, right. We both know that's a lie."

"Oh, Gemma." He sighs overdramatically, pressing his hand to his heart. "Your distrust wounds me so."

"If you're not here to tell me where my mom is, go away," I order, and Alex gives me this puzzled look.

"But I swear I really am here to help," he says, drawing an x over his heart with his fingertip. "I promise."

"What's he saying?" Alex asks, scanning the forest.

Nicholas's lips curl into a malicious grin as he steps in front of Alex and waves his hand in front of his face. "God, I hate you." He flattens Alex's hair with his hand. "And that stupid hair."

"Stop that." I glare at Nicholas. "And I like his hair."

"Why are you talking about my hair?" Alex asks, ruffling his hands through his hair.

I pull Alex out of Nicholas's reach then aim a finger at Nicholas. "Either tell me what to do or go away."

"Fine." He sighs, lowering his hand to his side. "You need to come with me."

I shake my head, stepping back until I can feel Alex behind me. "No way."

"You have to."

"I'm not."

"Yes, you are."

"No, I'm not," I argue. "And I can't, anyway. You're dead, and wherever the heck you're going, I can't go."

"And you'll soon be dead, too," Nicholas says simply. "Once you pick the way you want to die. Now, me personally, I'd pick a poetic way, like poison from a vile. But you, I'm guessing you'll go with something lame."

I gape at him. "What are you talking about? I'm not picking the way I'm going to die, not with you around, anyway."

Alex's hands find my waist, and he pulls me against him. "Let's get out of here."

"Just a second." I hold up a finger, keeping my

attention on Nicholas. "Start explaining from the beginning; otherwise, I'm leaving."

He yawns. "It's kind of a long story, one I'd really rather not waste time telling."

"Then give me the short version," I say through gritted teeth. "Just don't leave out anything important like you usually do."

He sits down on a rock, folding his arms. "Once upon a time, there was a beautiful princess," he starts and I glare at him. "You asked for the short version, and I'm giving it to you. This is how it starts."

Sighing tiredly, I sit down on a rock then signal for Alex to take a seat.

"What are we doing?" Alex asks as he sits down beside me.

"We're listening to a story," I explain, "that probably has no point."

"Like I was saying," Nicholas says, resting his hands on his knees as he leans forward. "There was a beautiful princess who was more extraordinary than any other princess because she liked to help the world. The problem was, she wasn't very good at helping. Every time she fixed a problem, she caused another until, one day, she caused a problem so great it cost the lives of many innocent people."

Alex whispers in my ear, "What's he saying?"

"I'll tell you when he's finished." I motion at Nicholas to continue.

"What the princess needed to realize is that to fix the problems she caused, she needed to save the lost souls of the innocent lives that were taken."

"And how do I save these lost souls?" I ask, even though I think I already know the answer.

"By going to the Afterlife and bargaining with the queen for their release." He flashes me his pearly whites, taking pleasure in my pain.

I frown, remembering the last queen I ran into—the Queen of the Underworld. "Why does it always have to be a queen?"

"Because it's much more fun that way." Nicholas smirks. "And her name is Queen Helena."

"And what's this queen like?" I wonder, picking at a hole in my jeans. "Is she as bad as the Queen of the Underworld?"

"No, she's much worse than the Queen of the Underworld." A grin plasters across Nicholas's face.

"How do I get her to free these souls if she's that bad? And how do I even get to the Afterlife to begin with? Because I can't die . . . Not when . . ." Not when I won't be the only one dying.

"Don't worry. Nothing's going to happen to your baby. You're not technically dying; your spirit's just leaving your body."

Even if what he's saying is true, I still don't understand how I'm supposed to make any of this happen.

"And to answer your other question," Nicholas says like he's reading my thoughts, "you get to the Afterlife by getting help from a Banshee."

I blink at him. "What's a Banshee?"

"It's an otherworldly woman whose cry signals death," Alex explains, watching me with concern. "She's also the spirit who carries the lost souls to the queen."

I blow out a breath, wishing I could just go home and sleep for like a week. "So we have to find a Banshee who'll be willing to help us."

Alex's forehead creases. "That's what we need?"

I nod and give Alex a quick recap of everything Nicholas just told me.

"You wouldn't happen to know any Banshee's just hanging around that might be nice enough to help us out?" I ask Alex with hope.

"Actually, I do." Snow falls from the sky as he stands up, frowning. "My mother."

My head whips in his direction. "Your mother's a Banshee? How did you . . . ? *What?*"

Nicholas snorts. "Oh, this is so fucking funny."

"There's nothing funny about his mom being dead," I snap at him, my emotions all over the place as the reality of what I have to do really, *really* sinks in.

My spirit has to leave my body.

"Oh, I'm not laughing because his mother's dead," he replies, grinning. "I'm laughing because she's a Banshee."

"I still don't get it," I admit.

"Banshee's are from the faerie realm," Alex says as if he knows exactly what Nicholas is saying. "I'm sure he thinks it's funny because I haven't been very nice when it comes to the fey I know."

"Oh." I frown. "But how did it happen? Has she always been one?"

He shrugs, scuffing his boot against the now. "Those journals of my mom's we found the night we snuck into my house, they talked about her fearing she was going to die. My mom worried my father was going to kill her if he learned her secret. She wrote something about finding a way to cross into the Afterlife if that did happen and becoming one of the queen's Soul Collectors, a Banshee. That way, she could still have a connection to earth and help us when the time is right. So I started poking around, asking some people, and I found out it's true. She's a

Banshee." He shrugs like that's that, but his eyes look a little watery.

I can't help myself. I want to kiss away his pain, so I stand up and press my lips to his. He seems surprised at first, but then he slips his tongue into my mouth, tasting me, feeling me, making me want so much more. I let myself get carried away for a second, not caring about the star or the world or anything, even the fact that Nicholas is watching us like a pervert.

When I start to want too much—feel too much—I break away, gasping for air, noting we have somehow melted the snow around us.

Alex's eyes are filled with untamed desire. He wants more and so do I. God, so do I.

"I think I'm going to throw up," Nicholas mumbles, looking royally pissed off.

"Then throw up." I raise my eyebrows at him, challenging him. "If it is that bad to watch, then you should've turned your head."

He sticks out his tongue. *"Then you should have turned your head,"* he mimics.

Alex turns in a circle, looking for something. "Hey, I have an idea. Why don't you shut it?" he says, searching for Nicholas.

When I nod my head, mouthing, *behind you,* he takes a swing, but ends up tripping and hitting air. Nicholas laughs, hunching over and cradling his stomach.

I sigh while Alex gets even more riled up. Then he stuffs his hand into his pocket and pulls out a piece of paper.

"This guy named Draven—the Lord of the Afterlife— he gave me this address. Supposedly, it's where my mom is."

I take the paper from him. "Reykjavik?" My eyes elevate to him. "*Iceland?* Your mother's in *Iceland.* God, it's good the snow's starting to grow on me."

"Actually, it's colder here than it is there," Alex explains, wiping a few snowflakes from his forehead.

I fold the paper back up and hand it to him. "It's good you have an address, but how are we supposed to get to Iceland without flying or something, since I've never actually seen the place?"

He cracks his knuckles, considering what I said. "Your Foreseeing thing only works if you can visualize where you're going, so maybe if you had a mental picture of how it looked, we could get there."

"But how do I create a mental picture? Because all I see when I think of Iceland is a big chunk of ice."

"Maybe if you had a picture, you could look at it then visualize it and take us there."

Maybe that could actually work.

"So where do we get the picture? Like, from the internet? Because we'd have to find a computer since my phone hasn't been working for over a week now."

"Yeah, mine, either. But we can't go back to the house," he says. "It's too dangerous."

"What about the library that was back by your college?" Nicholas interrupts, stepping between us. "They've got a ton of computers there, and they let the public use them. Plus, you spend a lot of time there, so you should be able to Foresee to the place without any problems."

I shove aside the fact that he somehow knows that about me and eye him over skeptically. "Did you just offer up something useful? Because it seems weird and makes me wonder what you're up to."

"There's a first for everything," he replies, but I know

there has to be more to it than that, something in it for him.

"What's he saying?" Alex asks, glancing around.

"He said we should try the library . . ." I trail off as Nicholas strolls away, whistling. Yep, something's definitely up. "I haven't been to town since all hell broke loose, so I'm not sure if anyone's still running things like libraries. Although, Laylen picked up groceries from somewhere, and Aislin picked up the . . ." I clear my throat, gesturing at my stomach. " Well, you know."

His eyes flit to my stomach, but thankfully, he doesn't look as freaked out as when he first found out. In fact, he seems oddly calm at the moment.

"We'll try the library, but we're going to be careful." He points a finger at me. "And I'm stressing the careful part. If anything goes bad, you have to promise you'll leave, even if it's without me."

It takes a lot of effort, but I manage a nod then extend my hand, preparing to take us back to the university I briefly attended.

Before we leave, I look over at Nicholas. "You never said what happens after I free the lost souls."

"Then the world returns to normal, you two go to the lake and sacrifice your lives, and everything is exactly how it's supposed to be," he says with honesty.

I press my hand to my stomach. "What about . . . ?"

He shrugs. "If you want to save your child, you'll have to figure something out."

"What'd he say?" Alex asks, a worry line forming between his brows

The heartbeat roars inside my eardrums as I blink at Alex. "He said . . . He doesn't know."

Alex presses his lips together as I reach for his hand,

electricity surging from the contact. As I shut my eyes, I make a promise to myself that, no matter what happens, I'm going to make sure our child survives this.

CHAPTER
FOURTEEN

Alex

I CAN TELL she is lying. Whatever Nicholas said to her is really, really bad. Getting her to fess up is going to be challenging, though, considering how stubborn she can be sometimes.

We land in an alley that runs right to the back of the entrance to the library. Snow is drifting from the grey sky, making the ground a sheet of ice and a death trap for Gemma. I run my hand across the hood that's over her head, sweeping away some of the snowflakes before threading my fingers through hers.

"I don't want you to fall," I explain, giving her hand a squeeze.

She surprisingly doesn't argue as we head to the back door. There are no windows around, so I can't see what is going on inside, but the area is almost too silent.

"You think it's open?" she asks, bouncing up and down on her toes, trying to warm herself.

I grab the door handle and give it a tug. "Nope."

She stops bouncing, staring at me with concern. "Alex, your skin's turning blue."

"I'm just a little cold," I lie. I'm not just cold. I'm freezing to death, and I don't think it's only from the cold. The longer I'm around her, the more I can feel myself fading as I fall more . . . well, in love with her. I don't want to admit it—know I can't—but apparently, love doesn't come from just announcing the word aloud.

Gemma reaches for the zipper of the jacket, but I grab her hand.

"Stop trying to give me the damn jacket back. I'm not going to take it."

Her worry magnifies as she encloses her hands around my wrist, her pulse slamming against her fingertips. She chews on her lip as she rubs her hands up and down my arm, creating friction, electricity, warmth.

"Better?" she asks.

"Yes." I inch closer to her. "What about you? Are you cold? Because I could warm you up."

"I'm fine, but thanks." Her cheeks flush, however, revealing what she truly wants.

I turn for the entrance door, smiling at myself, despite knowing everything going on between us is completely wrong. Then again, how can it be wrong when for the first time in my life, I feel . . . right? Like this is the person I was always supposed to be.

The thought bounces around in my head as we check the front door, which ends up being locked, too. I kick the living shit out of it, but nothing.

Gemma slumps against the brick wall, rubbing her stomach. "Now what do we do?"

"I don't know." I look at the restaurant next door.

"Think they'd have a computer we could use?"

She shakes her head. "The dude who owns it is a douche, so even if they did, they probably wouldn't let us use it."

I pop my knuckles. "We don't have to ask."

"No violence for the moment, please." She looks over her shoulder at the library window. "Maybe we should just break in."

"The alarm could go off and draw too much attention." I look around at the stores surrounding us. Most of them are closed, but a few blocks down, I spot the roof of the university. "I think I have an idea."

GEMMA IS EXTREMELY fidgety as we stand in front of the school. "I can't believe the school's open. You'd think they'd lock it or something."

"It's kind of hard to remember to lock up when the apocalypse is happening." I hold the door open, letting her walk in.

"Yeah, I guess." She bites at her nails, looking reluctant as she steps into the hallway, which strangely has a few people wandering around. "School's still going?" she whispers to me in shock.

"I guess." I shrug as we start down the hallway toward the student union. With each step, she seems increasingly distracted. "You know, I didn't really feel the way I acted that first day we met."

She nods, preoccupied with the few people walking around, heading to class. "I hope no one notices us here, especially if there are any fey, witches, or vampires around."

I pick up the pace, tugging her with me. "Let's just make this quick and get out of here."

My boots scuff against the tile as I weave past people while Gemma scrambles to keep us with me.

"God, this place brings back such bad memories of when I was . . ." She blows out a breath, shaking her head.

Suddenly, I realize why she's so distracted, and my heart literally aches for her. I'm not sure what to say to her that could take away the pain of years and years of solitude, especially when I helped cause it. As a result, I do the only thing I can think of—I hold onto her, entwining our fingers to let her know that I'm here, that she's not alone anymore.

And she clutches on for dear life.

"SO THIS IS what Iceland looks like, huh?" She frowns as she leans over my shoulder and studies the computer screen. "I thought you said it isn't cold there."

"No, I said it isn't as cold there as it is here." I tap my finger on the screen. "There's still snow there, though."

She tilts her head to the side, squinting at the photo on the screen. "What do you think that little road's for?"

"I don't know, but this is the clearest picture I can find." I try to ignore how close she is, but it's all I can think about. "Plus, there's a lot of bare space around, so we don't have to worry about the wrong people seeing us appear out of thin air."

"And then what do we do? We just roam around until we find the address? Because that seems like it could take forever."

"We'll get a taxi."

"Seems kind of amateur." She turns her head and smiles at me.

She rarely smiles, and it makes my heart skip a beat as I give her hair a playful tug. "Don't worry. I'm sure there'll be plenty of times we'll need your wonderful Foreseer power to take us around, but for now, yeah, I think a taxi is going to be the best way to find the address."

"Yeah, you're probably right." She clicks the mouse on the print button then turns around and waits for the printer to spit out the picture.

I spot a woman with blonde hair heading toward us with a strut to her walk. She looks vaguely familiar, but I can't remember her name.

"Oh, my God, Alex. Where the hell have you been!" she exclaims, strutting toward me.

Shit. I remember her now. She's the woman who gave me her number back when Gemma and I were in the library working on that stupid project. Although I never called her, she seemed to track me down at every class and party. She was a complete bitch to Gemma, treating her like a piece of garbage, and I hate myself for never saying anything to stop it.

I cough into my hand. "Code red. We need to get out of here."

Gemma stares at me like I've lost my mind. "What are you talking about?"

Pushing away from the desk, I snatch the picture from the printer, grab Gemma's hand, and stride for the exit.

"What's the rush?" Gemma jogs to keep up with me. "Wait, is there someone here who knows us?"

"Someone's here who knows *me*," I stress in a low

tone, "but not anyone who's going to take off and tell my father. They're just . . . I don't . . . I'm really sorry."

Her violet eyes skim the room filled with students, and then her lip twitches when she spots Blondie waving at me.

"Great," she mutters under her breath. "Just what I need."

"I never did anything with her," I feel the need to explain as I squeeze by a group of people.

She marginally relaxes as we approach the doors. "She still treated me like shit. You know, she came up to me after class once and told me I was a freak and a slut, even though I'd never had sex before. Hell, I hadn't even kissed you yet."

"I think she was probably just jealous that I was so focused on you." I open the door.

She doesn't step through the doorway. "I don't care why she did it. My entire life—at least the part I can remember—people like her were always teasing me and tormenting me."

She motions for me to walk out first then follows me. But she doesn't come with me when I head down the hallway.

"What are you doing?" I ask, but she only stares inside the union, holding the door open.

Blondie walks toward us, glancing from me to Gemma before sneering, "Oh, look, it's the tramp—"

Gemma lets the door swing shut in Blondie's face, and it hits her square in the nose.

"Ready to go?" Gemma asks, brushing past me and making a beeline for the doors.

Fuck, her confidence is totally turning me on.

Adjusting myself, I snag her sleeve and steer her

toward the exit. Once we're outside and around the corner of the building, out of watchful eyes, I back her against the wall and slam my lips against hers. Then I brace one hand to the side of her head while my other hand explores her body. My fingers slip up her shirt, and I cup her breast. Her nipple hardens under my touch, and I get rock hard. I know I'll have to stop soon, that my emotions will become too overpowering, but I push my limits like I always do, only pulling away when it feels like my lungs are being crushed.

"That was so hot," I whisper, grinding my hips against hers before stepping back and catching my breath.

Her chest heaves as she breathes raggedly, her eyes wild and filled with lust. "That felt good."

I don't ask her if she's referring to the kiss or slamming the door in that girl's face. If her answer is the first, then I'm pretty sure I'll kiss her again and end up killing us both.

"Ready to go?" she asks after her breathing settles down.

I nod, lacing my fingers through her. "Yeah, let's go to Iceland."

I don't bother telling her that, once I find my mom, I have every intention of convincing her I'm the one who's going to the Afterlife. I mean, there's no way I could risk Gemma's life like that or our child's.

Whether Gemma likes it or not, I'm the one who's going to die.

CHAPTER
FIFTEEN

Gemma

LETTING THE GLASS door hit that girl in the face like that might have been a childish thing to do; but, I'm not the weak girl I once was. The one who let people call her names and never stuck up for herself.

I try not to think about how guilty I feel for doing it as Alex and I make our way around the back of the school. I focus on studying the photo of Iceland, instead, trying to memorize every detail of the area, hoping I can get us there.

I'm almost ready to go when we duck behind the dumpster to Foresee away when I see something I wasn't expecting—a vampire feeding.

I gape at the scene in horror, realizing I know the victim.

"Professor Sterling?" I whisper. There's so much blood all over him and the snow on the ground. "Oh, my God. No."

This is all my fault, all of this: him being here, a

vampire feeding off him, the world being run by evil.

Alex swipes a stick from the ground and aims it at the female vampire with the triangle mark on her neck, feeding off the professor. She keeps draining the professor's blood as Alex stalks up behind her. With one quick motion, he stabs the stick through the back of chest, and her body obliterates to ashes that scatter across the snow.

Professor Sterling dazedly blinks up at us. "What happened . . . ? I don't . . ." He presses his hand to the wound as Alex helps him to his feet and guides him away from the garbage can.

"Go inside and tell the nurse you were cut," he instructs, pointing at the school.

Mr. Sterling deliriously nods his head then staggers for the back entrance of the school.

"Let's get out of here," Alex says, taking my hand.

I look down at the picture again, more determined than ever to get us there. I take in every detail from the snow lining the grass to the water in the distance to the shallow hills. Then I picture myself and Alex standing in the middle of it.

When I open my eyes, we're there, on that little road I pointed at. But something feels—

"Son of a bitch," Alex curses as the nose of an airplane dives for us.

I trip across the ice, almost getting taken out by a plane, but Alex's fingertips circle my wrist, and he swings me around in front of him and out of the way. We don't stop running until we reach the chain link fence enclosing the runway.

I slip my fingers through the metal links, staring up at the barbwire on top. "How do we get over it?"

Alex walks the line of the fence, searching for

another way out, while I check what's beyond the side of the fence—a parking lot and some cars. Getting an idea, I focus on a red car as I reach over and slide my hand up Alex's arm. I feel the zap, and then I Foresee us through the fence and next to the red car.

"Well, I guess that's one way to do it." He tries not to smile, but the corners of his mouth threaten to turn up. "You're amazing. You know that?"

I blush from the compliment. "Let's go find a taxi so we can track down your mom and stop more people from getting bitten by vampires."

Nodding, Alex takes my hand and hikes across the parking lot to the entrance doors of the airport. The doors glide open, and we step inside then start searching for the taxi station. I'm nervous about being out in the open, worried every single person we pass might be a witch or vampire in disguise.

Thankfully, we find signs that lead us to the taxi station without running into any problems. Of course, there's a line that we have to wait in, and Alex can't seem to hold still, nervous energy flowing off him and through me.

When I start to sweat, I decide it's time to distract him from whatever's got him all jittery.

"So, about that thing . . ." I have no clue why I decide to talk about *that* other than it just kind of slips out.

He glances at me with his head cocked. "Thing?"

I point at my stomach. "That thing."

His muscles tense, but the heat goes down a notch. "Oh."

"We don't have to talk about it if you don't want to," I say quickly, my words coming out in a nervous rush. "It just kind of feels like we should. I mean, I'm kind of freaking out . . . and you seem so . . . so quiet."

He relaxes, releasing a breath. "I'm freaking out, too."

A breath eases from my lips. I don't know why, but knowing he's nervous, too, makes me feel better, like I'm not crazy for being more worried than excited.

"What do we do?" I ask, touching my belly.

He looks down at my stomach and then with hesitancy places his hand over mine. I don't know if he can feel anything or still hear the beat of the heart, but a small smile touches his lips.

"We protect it," he says nervously, looking up at me. "We protect it more than anything."

A few tears escape my eyes. God knows why I'm crying other than I just feel so . . . warm and fuzzy inside.

"Gemma." He brings my hand to his lips and kisses my palm. "It's going to be okay. I won't let anything happen to you or the baby."

Strangely, I believe him.

THE TAXI RIDE is long, and the cab smells of old cheese and sweaty socks. I have to hold my breath most of the way just to keep from puking, although that's not the only problem. Squished in such a small space, it's like a lightning storm has erupted between Alex and I. The air is static charged, and all I keep thinking about is how long it's been since I've felt him inside me. Not counting the dream, it's been weeks since we've been together like that, and the kisses he keeps stealing only leave me wanting more.

Just when I think I'm going to pass out from the heat and the smell, the taxi pulls up to a curb on a street crammed with two-story houses.

Lampposts illuminate the falling snow as we hop out into the chilly air. Alex pays the driver before the taxi speeds off.

"Which one is it?" I ask as Alex puts his wallet away.

He takes the paper out of his pocket then walks up the street, glancing at each house before coming to a stop in front of a brown one with a tan roof.

"I think this is it." He stuffs the paper into his pocket then opens the gate.

Holding hands, we hike up the snow-covered path to the front door.

"Are we safe out in the open like this?" I ask, noting the stillness of the area.

"We're never safe when you really think about it. But hopefully, after we talk with my mom, we will be." He squeezes my hand before knocking on the door.

After knocking on the door two more times, he grabs the doorknob, but I swat his hand away.

He stares at me, partially confused, partially amused. "Is something wrong?"

"It just seems like every time this happens—every time someone doesn't answer the door—and we walk inside, things end badly."

"You want to wait out here while I go in and check things out?"

"No, I don't want anyone to go in." I clutch his hand. "What I want is for the door to open and your mother to be standing there, looking super happy to see us."

He chuckles. "You're so cute."

I narrow my eyes at him. "Would you please stop saying cute like that?"

"Like what?" He's even more amused

"Like it makes me sound special or something."

"But you are special." He kisses my forehead, his lips lingering there for a moment or two before he leans back. "Even without the star in you."

I sigh. "Fine. I'm cute. And special." I turn for the door and rap my knuckles against it. "Come on. Please, just answer." I beg the door.

"Yeah, I don't think that's going to happen," Alex says with a sigh.

"But wouldn't it be so nice if, just once, something was that easy?" I give him a hopeful look.

He gives me that look again, the one he gets whenever he calls me cute. Then, instead of saying something, he fishes out his knife.

"Stay behind me," he commands then opens the door and we step inside.

The house appears empty. The floorboards creak under our weight, and the walls are covered with a layer of residue.

I trace my fingers along the wallpaper as we slowly walk from the foyer to the living room. "It's ash," I say, cleaning my hands off on my jeans.

"It's weird that it looks burned on the inside but not on the outside," Alex takes note, looking around at the furniture covered with dusty sheets.

"Maybe the fire was put out before it spread?" I offer right as a wail resonates through the house.

We both go rigid, and Alex's arm immediately shoots out, holding me back protectively.

"What is that?" I whisper, gripping the back of his shirt.

He swallows hard. "I think it's my mother."

CHAPTER
SIXTEEN

Alex

I T'S THE KIND of sound that puts hairs on end, that raises the dead from their graves, that warns people of their approaching death. This is the second time I've heard the cry of a Banshee, and I can't help wondering if more years are shaved off my life each time.

As Gemma and I walk farther into the house, I keep my knife out, unsure how my mother is going to react when she sees me. Will she appear in her hag form and be as manipulative as the Banshee I met in the alley? Or will she look and act like herself?

I hear the thud of her footsteps coming down the rickety stairway, and I dodge to the side, positioning myself between Gemma and my unborn child and my mom, just in case.

The more the idea sinks in that I'm going to be a father, the more I feel an overwhelming need to protect it. It's the craziest thing ever, but strangely, it's starting to grow on me.

The figure descends the stairs, the moonlight hitting her face. She has long, brown hair and bright, green eyes that are so much like mine I swear hers have to be fake—an illusion created to confuse me. The more I stare at her, the more I start to question if that's what her eyes really look like. Maybe it's her Banshee form. Perhaps she's trying to play with my mind.

Her hand trails along the railing as she nears the bottom of the stairs. At first, she appears enraged, like I am nothing more than an intruder, but then she smiles and opens her mouth, letting out a wail

Gemma and I cover our ears as the sound rings against our eardrums.

"Sorry." My mom's voice turns angelic as she motions for us to put down our hands. "It's a habit."

By the time I lower my hands, she has her arms around me and is hugging me so tightly I can't breathe.

"You're so grown up. I can't believe it's really you." She stares over my shoulder at Gemma as she pulls away. "And who's this?" She grows quiet, catching sight of Gemma's eyes. "I can't believe it." My mother swings around me, opens her arms wide, and gives Gemma a brief hug. "I can't believe you've made it through everything. Although, with all the madness going on with all this mark nonsense, I doubt it's over yet."

"You know about the mark, then?" I ask and then shake my head. "Of course you do. You're fey now." Wait. She's fey. What if she's marked? I point the knife at her. "How do I know you're not marked?"

She rolls up her sleeves, lifts her hair away from her neck, and shows me all the places the mark appears. "All mark free. Even my Keeper's mark is gone now that I've died."

"You're lucky," I grumble, lowering the knife. "Sometimes I wish mine was gone."

She *tsks* at me. "You need that for now. It'll help you stay alive."

She's right, but then again, if I didn't have the mark to begin with, I probably wouldn't be standing here and neither would Gemma.

"We need your help with something," I tell her, keeping my knife out for now.

"I know." She tugs her sleeves down. "I've been waiting for you to show up."

I battle to keep my anger in check. "Then why didn't you just come find me?"

"I can't leave this place." She sighs as she looks around at the burned walls. "I was assigned to watch it after I died."

"Did this place burn down once?" I ask.

"No, this is death, sweetie," she says sadly.

"I'm sorry that you've been trapped here." I can't think of anything else to say. Seeing her here makes me feel so guilty that she's been suffering, and I never even knew.

"It's not your fault," she insists.

"But it's my father's fault," I remind her.

"Which has nothing to do with you." She smooths her hand over my head like she did when I was a child. "You're so different from him, so kind and caring and protective of the one's you love. I can see it in your eyes, in the way you look at her." She glances at Gemma, whose eyes widen.

Love, she mouths to herself.

My heart slams against my chest as I open my mouth

to deny it, but the lie gets caught in my throat. I do love her. I really do. Everything about her captures me, draws me in. I hate being away from her, hate seeing her in pain. I want nothing more than for her to live.

Then why am I still alive now that I've fallen in love with her?

"So, I'm guessing you need to get to the Afterlife to see the queen," my mom breaks the tension that has filled the room.

I nod, tearing my eyes away from Gemma. "We were told that's the key to getting rid of the mark and turning the world back to normal."

"It can be done, but it's not going to be easy." She lowers herself onto the bottom step. "There are certain things required in order for someone to enter the land of the dead without actually being dead."

"What kind of things?" Gemma asks, stepping toward my mom.

"Well, the first thing you already have." My mom eye-balls the ring on Gemma's hand.

Gemma fiddles with the purple stone on the ring. "And what else do we need?"

"To look like your dead," she says, "so much so that even the queen herself won't be able to tell."

Gemma winces. "And how do I do that?"

"Not *you*." I stride toward Gemma, closing the distance between us. "*Me*."

"No, not you, sweetie." My mom's gaze lands on Gemma. "It has to be her."

"No fucking way." My voice cracks, and it feels like I've swallowed a jar of needles. "I'm never going to let that happen."

"It has to be me," Gemma presses, her hands balled

into fists at her sides. "And it should be. This is all my fault."

"It's not your fault." I tuck a strand of her hair behind her ear. "None of this is. If anything, it's mine. I should have saved you earlier. We would've had so much more time to stop this."

"It doesn't matter," she says. "Whether it's my fault or not, it has to be me. I've seen it. I've seen myself dead in a coffin and Nicholas is waiting for me."

"You dreamed about this?" I rub my hands across my face, wanting to yell at her and kiss her at the same time.

She shrugs. "Since you left."

I shake my head and flex my fingers. "I don't give a shit how you dreamed it happens. We don't have to do it that way just because you saw it. We can make our own path, create our own future."

"She has to be the one who goes," my mom interrupts, rising to her feet. "She was given the ring, she has the connection to the ghost world, and she's the Foreseer who shifted the vision that turned the world into all of this. She has to be the one to fix it. It's the only way this will work." I start to protest, but she talks over me. "I know it's not fair—I know it's not her fault—but that's the way things are. If you do it any other way, it's not going to work. The queen won't accept you."

Gemma steps forward with determination. "So how do I make myself look dead?"

"She's pregnant," I sputter in desperation. "If she dies, then the baby could die, too."

"I thought I sensed another soul here." My mother smiles down at Gemma's stomach. "What an amazing gift, to bring life into this world."

"Will it . . . ? Will it hurt the baby if I go?" Gemma asks

tentatively.

My mom shakes her head. "We're only pulling your spirit out of your body. While you're gone, your body will be fine, the baby will be fine."

"This is such bullshit," I snap, but neither of them so much as look at me.

My mom places her hand on Gemma's belly and smiles.

Frustrated that everyone seems to be okay with Gemma pulling her spirit out of her body and paying a visit to the Afterlife, I move between them and do something I've never done.

I fucking beg.

"Please, don't do this," I plead with Gemma, clutching onto her shoulders.

"Alex," she says so softly, "I'll be fine. Your mom won't let anything happen to me."

I shake my head, panicking, a foreign feeling to me and one I'm not a fan of. "I can't lose you."

She places her hand on my scruffy cheek. "You're not going to, I promise. But I have to go. I'll never be able to live with myself if I don't save the world from the chaos I helped cause."

I feel so fucking helpless I want to scream as the two of them start making a plan.

"You'll need to have a funeral," my mom says, pacing the floor. "Helena needs to think you're dead."

Gemma nods. "I actually saw that in my dream."

"I think we need a different plan," I snap, "one where she doesn't have to die."

They don't even so much as glance in my direction.

"And we need a witch, one we can trust." She turns to me, looking hopeful. "What about your sister?"

"Aislin's marked," I say, still pissed the hell off. *I need another plan. I can't handle her dying.* "So she can't help us."

"Hang on. I think I might know someone who can." She spins around and whisks up the stairs.

I shake my head, irritated and on the verge of grabbing Gemma and running as far away from here as I can. I could always drain her of her energy, make her pass out, but that might hurt the baby.

"Stop looking at me like that," Gemma says, shifting uncomfortably. "It has to be me."

"No, it doesn't." I keep looking at her, letting the electricity get to her, hoping she'll lose focus of her sacrificial plan. "Give me the ring and let me do it."

She tucks her hand behind her back, shaking her head. "You heard your mom; I caused this. It has to be me."

"Stop being stubborn. We can at least try to do it with me." I face her, begging again, "Please don't do it."

"I'll come back," she promises. "I can't die completely, not without you."

"I'm not worried about you dying. I'm worried about you getting hurt. I can't stand the thought."

When she says nothing, frustration bursts inside me. I spin around and ram my fist into the wall, causing a crack to splinter across the sheetrock.

"Holy shit," Gemma says. "Are you okay?"

I cradle my hand, facing her again. "No. And I won't be until you promise me you won't do this."

"All right," my mother interrupts us as she jogs down the stairs, "my witch is on board, but you two are going to have to go to her place and pick it up."

"Pick up what?" Gemma and I say at the same time.

She hands me a piece of paper with an address on it, her body flashing for the briefest moment, and I worry she's about to transform into her hag form.

"The poison that's going to kill Gemma."

CHAPTER
SEVENTEEN

Gemma

I 'M GOING TO pretend I'm not scared out of my damn mind, but the very idea of dying is overwhelming enough. Adding poison to the mix has my heart racing a million miles a minute. But it's worth the fear, knowing soon I'll be able to fix the world to what it once was, without the possession of the mark. Everyone will be free, including Aislin, Laylen, and Aleesa.

I can't let Alex know I'm terrified, though. I have to play it cool, because he's already freaking out enough for the both of us.

Ever since his mother made the announcement about the poison, he went from a mad-crazy-begging Alex to a walking-silently-with-his-eyebrows-knitted-together Alex. He's contemplating something deeply—I can tell—and my bet is that it's a way for him to die instead of me.

Since Alex's mom can't leave the house, Alex and I make the journey to the witch's place alone. We silently walk down the snowy sidewalk underneath the glow of the lampposts as thick snowflakes drift from the cloudy night sky, and the cool air kisses my cheeks.

"Why do you think it's so quiet around here?" I ask as we turn south and head down a winding road that slopes toward more houses.

"I'm not sure." He tucks his hands in his pockets. "But I don't like it. At least when things are noisy, you know what's going on. When it's quiet, it leaves you guessing, and I hate guessing."

"I know you do." I look at the all houses around us. Are their families in them? Are they watching us? "It's just so different here. In Afton, there were vampires, faeries, and witches everywhere, but here, there's . . . nothing. Everything in the airport seemed pretty empty. It's like the apocalypse hasn't reached here yet or something."

"Maybe it hasn't." But his voice carries doubt. "Or maybe we aren't looking—" He suddenly snatches hold of my hand and jogs to the other side of the street. "We have to leave. Now."

I slip on the ice, struggling to keep up with him as he hunkers down and keeps running.

"What's wrong?" I ask, breathless.

He continues running down the sidewalk, reaching for his knife.

"Alex, tell me what's going on." I whisper as he slams to a stop near a large trashcan pressed up against the side of a house.

"Take us away from here," he says, pacing from left to right. "We need to go. Now"

I shake my head. "Not until you tell me why you're freaking out. Is this because of the poison?"

"No, it's because that wasn't my mom back there." He kicks the wall and curses.

"Yes, it was—"

He covers my mouth with his hand, shushing me. "Don't you think it's a little strange that this is all so easy? That we just walked in there, and she had all the information with a flawless plan?"

I wait for him to remove his hand. "Yeah, but I don't think your mom would lie to us. She seemed so nice and happy about stuff."

"When she first came downstairs, I thought she looked unreal. Her eyes were too similar to mine, and I don't remember my mom's eyes being like that. And then, when she gave me the paper with the address, I swear I saw her shifting into someone else. I thought it might have been her hag form, but it just came to me who she is." He lets out a long exhale, his head lowering as he pinches the bridge of his noise. "It's the Banshee that took me to Draven."

I slump my back against the house. "But she looked like your mom."

"Banshees can alter their looks, Gemma," he says, lifting his gaze to mine.

All my hope of fixing the mess I created is squashed in an instant. "Why would another Banshee do that?" I coddle my belly, thinking about how I let her touch it.

"I'm not sure." He grazes his fingers up my arm, trying to comfort me. "But we need to get as far away from here as we can until I can figure it out."

"Are you just trying to make it so I won't die and go to the Afterlife?"

"As much as I don't want you to go, that's not what this is about." He places an arm on each side of me. "But I'm not going to fucking lie to you. For now, I'm glad that wasn't my mom, because that means you're not going to the Afterlife."

My heart hammers inside my chest as he bends his arms, bringing himself closer to me.

"Alex, I still have to do it. I have to fix what I did."

"And we'll find a way"—he moves closer, closer, closer—"but it will be one where you don't have to temporarily die. I can't let that happen." He wets his lips with his tongue, all his attention zoning in on my mouth. "About what my mom said back at the house—"

Suddenly, garbage cans tumble over, and a dog howls. Alex spins on his heels, swinging the knife, ready to kill.

"Well, look at you two, hiding out by the trash cans like two frightened, little kids." Laylen's tall silhouette emerges from the shadows, and just above our heads, a porch light suddenly clicks on.

Laylen grins as the light hits his face. "Good job," he says to the air.

I want to run up and hug him, tell him I'm sorry this happened to him, but Alex pushes me back.

"Motherfucker," Alex growls, aiming the knife at Laylen's throat. "Where the hell did you come from?"

A grin creeps up Laylen's face, his fangs pointing sharply from his mouth. "I thought you'd be happy to see me like this, just the way you always saw me—as a killer."

Alex rolls his eyes. "Don't be overdramatic."

"I think he always saw you for what you were supposed to be." Aislin appears out of nowhere, rising from the night. Her golden hair blows in the wind, and an evil grin spreads across her lips as she walks up to Laylen and strokes his shoulder. "What we were both supposed to be."

Marking their forearms is a triangle outlined with a red, Greek-like symbol—the Mark of Malefiscus. The sight of it sends a shiver down my spine, and Alex notices my shudder.

"Get us out of here," Alex hisses under his breath, but I can't seem to take my eyes off them, like they've pulled me into some kind of trance.

"She's fixated by me," Laylen says, sweeping his hair back with his blue eyes trained on me. "She's remembering the bite and how good it felt."

I touch my neck as the memory sparkles in my mind. "I feel funny . . ."

"Gemma." Alex hooks a finger under my chin, and the nick of his sparks rips me out of the daze. "Don't look at him. Just get us out of here."

I hesitate. "We can't just leave them."

He looks me dead in the eye. "I know you want to save them, but right now, you need to take care of yourself more than others."

Even though it feels like it's going to kill me, I shut my eyes and picture the first place that comes to mind—Sin City. We've escaped there before. *That should work for now.*

But something feels wrong the moment I try to visualize Alex and I standing in the glittery streets. I open my eyes and catch Laylen and Aislin trading a knowing smile.

"They have praesidium on them," I say. "There's nothing we can do except run."

"You run. I'll distract them." With that, Alex spins around and rams into Laylen.

They collide and fall to the frostbitten ground, throwing punches and kicks.

My gaze darts to Aislin who's watching me like a hawk.

"Sucks, doesn't it?" She coils a strand of hair around

JESSICA SORENSEN

her finger as she strolls toward me. "Feeling so vulnerable, yet you can't do anything about it." Her expression hardens. "Like when I had to sit there and watch you bat your eyes at Laylen like some kind of lovesick girl"—her high-heeled boots click against the ice as she continues toward me—"watch the way he looked at you until it almost drove me mad—"she stops right in front of me—"but those days are almost over. Soon, you'll be gone—dead and rotting in the ground."

"We don't have to do this," I say, backing up against the wall. "You might not remember, but we're friends, and we care about each other."

"Friends?" She laughs, throwing her head back. "Oh, my God, what are we, like in sixth grade?" She clasps her hands in front of her, and her skin erupts in a green glow as she prepares to use her magic. "Oh, Aislin, please don't hurt me. You're my best friend in the whole wide world."

I attack, slamming into her and sending us to the ground. Her glowing skin fizzles out as we crash to the snow. I land on top of her, but I'm not sure what to do. This is Aislin, mark or no mark, and I don't want to hurt her. But when her eyes blaze red and she elevates her hands, I panic and slam my knuckles hard into her jaw.

"Oh, my God, I'm so sorry," I apologize, feeling like a jerk.

She barks a laugh, throwing her weight forward and flipping us to the side. My head smacks against the ground, and snow tumbles all around me. I reach for her coat pocket, hoping that's where the praesidium is, but before I can get a hold of it, she bites my hand, making me scream bloody murder.

More garbage cans topple over as Alex and Laylen roll farther away from us, and she bites me again.

Screw this shit!

"That's it. I've had enough. If you want to play dirty, then let's play dirty." I grab a fist full of her hair and tug on it while slipping my other hand into her pocket.

Jackpot!

I take the praesidium from her pocket, but she slaps my hand and sends the marble flying. She seizes my leg as I roll out from under her and scramble after it.

I flip over onto my back and kick her in the face. "I'm so sorry," I say as blood gushes from her nose. Then I shove away from her, scoop up the marble, and jog in the direction of where I last saw Laylen and Alex.

But Aislin wraps her fingers around my ankle again and flings me back down to the ground. I brace myself as I fall for the ice, protecting my stomach as much as possible. I roll over onto my back just in time to see an orb of red light flying at me.

I don't think.

I just go.

CHAPTER
EIGHTEEN

Gemma

W HEN I LAND on the black and white tile floor of Adessa's store, I'm instantly aware that I didn't make it here alone. I brought a crazed out Aislin with me, still gripping onto my leg, her eyes wide and murderous.

"I have to take you to him," she growls rabidly. "I have to take you to him." Her nails dig into my leg as she drags herself up my body.

"Adessa!" I shout, kicking at Aislin. *Please let her be home. And let her be* her.

By the scared look on Aislin's face, I think she knows she's in trouble if Adessa is here since Adessa is much more powerful. But when we both realize how quiet the house is, Aislin relaxes.

"Guess she's not home." She leaps to her feet and sticks out her hands. "Duratus!"

I scurry for the front door of the store, but the massive ball of light slams into my chest. My muscles immediately stiffen as I lose all control of my limbs and crumple to the floor.

My skull throbs as I lie there helplessly, and all I can think about is the baby inside me. Is it okay? Is it hurt? Can it feel all of this?

Aislin crouches beside me and reaches for my locket. "Guess it's not working anymore, or maybe my magic is stronger than sugilite now." She snaps the chain from my neck. "It's an immobilizing spell, by the way. Sucks not being the one in control, doesn't it?"

I open my mouth to beg her to stop, to remind her she could be an aunt soon, but no sound comes out. I try to Foresee my way out of here, but the spell secures me to the floor.

"I'm not sure what to do with you." She rises to her feet and roams around the room, running her fingers along the glass cases. She picks up a figurine of a woman with beautiful wings—a Black Angel—and turns it over in her hand. "You know, I'm supposed to take you to my father—the mark's begging me to—but I don't know." She thrums her finger against her lips. "I'd like to see you suffer a little before I do that." She glares at the figurine with spite. "Wait a minute. I have an idea." Excitement glimmers in her eyes as she sets the statue down. "I'll be right back." She grins. "Don't go anywhere."

With a swish of her hands, she vanishes in a vapor of smoke.

MINUTES GO BY, maybe hours, and still no Aislin. I'm glad, yet at the same time, I'm sick of helplessly lying on the floor, waiting for her to return.

Plus, Adessa has the most annoying faucet that keeps dripping and dripping and dripping. It's driving me crazy, but it's nothing compared to my worry over Alex and if he's okay.

Eventually, my eyelids grow heavy, and I somehow pass out.

"How did we get here?" Alex asks me, glancing around at the field of flowers surrounding us.

I shrug. "I don't know. I was thinking of you before I closed my eyes. Maybe that's how."

"You're worried," he states, picking a violet flower from the field, "about me, about Laylen, Aislin."—he tucks the stem of the flower behind my ear—"the baby."

I nod. "I just want everyone to be okay."

"You're always worrying about everyone else." His arms circle my waist. "You need to worry about yourself sometimes."

"I'll try," I promise, "but I need to know if you're hurt . . . if Laylen hurt you."

He simply smiles then leans in to kiss me, causing my heart to flutter in my chest. When he pulls away, I'm breathless and lightheaded, and I grip on to him to keep from sinking to the ground.

He drops his lips to my ear. "Everything's going to be okay," he whispers, "but you need to wake up now."

My eyelids shoot open right as a thump echoes through the store.

This is it. She's going to kill me.

All I can do is I cross my fingers that somehow Aislin's returned to her normal self during the time she's been gone. I hold my breath as someone walks into the room, but when I see who it is, I breathe in relief.

Adessa's golden, cat-shaped eyes land on me as she slams to a stop in the doorway. "Gemma? What are you doing here?"

I try to nod, but my head won't budge.

"Why are you . . . ?" Her eyes sweep the room before she kneels down beside me, inspecting me then yelling, "Liberum!"

The numbness leaves my body, and I jump to my feet, wanting to get as far away from this place as possible. "We have to get out of here. Now."

"What's going on?" she asks, rising to her feet.

I give her a quick recap of what's going on with Aislin, biting my nails the entire time, worried Aislin is going to show up.

"So she's marked, but she can remove the mark. Interesting." Adessa considers the situation while pacing the floor. "And you don't know where she went?"

I shake my head then head for the front door. "But with how pissed off she is, I'm guessing it has something to do with a torture device or a crazy-ass spell that will turn me into a rodent or something equally as gross."

Adessa captures my sleeve before I make it very far. "I can fix this, take the mark off her."

I scrutinize her as my muscles wind into knots. "How do I know you're not marked?"

She rolls her sleeves up then sweeps her hair to the side and shows me her shoulders and neck.

Satisfied, I lean against the doorway. "You think you can remove the mark, then?"

"If you can remember how Aislin removed the mark," Adessa says, twisting a pendant around her neck.

"I think I can."

"Tell me, then. And try to remember every little

detail."

After we sit down on the velvet sofa in the living room attached to the store, I get really fidgety. "Aislin could come back any minute," I warn. "We should probably go somewhere else and talk about this."

"If we go somewhere else, we'll have to track Aislin down again." She stretches her hand toward the ceiling. "Me tenebris et tueri nos." A dark cloud funnels from her hand. "There, that'll keep her away for a bit." She dusts her hands off. "Now go ahead and explain the spell to me."

I feel the slightest bit better. "Well, the first thing she did is go to the graveyard to summon some kind of witch spirit to give her more power. Then she created the spell itself. First, she cuts into the middle of the mark so blood drips out."

"To bleed out the evil." Adessa nods her head. "That makes sense."

"Then she inserts some kind of potion—I think she called it Vitis . . . vinifera—which is supposed to free them from the evil connection. Then the last thing she does is chant some sort of spell . . . liberare vos . . . ligaveris, I think."

Adessa springs to her feet and lifts open the top of the apothecary table. Inside are bags filled with various kinds of herbs. She takes one out and shuts the lid.

"Does this look like what she used?" she asks, holding a bag of crushed green leaves in front of my face.

"I think so." I squint at the bag. "But it doesn't matter if you have all the stuff. You need the power of that ghost flame woman."

Adessa smiles warmly. "Has Laylen ever told you anything about me?"

"Um . . . a little."

"Well, did he ever mention how old I am?"

I shake my head, remembering how pissed off Sophia used to get when someone assumed her age.

My heart suddenly squeezes in my chest as I remember all the soulless years I spent with Sophia and how confused I felt when Aislin broke the news to me that Sophia and Marco might be dead. Aislin discovered that information when she was trying to locate Keepers with a Tracker Spell; only, the spell informed her they no longer existed, which more than likely means they're dead.

"I'm two-hundred fifty-eight," Adessa sates proudly. "And do you know how I've lived this long?" She stands up with her shoulders squared and her chin elevated. "Because I'm that powerful."

Without warning, she spans her hands out to her sides and tips her head back. "Isabella, come to me!"

A roaring fire ignites in the middle of the room, and a flaming woman materializes in the center of the flames. She lets out a deafening wail, and I cover my ears as Adessa chants under her breath, settling the fire woman down.

"You've been hiding something from me, Isabella," Adessa says sternly. "Is there something you'd like to tell me?"

The fire woman hisses at Adessa, blowing smoke into her face.

"Don't take that attitude with me," Adessa says. "You've been lying to me for a very long time."

The flame woman tips her head back and screeches again.

"Stop being a pain in the ass and hand it over." Adessa sticks out her hand and waits.

The fire woman huffs. Then, with a scowl, she blows a

breath of smoke into Adessa's palm.

"Go now." Adessa flexes her fingers.

When the fire woman dissipates, Adessa turns to me, grinning. "Now that I've taken care of that, I think I can make the spell work, but I'm going to need your help with something first. It's very dangerous, but very important to me. I'm going to be straightforward with you, Gemma. What we're about to do is very risky."

I look down at my stomach, remembering what Alex said, that I needed to take care of myself.

"I'm not sure I can."

Adessa tracks my gaze, and her brows shoot up in surprise. "You're with child?"

I nervously nod. "I think so."

She considers something before stepping forward and reaching for my belly. "May I?" she asks and I nod. She gently places her hand on my belly, and a smile touches her lips. "She's a strong one."

"*She?*" My heart hits my chest hard. "How do you know it's a she?"

"It's one of the gifts I have, among many others." Her brows knit as she continues to stare at my belly. "Do you want to protect her?"

"I do, but it's unbelievably hard when everything around me is so dangerous." Tears burn at my eyes. "I've been hit by so many spells, fallen so many times . . . I'm getting worried."

"She's fine." She glances up at me. "And she can be fine, even when you're not."

I wipe the tears away with the back of my hand. "What do you mean?"

"I mean, I can put a spell on her that will allow her to survive even if something happens to you. I can help you save the one you care about the most," she says, "and in return, you'll help me save what I care about the most."

I'm surprised how easily I agree. With a simple nod, I protect my daughter and put myself in danger again.

But somehow, it feels like the most right thing I've ever done in my life.

CHAPTER
NINETEEN

Alex

I 'M GOING TO fucking kill him, strangle him to death. At least, I want to. But I can't. Killing Laylen would nearly kill Gemma, and she'd hate me for it. Besides, that would be stooping to my father's level, and no matter how hard he's tried to turn me into one of his murderous soldiers, I refuse to be that horrible person. I'm stronger than that. I have to be for the world, for Gemma, for my child.

I hold back on the strangling and, instead, knock Laylen out with a snow shovel. Once he collapses to the ground, I drag his body under a tarp beside a pile of firewood so no one will find and hurt him. Then I try to come up with some kind of plan to salvage this mess.

I have an unconscious, killer vampire on my hands, and the two people who could help me are missing. Not to mention, one of them is bat-shit crazy at the moment.

In the middle of my plan making, I somehow end up

in a field with Gemma. Initially, I'm confused, but then I remember the last time we met like this, and I smile to myself. She's dreaming of me.

After I leave the dream, I thrum my fingers on the sides of my legs as I pace back and forth in front of the woodpile. I don't know how this happened, how Aislin and Laylen found us, but it seems way too coincidental that, the moment we left the Banshee's house, the two of them showed up. There has to be a connection

Either I can run away, go back to the airport and fly home, or go back and see what the Banshee knows.

WHEN I ARRIVE back at the house, she's wailing her cry of death. I barge in without knocking, and the pleased look on her face is enough that I see red.

"Good. You're alone," she purrs. "Just what I wanted."

I stride toward her and shove her against the wall.

"Who are you?" I demand, pushing her again.

She trips back and lands on the floor, wincing as she twists her ankle. "Don't you think I should be asking you the same thing?" she growls.

"You don't get to ask questions." I crouch down in front of her and press the tip of my knife to the base of her throat. "Now, who are you?"

When her lips remain sealed, I press the tip of the blade into her skin just enough to draw a few drops of blood. She winces then, with a venomous growl, the color of her eyes turns from green to blue and her hair from brown to blond, transforming into the Banshee from the alley

I shake my head. "I knew it."

"You didn't think Draven would just hand you the information without a price, did you?" she snaps, baring her teeth then trying to bite my hand.

"I did pay a price." I poke her again with the knife. "Remember, he gets a year of my life."

"Like that matters to him. What he really wants to know is why you're seeking a Banshee." She scoots across the floor and backs herself into the corner. "Who are you really? And why do you need the help of a Banshee?"

"I'm not telling you anything," I say calmly, standing up straight. "Not until you tell me why you brought me out here. What was the purpose of tricking me into coming all the way out to Iceland? Because I know there has to be a reason when it comes to Draven. He doesn't do things just because."

"This is the entrance to the Afterlife," she says simply, gesturing at the walls. "This is where you cross over."

"I'm not going anywhere."

"You don't have a choice. You owe Draven."

"I owe him nothing," I snap, the floorboards creaking below me as I stalk toward her. "That deal was made based on the assumption that the address I was given would take me to my mom, so unless you want to tell me where she is, I'm not handing over a year of my life."

She crawls on her hands and knees for the window and pulls herself up by gripping onto the sill. "We don't just give away information about our kind, not unless we fully understand why someone seeks one of us."

In three long strides, I'm in her face. "Where's my mom? You have to know where she is . . . She's one of you."

Her eyelids narrow to slits. "If you really want to

know, then fine. She's in hiding in a place where no one wants to hide."

I wrap my fingers around her throat. "Where. Is. She?"

"I'll tell you." When she grins, somehow I know I'm about to make another bargain, probably one I can't afford. "But it'll cost you."

CHAPTER
TWENTY

Gemma

"TESHA'S A FRIEND of mine," Adessa explains as we hunker down behind a car parked in front of a building with flashing neon lights. "If we can get back to the house, I can take the mark off her, and then we can start removing it from everyone else."

I peek over the hood of the car to glance at the female vampire with chin-length hair and pointy ears that I'm supposed to help Adessa save. According to Adessa, the two of them are really close friends, but after listening to Adessa talk about her while we walked to this place, I wonder if they might be more than that.

"But what if the spell doesn't work on her? I mean, you haven't tried it on anyone else yet," I point out, scanning the area for any sign of vampires, witches, or fey who might be lurking around in the shadows.

"You're doubting my magic?" Adessa questions, pressing a glance in the direction of my stomach.

After Adessa performed the spell to protect my

daughter, the sound of her heart has been crystal clear. And all that worry I felt about her being hurt has vanished. Somehow, I can feel the spell working, reassuring me that she's going to be okay, even if I'm not.

"Do you have a game plan?" I ask, sneaking a peek over the hood of the car again.

Tesha is now chatting with a man twice her size with fiery red eyes and skin as white as snow. My bet is that he's a vampire, too. Great. Things just got even more complicated.

"I'm not sure," Adessa says with a sigh, leaning back against the wheel of the truck. "I've been trying to get to her for weeks, but it's useless. She either runs away from me or tries to kill me."

"What about another spell? Like a summoning one?"

"She's protected from most of my spells, thanks to me. She can even sense when I'm coming after her, thanks to a stupid connection spell I did a long time ago. At the time, I thought it was a fantastic idea, but now I realize it was stupid." She crosses her arms. "We probably have maybe three or four minutes before she senses me."

"Okay, so what do you want me to do? Because I'm guessing there's a reason you brought me with you."

Adessa gathers her hair into a low ponytail and fastens it with an elastic on her wrist. "Well, you're a Keeper and a Foreseer, which makes you both very powerful and very strong. Plus, you can appear out of nowhere, and since Tesha has never met you, she shouldn't be able to feel your presence."

"Shouldn't be able to?" I question, arching my brows.

"You'll be fine." She pats my hand. "You're stronger than you give yourself credit for."

I'm not sure if she's telling me the whole story, but it

doesn't really matter. My daughter is protected, and I owe Adessa for that.

I peer around at the cars, the street, and then the building. "I'm going to Foresee my way over there, grab her, and blink us back here. You better be ready to do the spell because I'm betting that I'm not going to be able to hold her for very long."

Adessa nods, opening up the bag of herbs she brought with us. "Be careful. And don't hurt her."

"I'm not going to, but I'm not going in unarmed, either. I need a weapon."

Reluctantly, Adessa reaches into her pocket and draws out a pocketknife. "It's all I have."

I flip open the dull blade. "I guess it'll have to do."

"Please, don't hurt her," she begs again. "No staking her in the chest or anything like that."

"I'll try not to." I start to close my eyes when she grasps onto my arm.

"Gemma, I love her," she whispers, her eyes pleading with me.

I nod my head, my thoughts briefly drifting back to Iceland and how Alex's mom—or who I thought was Alex's mom—said Alex loves me. It terrifies me to my very soul, but in the craziest, most breathless, overwhelming way possible. I know there's no way he could love me since I'm still alive. Or maybe he does, and I don't feel the same way for him yet.

I shake the thought from my head.

"I promise I won't hurt her."

Adessa lets go of my hand. "You'll have to be the one to puncture her mark. It's on her left wrist."

Nodding, I shut my eyes and picture the front door of the casino, and just like that, I'm standing in front of

Tesha and the tall man with fiery red eyes.

"Well, what do we have here?" Tesha says, eyeing me over with hunger in her eyes.

"A treat," the man says, lunging for me.

Slamming my hands against his chest, I shove him back with all my strength. He barely stumbles, but it gives me enough time to grab Tesha's arm, shut my eyes, and whisk us back to the car where Adessa is waiting.

As soon as we land on the asphalt, I push Tesha down. Her fangs snap out, and she nicks my arm with one of them. Grabbing her wrist, I wrestle her down and make the incision across the triangular mark on her arm. She snarls, trying to bite me, but then, as if she can't resist herself, sinks her teeth into her own arm where the blood is seeping out.

"Adessa!" I shout, trying to pin Tesha down. "Do it now!"

Adessa frantically kneels beside us, her hands trembling as she opens the bag of Vitis vinifera. She sticks some flakes into the open wound, mixing it with the blood. Tesha bites at my arm again, and pissed off as hell, I slap her.

She blinks, stunned, and then her eyes turn murderous. "I'm going to kill you for that," she growls.

"No, you're not," Adessa's says, raising her hands. He skin blazes with a flame so powerful I can feel the energy flowing through my own veins. "Liberare vos ligaveris!"

The flames roar and Tesha screams as the mark slithers off her skin and melts into the ground, liquefying into the asphalt.

I'm so relieved it worked. Now Aislin and Laylen can be saved, too. That is, if nothing has happened to them already.

I sit back on my heels and take a few measured breaths, trying to ease the wooziness that suddenly overcomes me.

"I'm so sorry." Tears pour down Tesha's cheeks as she crawls over to Adessa and wraps her arms around her

"It's not your fault." Adessa rubs her hand up and down Tesha's back.

Nope. It's mine. All mine.

Unable to stop myself, I crawl away from them and throw up in the grass. After I've emptied my stomach, I sit down on the curb and rest my head on my knees until Tesha and Adessa walk over.

"And who is she?" Tesha asks, looking down at me, and Adessa smiles at Tesha in a way that makes me grin.

After Adessa gives Tesha the details of who I am, I Foresee the three of us back to Adessa's store. The moment we land in the living room, we're faced with another huge problem.

Adessa sees Aislin standing in the shadows of the room, and she immediately elevates her hands into the air, ready to fire.

"I wouldn't do that if I were you," Aislin warns, straightening her stance. "Otherwise, we all die."

"You did a Magic Binding Spell?" Adessa's voice carries both horror and awe.

Aislin shrugs. "I've gotten way more powerful since the last time you saw me."

Adessa eyes her over, her gaze lingering on the mark. "I can see that."

Aislin's lips curl into a grin as she emerges from the shadows and steps into the light, towing a chain with her. "Remember these," Aislin asks, jerking at a chain.

A woman with black hair emerges from the shadows

right behind Aislin. She's wearing a corset top, lace-up leather boots, and sprouting from her back are a pair of wide, black-feathered wings.

"A Black Angel?" I gape at Aislin. "How did you get one of those?"

"Wouldn't you like to know?" Aislin sneers, tugging on the chain again.

The Black Angel trips forward, a low growl rumbling from her lips as she glares at me. I try not to look her directly in the eyes as I circle the room, my Keeper instincts kicking into high gear.

Aislin lets the chain go and stalks toward Adessa. "Let's get this over with." Her palms ignite as she raises her arms above her head.

The Black Angel tracks my movements, snarling at me, so I move to the right, as does it, skittering around and blocking the exit.

I dare a glance at Aislin and see Tesha tackling her while Adessa chants a spell. Aislin claws at her face, and Tesha's hair lights on fire. She screams, and Adessa's skin pales. I run for them, but the Black Angel mimics my move and gets in my way. She flaps her wings and the wind howls. I shield my eyes as glass and papers funnel around the room. Then the Black Angel growls again, snapping her teeth, as she races forward and stands before me.

Our gazes collide, and just like that, I'm paralyzed, helpless again, bound to her by a trance. She creeps toward me, dragging the chains behind her, silently whispering for me to free her. My hands raise, my limbs no longer under my own freewill. I fight not to do it, battle to keep control of myself, but I end up reaching for the cuffs around the Black Angel's wrists.

Using my Keeper strength, I snap the metal into pieces and free her from her imprisonment.

I scream at the top of my lungs, knowing what's about to happen, and the Black Angel cries with me as papers and glass continue to fly through the air.

Then everything grows really quiet.

My knees buckle, and I collapse to the floor, landing on my side. I lie there for what feels like forever until I can finally move again. Pushing to my feet, I dust myself off, feeling fine.

"I'm okay," I breathe in relief.

Then I catch sight of Aislin, Adessa, and Tesha. Aislin looks fine, and I notice the mark is no longer on her. I want to celebrate, but the fear in their eyes stops me.

"What's wrong?" I ask, brushing the pieces of glass out of my hair.

Before anyone can answer, I hear heavy breathing from the side of me. Instinctively, I spin around.

A tall woman wearing a blue dress smiles at me.

"See you in hell, Gemma." She winks at me then disappears into thin air.

I start to put two and two together, and my gaze drops to my arms. The same symbols that traced Laylen's arm now trace mine.

I trace my finger along the ink. "The Mark of Immortality." I gasp, rapidly reaching around behind me. My eyes snap wide as my fingertips brush soft feathers. "Oh, my God. I have wings."

CHAPTER
TWENTY-ONE

Alex

THE BARGAIN I just made is going to cost me a lot more than before. More than my life. More than a year working for Draven.

The damn Banshee wants my soul. It's the reason she led me out here, thinking if she somehow got me alone, she could trick me into handing my soul over to her. When Gemma showed up with me, she saw an even better opportunity. Apparently, when someone sacrifices their own life, their soul is more valuable. So if Gemma had drunk the poison, her soul would belong to her and give her more power.

Thankfully, that never happened, but the Banshee is still convinced she's going to somehow get my soul. What she stupidly doesn't realize is that my soul belongs to Gemma. Literally. It's something I haven't told Gemma yet, that when we made the forever blood promise, I actually gave her a piece of my soul.

That's why I can't make the deal with the Banshee woman, no matter what she tries to bribe me with. It doesn't mean I am going to give up, though. If she knows where my mom is, I have to get the information out of her. I just need some time to figure out how to do that.

I leave the house with the Banshee wailing at me to come back. I head back to the woodpile to check on Laylen, finding him still lying unconscious underneath the tarp, drooling all over himself.

"What am I supposed to do with you?" I mutter, crouching down beside him. "I'd just leave you here, but I'm pretty sure Gemma would hate me if I did that, and I can't deal with her hating me."

"I can fix him," Aislin's voice sails over my shoulder.

I jump up and whirl around with my knife out. "What did you do to Gemma?"

Aislin sticks her hands in the air. "She's fine. I'm fine. Everything's fine now." She nods at her arm that's no longer marked.

"Gemma freed you?" I ask, impressed. "How?"

"She went to Adessa's and got her help," Aislin explains, her hands falling to her side. "But not without running into a few other problems."

I sigh heavily. "What happened now?"

"I'd rather you just come with me and see for yourself," she says, picking her fingernails, a nervous habit of hers.

I nod at the woodpile. "You want to take care of him first."

She smacks herself in the forehead. "Oh, yeah, duh." She rushes over to Laylen and quickly works her magic, removing the mark from him.

When Laylen wakes up, he's extremely disoriented.

"What happened?" He clutches his head. "And why does it feel like someone punched me in the head."

"No one punched you in the head." I pull him to his feet. "I just clocked you over the head with a shovel."

He blinks dazedly at me, and then his expression plummets. "Shit . . . I was . . ." He looks down at his arm where the mark used to be then shakes his head, looking disgusted. "What did I do?"

I could tell him everything he did—how he attacked us, drank Gemma's blood, and tied her up—but for some crazy reason, I don't want to make him feel guilty. Maybe it's because I'm tired, or maybe Gemma's kindness is starting to rub off on me.

"Nothing too bad," I lie.

He looks unconvinced but doesn't say anything.

"We need to get back to Adessa's," Aislin announces. "Like now."

"You're starting to worry me," I admit to Aislin, tucking the knife in my back pocket.

She opens her mouth, worry written all over her face. "Let's just get going, okay?"

My heart races in my chest. "Please, just tell me she's not hurt."

"Not with any injuries," she replies, avoiding eye contact with me.

"What about the . . . ?" I rake my fingers through my hair and lower my voice. "The baby?"

Aislin looks taken aback. "You know about that?"

I nod. "Tell me it's okay."

"Well, turns out, it's a she," Aislin says. "And yeah, she's okay."

"*She?*" I blink. "I'm having a daughter."

Aislin smiles tensely. "You're having a daughter, and

I'm going to be an aunt."

My mind is racing a million miles a minute as the three of us huddle together, preparing to go to Vegas.

"I need to warn you to prepare yourself," Aislin suddenly says.

I open my mouth to ask why, but she's already taking us away.

CHAPTER
TWENTY-TWO

Gemma

WHEN AISLIN, LAYLEN, and Alex materialize in Adessa's living room, I immediately duck behind the sofa, embarrassed over how I look.

"What was that?" Alex asks with a hint of repulsion in his voice.

I want to cry, but at the same time, I want to kick him for being such an asshole.

"Gemma, you can come out," Aislin says tentatively. "No one's going to hurt you or judge you. I promise."

"I'd rather just stay here until this is fixed," I say, curling up in a ball.

"I don't get it," Laylen says softly. "Why did it look like she has . . . wings?"

He sounds like his old self, thank God. At least one good thing came out of all of this.

"Gemma, please come out," Aislin says. "I can't help you if you don't."

Heaving a sigh, I rise to my feet. I feel like an animal

in a zoo as Alex and Laylen gawk at me. Their eyes are wide and full of horror, and I feel so ashamed of how I look.

On top of having huge-ass wings sprouting out of my back, I'm also stuck in the corset dress the Black Angel was wearing when I freed her. The fabric barely covers my ass. Not to mention, I'm stuck in heels I can barely walk in.

Laylen gives me a once over, and then his blue eyes meet mine. I want to run up and give him the biggest hug I can muster.

"You're back," I say, smiling.

He smiles, but there's a drop of sadness in his eyes, probably guilt over the stuff he did. "Yeah, I'm back."

I avoid Alex's eyes altogether, because I won't be able to handle it if he even so much as has a speck of disgust in his gaze.

"So, there was an accident," I utter quietly.

"What kind of accident?" Laylen asks with caution in his tone.

"It's my fault." Aislin bursts into tears. "I brought the Black Angel here."

"It's not your fault," I tell her. "You weren't yourself."

Tears cascade down her cheeks. "Yes, it was. I did this. And I was so mean about it. God, the evil me is such a bitch."

"Yeah, but if it wouldn't have been for me, the mark would have never gotten so out of control," I remind her.

While she shakes her head and continues bawling, Laylen puts his arms around her and allows her to cry against his chest. I stare at the wall, even when I feel Alex move toward me. My senses are even more tuned to him somehow, and I can feel his every movement, sense it through the sparks.

He doesn't say anything as he stops in front of me. I tip my head down, mortified, but he hooks a finger under my chin and forces me to look up at him.

His eyes skim every inch of me, drinking me in. "You're going to be fine," he says. "We still have time before this turns permanent."

"But I don't want anyone to have to take my place." I frown. "I don't want to trap someone like that."

"Don't worry. We'll find another way to get those wings off you." He offers me an encouraging smile. "But we have to hurry. You're still you right now, but you won't be for long if we don't move quickly." His gaze sweeps across my body, and his eyes fill with hunger as he wraps an arm around me and cups my ass. "You should keep the dress, though." His breath is hot on my arm. "You look so fucking sexy right now." His teeth graze my earlobe, and I shudder. "I missed you."

"I'm glad you're okay," I whisper. "I was scared when I didn't know what was happening to you."

"I know you were," he says. "You said so in your dream."

A faint smile graces my lips. "You were there again?" I ask and he nods. "I wish I could just keep us there forever, trapped in a dream. It'd be so nice."

"It would, but then again, you wouldn't be really living life," Alex says softly. "And, Gemma, you're going to live your life, no matter what I have to do."

I lean into him instead of arguing, knowing there's no point. No matter what I say, he's always going to be determined to save me.

He shifts his weight, and his fingers fumble as he traces the length of my spine. "So, a girl, huh?"

I pull back. "How'd you know?"

He looks a little guilty. "Sorry, but Aislin kind of has a big mouth."

"It's okay," I tell him. "And I mean that. The baby's going to be okay. Adessa did a spell on her that's going to protect her no matter what happens to me."

"Nothing's going to happen to you," he assures me. "You're going to live, and we're going to get those wings off you, but I'm going to need Adessa's help."

"Sorry, but she left," Aislin interrupts, stepping out of Laylen's arms. She wipes her red, swollen eyes with the sleeve of her shirt then tries to comb her tangled hair into place. "She and Tesha took off. They said they were going into hiding until all this shit with the mark is over."

"Which will be soon," I say, wrapping my arms around myself to try to cover up my chest that's nearly bursting out of my top. "Alex and I found a way."

Alex shakes his head. "No, we didn't. I still haven't found my mom."

Aislin's eyes pop wide. "Wait a minute. Our *mom?*"

I shoot Alex a dirty look and nudge him in the side. "You didn't tell her you're looking for your mom?"

He winces, clutching his ribs. "Fuck, that hurt. You're like freakishly strong now."

"And immortal." I stick out my arm, showing him the mark that matches Laylen's.

Alex pulls me closer and blinks at the Mark of Immortality. He mutters something under his breath, and then he's storming for the door.

"Where are you going?" I chase after him, my wings slamming into the walls and shelves.

"To find a witch who can help us get those things off you," he all but growls.

"Hello, Aislin can," I remind him.

He slams to a halt, and I crash into him. "We're going to need more than one witch in order to pull this off."

"I'm going with you," Aislin says, grabbing her jacket from the back of the sofa.

Alex looks back and forth between Laylen and me. "Are you going to be okay here by yourself?"

"I'll be fine. I'm super strong right now and immortal. Plus, Laylen can stay here with me, but Aislin should go with you. I don't want you going alone." I look over at Aislin as something dawns on me. "Wait a minute. How'd you even get the Black Angel out of the cage without changing into one yourself?"

Aislin frowns. "I used magic . . . a spell I didn't even realize I know." She slips her arms through the sleeves of her jacket. "It was so weird, but somehow, I knew a lot of spells, darker spells." She sighs, reaches in her pocket, and retrieves my locket. "Sorry I took this."

"It's okay." I put my locket back on and then give Alex a heavy stare. "Hurry back, okay? It's becoming more . . . difficult when you're gone."

He lightly touches the feathers on my wings, and I shiver. "I'll be back soon."

They head out, shutting the door behind them and leaving Laylen and I alone.

"So," he starts, sinking into the sofa, "how bad was I?"

"You don't remember what happened?" I ask, sitting down beside him.

"I remember some stuff . . ." he trails off, scratching at the back of his neck. " I'm just asking because . . . You're the one I hurt."

My fingers wander to my neck where the bite marks once were. "It wasn't that bad."

His shoulders sag. "Please don't sugarcoat it for me. I don't deserve that."

I twist to face him and put my hands on his shoulders. "You know what? You're right. It was bad. You scared the shit out of me. But we've all done things we're not proud of, and we just have to live with it and move on. Our mistakes don't define us; it's what we do afterward—how we grow—that makes us who we are."

"When did you get to be so insightful?" he asks with a soft, shocked laugh.

I grin. "I learned from the best."

His smile grows, and then he hugs me, wings and all.

CHAPTER
TWENTY-THREE

Alex

I HATE LEAVING her, but there's no way I'm going to let her come with me. Her violet eyes draw enough attention, but now she has wings.

"How do you know about this spell, but I don't?" Aislin jogs after me as I shove my way down the crowded streets of Vegas.

The neon lights flash across every person's face, and the slot machines ding from inside every building.

"I know a lot of things you don't," I tell her, squeezing past a guy dressed like a cat who's really a vampire. In fact, most of the people around here are otherworldly creatures.

"Yeah, but I'm a witch. You'd think I'd know there's a spell to remove the wings of a Black Angel without sending them to hell." She casts a glance around the crowded sidewalk. "I wish it only took one witch. It'd be so much easier."

"You need a witch for each wing. So this is where all the vampires, fey, and witches migrated to." I intentionally change the subject, worried if she finds out how I know about the spell, she'll get upset.

When I was younger, before our mom vanished, she used to teach me all kinds of stuff, including spells, even though I'm not a witch, like how to slay a Death Walker and the location of the City of Crystal. She also taught me how to turn a Black Angel back into a human. Sometimes, I wonder if she knew all of this was going to happen and was preparing me for it.

Aislin shakes her head and crosses her arms. "I can tell when you're lying."

"I know I am." I scan the crowd for a witch who isn't marked. "But right now, all I care about is getting those damn wings off Gemma." I spot a witch not too far away with her head tipped down and her gaze fastened on the ground. She looks terrified out of her damn mind, and I'm betting it's because she's not marked.

"You know we have a ton of other problems, right?" Aislin reminds me. "Like the fact that Aleesa's still missing, and we need to find her."

"We will." I slam to a stop, and Aislin runs into me. "There we go. An unmarked one."

Aislin assess the woman I point at.

"Maybe I should handle this so you don't piss her off."

"Hey, I can be charming when I need to."

"No, you just think you can," she says. "Give me a few seconds to talk to her, okay?" Then she marches up to the witch with her shoulders held high.

They talk for a minute or two before they both push their way through the mob, heading toward me.

"This is Emilia, and she's going to help us," Aislin

says, "as long as we offer her protection while she does."
I nod. "Let's hurry, though, before we're too late."

THE MOMENT WE step inside the store, I freeze at the
lack of electricity in the air. A rush of cold hits me next,
and I know the Death Walkers have been here.

I sprint into the living room as rage floods my body.

The table, the chairs, and walls are all glazed over
with ice. And lifelessly lying on the floor is a Death Walker
with a gaping hole in the center of its rotting chest

"Dammit!" I kick the tipped over table. "I'm so sick
of this shit! I'm so sick of losing her! I just want to fucking hold her in my goddamn arms and not have to worry
about Death Walkers, Black Angels, and my father. I just
want us to be . . . normal!"

Aislin and Emilia come rushing into the room.

"What on earth is this?" Emilia asks, horrified. "I
didn't sign up for this." She backs toward the door, her
eyes wide as she gapes at the dead Death Walker. "You
said I'd be safe. This isn't safe."

Aislin shakes her head, her eyes watery. "They made
it out alive," she whispers more to herself. "They had to."

I point my knife at the dead Death Walker. "Who
killed that, though?"

Before Aislin can answer, Emilia screams at the top of
her lungs and runs out of the room.

"I'll go get her," Aislin says before racing after her.

I crouch down to examine the Death Walker. The
only thing that can kill a Death Walker is the Sword of
Immortality. I can see where the blade pierced its chest,

but what I don't get is where the sword came from, because the last time I checked, my father had it.

"Gemma, where are you?" I stand up and circle the room.

Everything is frosted over except for the front window, which strangely is open. I walk over, sticking my head outside, and spot a single purple flower sitting on the windowsill, the same kind of flower that was in the field where we met while Gemma was dreaming. And it's the same kind of flower I used to pick for her when we would walk out to our hideout.

I shut my eyes, and just like that, she's pulled me into a dream. Only this time, it's not a dream filled with kisses and touching. This time, there's nothing but chaos as she shows me the horror that happened . . .

I'm standing at the side of the room, watching as Laylen and Gemma sit there and chat on the sofa. I try to say something to her, but unlike the other times we've met in her dreams, she doesn't seem to hear me.

"You know what? I think I kind of like the wings."
Laylen caresses the feathers on her back, making my blood boil.

"Don't be weird," she jokes, pulling a face at the wings.

"I'm not being weird." He gives her a teasing smile. "Hey, what if you can fly?"

"I can't fly," she says, but then her brows knit together in that cute way that means she's thinking deeply about something. "Can I?"

"You should try it," Laylen encourages.

She only sighs, leaning back against the couch. "This sucks. I should be trying to find a way to get into the Afterlife, and instead, I'm stuck here."

"We'll get it all fixed," he assures her. "We always do."

"I hope so." She kicks her boots up onto the table. "Although, sometimes I wish we could just take off and run away from it all like Adessa and Tesha."

Laylen leans back, resting his arms behind his head. "I still can't believe they bailed."

"Wouldn't you run away if you could?"

"Maybe," he says, pondering something. "Do you think maybe in another life, if we'd been born human, without marks, without all of this, we could've lived normal lives?"

"Maybe." But she doesn't look too convinced.

"Do you think you and I would still be friends?"

She laughs, her eyes lighting up. "I think, no matter what, you and I will always be friends, Laylen."

My heart aches while I watch the two of them talk. The air between them is so light, and everything just looks . . . well, easy. It's the complete opposite of the intense conversations and moments Gemma and I share. Also unlike us, the two of them are able to relax and not have to worry about killing each other.

"What about you and Alex?" Laylen asks. "Do you think you two would've been together if the star and the promise never existed?"

I hold my breath, waiting for her answer.

She traces the scar on her hand then shuts her eyes. "Yes," she whispers.

I exhale loudly and lean back against the wall, smiling for some goddamn weird reason.

Laylen puts his shoes on the table and then moves his feet to the floor again, seeming uneasy. "Maybe one day that world will exist."

Gemma smiles, but then she suddenly leaps to her feet and bolts for the door. Laylen hurries after her and so do I, chasing her outside.

"What are you doing?" he asks Gemma as we stop on the porch.

Checking left and right, Gemma spans her wings. "Seeing if I can fly. It might be my only chance."

She flaps the feathers back and forth, back and forth until they lift her off her feet. Then she hovers in the air for a while before her feet touch the ground again. She looks so happy, so free, exactly what I want her to have for the rest of her life.

"See, not so bad," Laylen says, grinning.

She curls her wings back in. "I guess not, but it doesn't mean I want to keep the wings."

They exchange a grin before she plucks a violet flower from a pot hanging by the front door. That's when I hear a crackle from inside the house.

The two of them must hear it, too, because they dive into the bushes and peer through the open window into the living room.

I move beside them and look inside the house, too.

"Where are they!" my father growls. "They are supposed to be here."

Death Walkers surround him as he paces the floor with the Sword of Immorality clutched in his hand. He looks like he's panicking, completely out of control. I've never seen him look like this before, and it has me wondering what's causing it. What's got him so scared?

As he continues to chew out the Death Walkers, I spot a girl cowering next to him with dark, curly hair and yellow-eyes.

"Aleesa," Gemma and I mutter simultaneously.

My father growls at the Death Walkers, his face turning bright red "You all failed me!" He swings back the sword and plunges it into a Death Walker's chest. It lets out a sharp cry, the light in its eyes dimming.

Laylen and Gemma exchange a look. "Maybe's he's worried he's not going to be able to pull off opening the portal," Laylen whispers.

"Maybe," Gemma says then frowns. "We should help Aleesa."

The window suddenly explodes, and glass flies everywhere. My father marches for the window with the Death Walkers tailing at his heals.

"Time to go," Gemma says, grabbing Laylen's hand.

But it's too late. Death Walkers are marching out the front door and surrounding the bushes as Gemma and Laylen stumble out.

My father strides right for Gemma with that stupid grin on his face that he always gets whenever he thinks he's won something.

"Well, well, well, what do we have here?" He looks her over, smiling at the wings. "Looks like you ran into some trouble."

I grit my teeth and lunge for him, but I fall right through him like he's a ghost. Rolling on my back, I see Laylen shift in front of Gemma, trying to protect her.

My stupid asshole of a father looks up the street. "Interesting choice of places to hide, especially since you've hidden here before." He releases an exhausted sigh. "I wish you'd just give up. It'd make my life easier. But I guess I can't be too upset with all of this. It's amazing how good I'm getting at creating marks."

"It's not over," Gemma says, her voice surprisingly even. "And do you want to know why?" She leans in.

"*Because Alex and I our going to kill you.*" Then she does something freaking badass as hell.

She punches him in the face.

My father clutches his nose, tripping backward as blood gushes from it. "Get her!"

Death Walkers close in on Laylen and Gemma, but Gemma extends her wings and twirls around in a circle. The powerful feathered wings hit the Death Walkers, and they drop to the ground like dominoes. Gemma grabs Aleesa's hand then Laylen's before she kisses the flower and tosses it onto the windowsill.

"You know where to find me," she whispers, and then the three of them disappear.

CHAPTER
TWENTY-FOUR

Gemma

"I THINK MY wing's broken," I complain, tucking the feathers inward. "I think the Death Walker's ice did it or something."

We're in my old, childhood hideout with candles lit along the narrow room hidden inside a hill. Laylen is inspecting my wing while Aleesa lies on the floor, passed out from exhaustion.

"Does it hurt when I do this?" Laylen brushes his fingers along the tips of the feathers.

"Yeah." I wince, my muscles tightening as pain shoots through the wing.

Laylen sighs then rests back against the dirt wall. "I'm not a doctor or anything, but I'm guessing it might be broken. Let's just hope Aislin and Alex show up soon so we can do the spell and turn you back into you." He pauses, rubbing his jawline. "Although, I still don't get why you think they'll be able to find us here."

I shrug, leaning back against the wall. "It has to do

with the flower I left in the windowsill." I'm just hoping Alex will be able to find it.

I think he did . . . I had a dream that he did, anyway.

"What are we going to do when Aleesa wakes up?" I ask, yawning and stretching my arms above my head. "She's going to act crazy."

"I think we should find a place to lock her up until Aislin removes the mark." He massages his arm where his Mark of Malefiscus used to be.

"Yeah, I guess." But I'm starting to run out of ideas of places we can hide.

"Nice punch, by the way," Laylen says with a proud smile. "I've been waiting for someone to do that to Stephan for a long time."

I flex my fingers. "It did feel kind of good."

As more time drifts by, I grow concerned that Alex didn't find the flower and that my dream was only a dream. But about an hour later, smoke funnels around the room, and then Alex and Aislin appear in front of us.

My skin hums as I jump to my feet, so overwhelmed to see him that I start crying.

"You found us." I throw my arms around him and hug him tightly.

"Of course I found you." He buries his face into the crook of my neck. "I knew the moment I saw the flower that you probably came here."

I suck back the tears and lean away to look at him. "Did you find a witch to help me?"

Alex shifts uncomfortably, keeping a firm grip on my hips. "We kind of ran into a problem with that."

My elation crashes to the ground. "What kind of a problem?"

Aislin raises her hand, showing us a giant red X

tattooing her flesh. "This kind of a problem."

Alex sighs tiredly. "She's been branded, which means no other witch will work with her again."

CHAPTER
TWENTY-FIVE

Alex

THE LOOK ON Gemma's face when I tell her the heart-crushing news that we don't have a witch is enough to kill me.

I'm still pissed off that Aislin managed to get herself branded.

After I left Gemma's dream of her escaping Stephan, Aislin and I went to track Emilia down so we could still do the spell when we came to the hideout. Turns out, Emilia had gathered her own mob of witches who blamed us for the Death Walkers showing up in Sin City. To punish Aislin, they marked her with the x so no other witch will ever work with her again.

"So I'm stuck like this forever?" Gemma sucks back the tears, her wings curling inward as her shoulders slump.

"We'll find a way to fix this," I promise her, cupping her face between my hands and wiping away the tears.

"I'm not going to let anything happen to you. You know that."

She sniffles. "I know you'll try, but not everything's in your hands, Alex. Sometimes shit just happens, and you can't do anything about it." As she starts to step away from me, one of her wings clips the wall, and she winces

"What happened?" I touch the wing, noting it looks crooked.

"It's been like that ever since the Death Walkers and your dad showed up," she says, frowning over her shoulder at the wing. "I'm not sure if it was the ice that did it or what."

"I'm sorry you had to deal with him." I press my hand to her cheek, turning her head so she'll look at me. "But I'm proud of you."

Her forehead creases. "For what?"

I smile. "For punching him in the face."

She smiles back at me. "I'll admit, it felt good."

Unable to help myself, I dip my head, moving in to kiss her.

"Holy shit! I can fix this." Aislin announces, and I sigh, leaning back. "I can remove her Mark of Immortality and her wings! I just need a little bit of time."

"We don't have time," I tell her, pulling Gemma against me.

"She's still her, so we have a little bit of time," Aislin says. "And this is what we're going to do."

CHAPTER
TWENTY-SIX

Gemma

"BLACK MAGIC?" ALEX says flatly to Aislin. "That's your brilliant plan?"

"It's better than your plan," Aislin snaps, her nerves frazzled and on edge, "which is nothing."

She wants us to go to a black magic store so she can collect some items that will allow her to create a spell to steal another witch's power. Then she'll have the power of two witches, which she thinks will free me from the entrapment of my wings. Plus, she needs some stuff from there to complete the spell she's been working on that will remove the Mark of Immortality from Stephan, which is the same spell she plans on using on me.

"Black magic's dangerous," Alex warns Aislin while keeping his hand on my back. He hasn't stopped touching me since he showed up, as if he's afraid he's going to lose me. "You've told me that a thousand times."

"Life's dangerous." She gestures at me, at Laylen, and then at Alex. "I mean, look at us. We're shit deep in danger all the time. It's who we are, and I think it's time we start embracing it."

Alex rolls his eyes. "So what you're saying is we just stroll on into a black magic store and order these witches to give us the stuff so you can take away the power of another witch. Because I'm guessing witches aren't going to be too willing to help us, especially with"—he points at her hand—"that."

"I'll wear gloves," she says, tucking the branded hand behind her back. "And I'll take Gemma with me to the store. Not you."

I lift my head from Alex's chest. "Why me?"

"You're an Angel from Hell. Dude, you have clout in the evil world," she says.

"Is that a good thing?" I ask.

"Right now, it is," she replies.

"I'm not agreeing to this," Alex talks over me.

"Good thing you're not the boss," Aislin replies haughtily.

"According to Gemma, I am," Alex says, giving me a look that makes my skin heat.

"Dude, TMI," Laylen says from the floor.

"And while we're doing this," Aislin says, pulling her hair into a messy bun on top of her head, "you can go find Mom. Besides, the two of you need space, remember?"

Alex's fingers tense on my back. "The last time I checked, you weren't in charge."

"I think we should vote," Aislin says with a smirk.

Alex pulls me closer to him. "No way. I already know where everyone's votes lie." Still, he looks at Laylen with hope.

"Sorry, but I'm with them on this one," Laylen says, stretching his arms above his head as he rises to his feet.

Alex lets out a deep grunt. "Whatever." He shakes his head, pulling me closer. "Let's just hurry and get this fucking over with."

I look up at Alex. "Meet you back here soon, okay?"

"Hold on a second," Laylen says. "You guys are forgetting something really fucking important." He nods at Aleesa lying on the floor.

"Shit," Aislin mutters, rubbing her branded hand. "I think it might be time to take her to the Faerie Realm. She'll be safer there."

"But I thought, since she's half Keeper, she is forbidden in the Fey Realm?" I ask.

"They won't hurt her," Aislin promises me. "It's the best place I can think of to hide her while we take care of the apocalypse and my father. And I have a friend there who will watch her."

After we all agree to the plan, Aislin vanishes with Aleesa to take her to the Fey Realm.

"She's letting this power thing get to her head," Alex mutters as he sinks down to the floor, pulling me with him.

"I'm sure she knows what she's doing, Alex," I say, crisscrossing my legs.

Alex snorts a laugh "The last time she ran off by herself, she was chased down by a mob of witches who branded her."

"She'll be fine," Laylen says more to himself. Fidgety, he reaches for the lighter I lit the candles with and starts messing around with it.

"So what exactly happened back in Iceland?" I ask Alex. "Did you ever go back and see if you were right about the Banshee not being your mother?"

Alex slumps back against the wall, rubbing his

bloodshot eyes. "I went back to check, and it wasn't my mother."

"So how are you going to find your mom?" I ask.

He shrugs. "Go back to Draven, find out why he didn't give me the right address in the first place, and if all else fails, I'll beat the shit out of him until he gives me the correct one."

I place a hand on his arm. "I don't want you getting hurt."

"I won't. I promise I won't." His eyes burn fiercely with passion as his hand slides around the back of my neck. "I just want to touch you right now, so fucking badly."

My heart slams against my chest as I shut my eyes and breathe in Alex's scent. I want him so badly, too.

Laylen clears his throat as he gets to his feet. "I think I'm going to go get some fresh air." He rushes for the ladder and hastily climbs out of the hole.

The second we're alone, Alex tugs on the ribbon lacing up the front of the corset. My breasts spring free, and his lips cover my nipple. He sucks hard, and I cry out, my back arching into him. Then he groans, gently biting down, and I nearly lose it.

"I just want things to be like this," he whispers as he kisses a path up my neck to my chin, "forever."

Suddenly, he blinks and his head wobbles like he's about to faint.

I cup his cheek. "Are you okay?"

He nods, blinking. "I'm . . . fine . . ." His brows dip in puzzlement as he studies me, looking at me in a way I don't quite understand.

"Can we just lie down for a minute?" he finally asks.

I nod, feeling completely lost, but I do what he asks and lie down on the dirt beside him. After I lace my shirt back up, I rest my head against his chest. I can hear his heart beating wildly, but the longer we lie there, the fainter it gets. When I glance up at him, he has fallen asleep. For some reason, that makes me smile. He looks so peaceful at the moment, more content than he ever has.

"I want to stay this way forever, too," I whisper then rest my head on his chest, listening to his heart thudding until I fall asleep, too.

I WAKE UP when Aislin returns, and Alex jolts awake a split second later.

"What time is it?" Laylen asks, sitting up and stretching his arms above his head.

"I have no idea," Aislin says. Her hair is wild, and she's breathing heavily. "What I do know is that faeries are mean. Like really, really mean." She plucks a leaf out of her hair and flicks it to the floor. "And to make this whole thing even more complicated, I now owe Luna a magic spell."

"Who's Luna?" I sit up, arching my back as I stretch.

"She's the Empress of the Fey Realm." Aislin rubs some dirt off her cheek. "And she's not very nice."

"The fey never are." Alex sits up, rubbing his hands up and down his arms like he's cold. Even though he slept, he somehow looks more tired, the bags under his eyes more prominent. "All right, let's get this over with. I don't want to waste any more time."

"Are we just going to meet back here?" I ask him, growing even more concerned when he yawns.

He shakes his head. "No, let's meet at your house.

There's something I need from there, anyway." He reaches for my hand. "Can I borrow your ring?"

"Why do you need it?" I ask.

"In case my mother's in her ghost form," he says. "I promise I'll give it back, Gemma. Just trust me."

"I do trust you," I say, realizing how true my words are. I trust him with my life, with everything.

I slip off the ring and set it in the palm of his hand.

"Thank you." He kisses me quickly on the cheek, and I hear him gasp.

"Are you sure you're okay?" I ask, leaning back to catch his gaze.

He nods, slipping the ring on his pinkie finger. "I'm more than okay."

I'm not sure I believe him, but I don't have time to pry the truth out of him.

AFTER AISLIN DROPS Laylen and Alex off at my house, we transport to The Evil Side, which is the closest black magic store Aislin can find.

It's late by the time we arrive; the stars and moon are out, and the air has a nip to it. The store looks as dark as the sky, but that might be because the windows are covered with grim.

"Ready for this?" Aislin asks me as we hike across the parking lot for the store.

"I guess so"—I wrap my arms around myself—"but I think we should have a game plan just in case something goes wrong."

"We already have one—you. Black magic witches

worship you. You're like their god or goddess."

"Still, I'd feel better if we had an escape plan. I can already sense the praesidium inside, so my Foreseer power is a no go."

She brushes her bangs out of her face. "Well, if all else fails, I'll transport us out of there." She grins. "Because I can now do that, no assistance needed."

My heels crunch against the gravel as we approach the front steps. "Yeah, how did that happen?"

She shrugs. "My magic's just getting stronger. It happens."

We trot up the steps, and a bell dings as we enter. The air reeks of burnt herbs, cigarette smoke, and weed. Around the room, there are rows and rows of jars filled with a gooey, yellow liquid and what looks like animal parts.

"So gross," I mutter under my breath.

Aislin puts her fingers to her lips and mouths, *They're listening.*

I cringe and mouth, *Sorry.*

"Can I help you?" A woman with golden eyes and hair as pale as snow ducks through a curtain of beads at the back of the store. She gives me a once over, quickly notes my wings, and then bows her head. "We're so honored to have a Black Angel in our store. How can I assist you?"

Aislin hands her a piece of paper with the items she needs. "We need everything on this list."

The witch ignores her. "Is that why you've come here? To collect the items from this list?" she asks me.

I nod, trying to convey more confidence than I have. "Yes."

She bows her head again, snatches the list from Aislin, and ducks back through the curtains. Another woman enters moments later, her hair as orange as fire.

"It's a pleasure to have you in my store." She curtsies at me, and it looks so awkward I have to stifle a laugh. "I'm Catalina, and if you need anything at all, just let me know."

"Thanks," I say, carrying my shoulders high.

She frowns, her expression turning icy. "She hasn't even transitioned yet." She storms for the curtains right as the other witch steps back out. "That's not a Black Angel, only a mere human with wings."

"Watch it. You know they're still powerful, even when they haven't transitioned," the woman with pale hair warns then begins collecting items off the shelf

As they argue some more, Aislin and I wander around the store, crossing our fingers that this will go smoothly.

"I wonder what this is for," Aislin mutters, reaching for a glimmering rainbow candle on the shelf.

I smack her hand away. "Don't touch it if you don't know what it is. Trust me. The last time I did that, I ended up falling into a Foreseer ball."

"That's just the Power of Entrapment candle." The paled-haired witch appears behind me, startling Aislin and me. She picks up the candle and turns it in her hands. "It traps the power of a witch inside their own body, at least while the wick burns."

"What about other kinds of power?" I ask, my voice a little uneven. "Or is it solely for Wicca power?"

"That depends on what other power you're talking about." She waits for me to explain.

I shrug, not even positive why I asked.

Because you think you love Alex and want to tell him. And if you have the candle, it might protect you from the star's power killing you.

I shake the thought from my head.

"How much is it?" Aislin asks, reaching to unzip her purse.

"Oh, it's not for sale," she replies, tightening her hold on the candle. "Catalina only makes trades for things as powerful as this, and it has to be a very enticing trade."

"And you two have nothing I want," Catalina grumbles from across the room.

The paled-haired witch sighs. "Sorry, she lacks people skills." She eyes us over before her fingers float toward my locket. "For this, I think she might be willing to make the trade."

I step back, shaking my head. "I won't trade that."

"Catalina, come look at this," she calls out, her eyes fixed on my locket. "This one's got sugilite on her."

Catalina whisks over to us in the snap of a finger and puts her hand on my necklace without permission. "And it's coated in silver." She looks at the candle and then at me. "If you want the candle, give me the necklace."

I clutch onto my heart-shaped locket, shaking my head.

She snaps the chain from my neck and drops the candle at my feet. "It's not really a choice. I'm taking the necklace. You can have the candle if you want."

I'm sorry, Aislin mouths, looking like she's a step away from bursting into tears.

"It's okay." I scoop up the candle and hold it in my arms, trying to figure out if I'm really ready to use it, ready to open my heart like that.

The silence of the prickle on the back makes me wonder if I'm not.

CHAPTER
TWENTY-SEVEN

Alex

I'M NOT SURE if the ring will work, and I really don't want to fucking talk to him, but this isn't about me. This about saving Gemma, and if that means talking to Nicholas, I'll do it. I'm just hoping, since his fey blood connects with every breed of faerie in the world, he'll know a thing or two about Banshees.

"So what exactly are we doing here?" Laylen asks, glancing around at the tan walls of Gemma's bedroom.

I crack my knuckles. "Looking for Nicholas."

"Come again?" Laylen does a double take.

"He's fey." I shrug. "He might know something about my mother. Plus, Gemma said she saw him in her dream where she died, that he took her to the Afterlife."

"Okay." Laylen clears his throat and shifts his weight, leaning against the doorway. "Is he here?"

I shake my head, inching into the room. "I'm not even sure the ring will work on me."

Minutes tick by and still no Nicholas. I sigh, about to give up, when I hear a soft thud from somewhere in the room.

"Look at you," Nicholas's voice floats around the room. "Got you a fancy little ring, huh? Sure does look pretty."

I roll my eyes. "Show yourself."

"You first," he says with a laugh.

I take a few calculated breaths, trying to keep my temper under control. "Where is she?"

"You'll have to be more specific," Nicholas says. "Because the list of people you're looking for is endless. I mean, there's me, the lovely Jocelyn who might not be so lovely anymore . . . and of course, your dear old mom, Alana."

"Tell me what you know." My eyes skim the ceiling and the walls as I draw out my knife.

Laylen turns in a circle and accidently bumps into the desk, knocking a CD onto the floor. "He's not by me, is he?"

I hold up a finger. "Not yet . . . but . . ."

"I have nothing to say to you," Nicholas says. "Now go away and don't come back unless Gemma's with you. I miss our little talks and watching her undress."

"Goddammit." I grunt in frustration, wishing I could beat the living shit out of him.

"Keep it together, man," Laylen says, scooping up the CD off the floor. "He wants you to get pissed off. It's just like when we were kids, and he stole all our stuff just to watch us struggle to find it. He likes torturing people. It's his thing."

Laylen's right. I need to get my shit together; other-wise, I won't get anything out of Nicholas.

"I'll tell you what. Show yourself and I'll make a bargain with you," I try to entice him, knowing it's risky, but I'm desperate.

"What kind of a bargain?" he asks, his curiosity piquing.

"The kind where you can live again," I say, circling the room.

Laylen shoots me a what-the-fuck-are-you-doing look, but I swiftly shake my head, warning him to keep quiet.

Nicholas appears in front of the foot of the bed with his eyes narrowed and his arms folded. He looks the same as he always did except I can see through him.

"This better be good," he says.

"It is, but I want your info first." I toss and catch the knife before pointing the tip of the blade at him. "Starting with the location of Jocelyn and then move on to my mother."

Nicholas eyes the knife. "You know that can't hurt me. I'm a ghost."

"Then I guess you have nothing to worry about." I stop tormenting him with my knife and set it down on the dresser. "Answer my questions."

"First, you're going to bring me back to life," he demands.

I shake my head. "Nope. You first."

We stare each other down, a challenge between the dead and the living. I remember the days when I used to beat the shit out of him to get him to talk. I really do miss those days.

"Jocelyn's gone," he tells me, "but I'd like to point out that I warned her they don't like me down in the Afterlife because I'm a half-breed."

I want to rip his head off. "What do you mean, 'gone'?"

He shrugs, sitting down on the bed. "When we showed up in the Afterlife, Annabella collected her essence and forced her to cross over. She's moved on, past the ghost life."

A lump forms in my throat, and I have to force it down before I speak. "So Gemma won't ever see her again?"

"Jocelyn was never supposed to be here," he says with an eye roll. "I already told you this. She had a brief gap between her death and crossing over where she could roam free, but unlike me, it was her time to go, and Annabella made sure she went."

God, how am I going to break the news to Gemma? She was so determined her mom was going to come find her again, and now she's never going to see her.

As my worry for Gemma swells inside me, I feel my life fading away. It's the same thing that happened when I was kissing her in the hideout. I almost died, and I know why.

Because I'm falling in love with her.

"And what about my mom?" I ask cautiously, trying to keep my emotions intact. If I lose control, that might be it for me, and I can't die yet. I have to save her. "Do you know where she is?"

"I thought she was dead, too."

"Watch it," I warn, aiming the knife at him again. "It's your life at stake here. If you don't help me, then I don't help you."

"Oh, I beg to differ." He laughs at me. "This is so funny—watching you stress out because I know where your mom is and you don't."

Something snaps inside me, and I lunge for him, sailing right through him and landing on the bed, bouncing on the mattress and hitting my head against the headboard.

"What the fuck are you doing?" Laylen asks, gaping at me like I've lost my damn mind

"Trying to kill a ghost," I growl, springing from the bed.

Nicholas laughs again as he dances around the room and spins circles around Laylen. "This is so much fun."

I storm for the door. "Fuck you. I'm tired of this shit. Laylen, let's go."

"Wait," Nicholas calls out in panic.

I smile to myself because he took the bait. "What?" I snap as I turn around.

"I might know where Alana is," he says, stepping away from Laylen. "She's trapped in a place where you yourself were once imprisoned."

"What are you . . . ?" A revelation clicks, and it's brutally painful, like a knife to the heart. "The City of Crystal . . . She's trapped in that massive crystal. But how is that possible? She's a Banshee."

"Banshees, fey, vampires, all kinds have been trapped there at one point or another. And otherworld creatures give out the best power." A shit-eating smirk comes across his face. "Amazing, isn't it? You were once trapped there with her, and you didn't even know it."

"Take me there," I demand as guilt piles on my shoulders.

She was there the whole time. How did I not know?

"Not until you tell me how to bring myself back to life," he says, crossing his arms.

I flip the knife closed and shove it into my pocket. "When I free the lost souls from the Afterlife, I'll make sure to include you."

"You say it like you're the one going." He shakes his

head and rolls his eyes. "That's never going to happen, no matter how much you want it to."

I gesture around the room. "Gemma's not here, is she? And I have the ring, and as soon as I get my mother out of the City, I'll have my ticket to the Afterlife."

He erupts in laughter, hunching over and gasping for air. "You still don't get it," he says as his laughter dies down. "It *has* to be Gemma. It always has been and always will be. All of this was planned out before she was even born."

"Well, I'm going to change it," I say. "Like she changed her vision, I'll change her future by taking her place."

Laylen throws his hands up in the air and walks out of the room, muttering, "This one-sided conversation is too much. It's giving me a fucking headache."

"It'll never work," Nicholas says. "You can't change the future. You're not a Foreseer."

"It sounds pretty possible to me. I go to the Afterlife; therefore, I change her future."

"You're still not getting it. You can't just change how it's supposed to be. That's what you mere humans don't get. Us Foreseers understand everything happens for a reason, even mistakes as great as Gemma's father committed. We are who we are. There's no changing it. It has to be Gemma. She is the one born with the Foreseer gift, the one destined to change the vision. And she's the one who has to make the bargain with Helena because she's responsible for the lost souls. Any other way won't work."

"But she didn't trap the souls on purpose," I say. "She was only fixing her father's mistakes."

He shrugs half-heartedly. "Doesn't matter. This—all of this—was what she was destined to do since the day she was born."

"And what about my mother?" I snap, seething mad. Not at him, but at destiny. At my father for making all this happen. At myself, because no matter what I do, I can't seem to make anything right. "What does she have to do with this? Because I'm guessing she has some role to play in this stupid fucking destiny game."

"You can ask her yourself." He retrieves a miniature crystal ball from his pocket. "In the City of Crystal."

"What's going on?" Laylen asks, sticking his head into the room.

I shake my head. "This is such bullshit. None of this is fair. Gemma . . . She's already been through enough."

"We all have to endure difficulty in our life," Nicholas says, "some more than others."

CHAPTER
TWENTY-EIGHT

Gemma

"STOP PICKING AT your feathers," Aislin scolds while mixing a bowl of green goo and leaves.

"But they itch like crazy," I whine, continuing to scratch my wings and causing more to fall to my bedroom floor.

After we left The Evil Side, we transported to my house. Since Laylen and Alex aren't back yet from their search for his mother, Aislin jumped straight into witch mode, mixing potions, while I sit on the floor, itching at the feathers and staring at the rainbow candle, trying to figure out if it's worth lighting, if I love Alex.

I touch the back of my neck, willing the prickle to tell me, but then quickly panic, realizing without the use of the candle, my power might die with the revelation and take me along with it.

"You're molting," Aislin observes while smashing the wooden spoon against the goo in the bowl.

I glare at her. "I'm not a bird."

"I know," she says, tucking her feet under her butt as she sets the bowl down on the carpet. "But you do have wings."

I pluck another feather from my left wing and flick it to the floor. "How long is that going to take to make?"

She peers into the bowl. "Not too much longer, but I still have to steal a witch's power, and that might take a little bit of time."

I motion at the boarded window. "There's a ton out there. Just take the power from that creepy one that was hanging outside by the mailbox."

"We can't steal the power from one nearby. When I take their power, whoever they are, they're going to try to kill me, so it needs to be someone who has no clue where I'm going to go."

"Have anyone in mind?" I massage the tip of my wings as they start to cramp. "Because it kind of sounds like you do."

"Yeah, I have an idea." She stares down at the palm of her hand.

"Is this some kind of revenge plot or something?" I kneel up, wiggling my wings, trying to shake the cramps out of them.

She shakes her head. "Why would I ever do that?" she says.

I aim a finger at her. "This *is* a revenge plot."

"She branded me, barring me from the witch world," she gripes. "She deserves it."

"Fine, have your revenge, but just be careful." I lie down on the floor on my side. "I should go with you. It's too dangerous to go alone."

"You draw a lot of attention. Plus, you need to rest, take a shower, and eat something. Take care of that little one growing inside you."

I listen to the baby's heartbeat. "Why do you think I can hear her heart beating?"

"I don't know." She stands up, picks up the bowl, and balances it on the computer desk. "Maybe it's because of the star or something, like how you can feel the electricity with Alex."

"Do you think"—I drape my arm over my stomach—"she's normal?"

She kneels down beside me, brushing my hair out of my eyes so I can see her face. "Gemma, of course she is. And do you want to know what else I know?"

I nod.

She smiles. "That she's going to grow up living a happy life, full of love and rainbows and all that fun stuff."

"I hope so."

"Well, I *know* so." She stands up, opening and closing her hands. "Now wish me luck."

"Good luck," I say. "I'll just stay here and work on my nest until you get back."

She snorts a laugh, and I laugh with her, sharing this weird, normal moment. Then she chants a spell, creating a cloud of vapor that carries her away, leaving me alone in an empty house.

After I eat a sandwich, I take a shower, and the water feels really odd against my wings. When I try to put on different clothes, though, the corset and boots appear on my body.

I pass the time by scrounging through Marco and Sophia's room, looking for signs that I missed growing up. How could I have not known all that time what I was? Who they were?

I flip open a trunk at the foot of the bed and take out

all the photos, none of which include me. I look at my birth certificate and think of my father trapped in his own mind, perhaps with the Death Walkers. My mother sneaks into my thoughts, her life spent in The Underworld. And now she's dead, and I have no idea where her ghost took off to.

"Mom," I call out to the empty room. "You're going to have a granddaughter. You have to come back; if not for me, for her."

The only answer is mine and the baby's heart beating.

I curl up in a ball, curl my wings around my body, and cry until my eyes run dry.

CHAPTER
TWENTY-NINE

Alex

I'VE NEVER BEEN a fan of the City of Crystal or the Foreseer leader, Dyvinius, so being back here fucking sucks. It's not just the place itself that I dislike, but what the place's power represents. The people here know everything about you: your pasts, the sins you've committed, when you're going to die.

But as Laylen, Nicholas, and I walk up the glass path above the river and past the crystallized walls, I have a sudden, crazy-ass urge to turn, march up to Dyvinius's throne, and demand to know if Gemma and my unborn daughter survive. But I fear what I might see, fear looking ahead might mess up the future more, so instead I follow Nicholas to the massive crystal ball that flames in the center of the city and feeds power to the Foreseers.

Laylen sighs as Nicholas reaches to open the door. "I was hoping I'd never have to come back here again. This place gives me the creeps."

"Me, too, man," I agree, glancing around at the crystal columns and icy path behind us, searching for signs of Dyvinius or anyone else who might be pissed off that we're here.

After Nicholas opens the door, we step inside the room where the fireball of energy burns fiercely. Lifeless bodies are chained to the massive orb with tubes running from their skin to the crystal ball.

Nicholas strolls up to the crystal, crossing his arms while whistling, acting way too casual for the situation. "It's such a fascinating thing, watching the crystal drain life from humans."

"It's a pointless sacrifice," I snap, shielding my eyes as the crystal balls blazes brightly and blinds me. I skim the faces of the people, looking for my mother, but it's been so long since I've seen her I'm not even sure I'll recognize her. "No one needs to see what happens in the future, and if it hadn't been for a Foreseer fucking around with stuff, we wouldn't even be in this mess to begin with."

Nicholas tugs on one of the chains securing the bodies. "Oh, your father would have found another way."

"That might not be true," I say. Where the hell is my mom? "Without Foreseers, my dad would've never found out about the star to begin with."

Nicholas lets go of the chain and steps back. "Well, maybe one day someone will free all of them and destroy the crystal ball."

I have no idea why he's being agreeable, and honestly, I don't like it. It makes him seem even more sketchy and untrustworthy than he already is.

"Where's my mom?" I ask Nicholas.

He gives a shrug. "How should I know? She's *your* mother. I just know she's here, not what she looks like."

Shaking my head, I turn to Laylen. "Do you want to look left, and I'll take the right?"

Laylen nods then disappears around the left side of the crystal ball while I head right.

"What about me?" Nicholas calls out after me. "What should I do?"

I ignore him, scanning the features of each person I pass. The longer I search, the more I question if this is just another one of Nicholas's games, some stupid trick like the ones he used to pull when we were kids.

When we were younger, I always hated when he visited the Keepers' castle. Everything was a joke to him, and he constantly teased Gemma. There was one specific time when he almost convinced her to go swimming in the lake when she couldn't swim. That day, I lost it and made a plan to get rid of him. Gemma and I had stolen the Cruciatus diamond—the Queen of The Underworld's diamond—and when my father went looking for it, I blamed Nicholas, said he took it. My father was so furious he never allowed Nicholas back into the castle. He's had a grudge against me ever since, but the feeling is completely mutual.

I abruptly slow to a stop as I catch sight of someone who resembles my mother. Her skin is much paler than I remember, and her dark hair has thinned, but beneath her weakened state, I can see it—the person who used to take care of me.

I hurriedly yank out the tubes and snap the chains, catching her weight as she slumps against me.

Her eyelids lift open. "Is it time?"

"Yeah, it's time. I'm going get you out of here." I shift her weight, leaning her against my shoulder as I wrap my arm around her. "Just hang on."

Blood drips from her skin where the tubes were. "But

it's time, right? For Gemma to go to the Afterlife?"

I almost drop her on the floor. "You know about that?"

"Of course I know," she says, her voice feeble. "That's what I've been waiting for. It's kind of the whole point of all of this."

I have a ton of questions, but I shove them away for now. "Let's get you out of here, okay?"

Laylen races over and drapes my mom's arm around his neck. Then the three of us all head for the door.

Nicholas bows his head as we approach him. "Alana."

My mother smiles weakly at him while I shoot him a death glare.

"Wait? How can you see him?" I ask.

"I'm part of death now, Alex," she answers, her head slumping to the side.

"Oh, yeah, I guess that makes sense." I balance my mom against me, and we follow Nicholas out of the room.

Once we get far enough away from the enormous crystal ball, Nicholas takes out the miniature traveling ball. "Do I need to ask where we're going?"

"You already know," my mother replies, leaning against me. "To Gemma. Take us to Gemma now before it's too late."

"Too late for what?" I ask.

"Let's hope you don't ever have to find out," she says.

Nicholas sticks out his hand with the crystal balanced in his palm. "All right, who wants to go—?"

"Put the crystal down," Dyvinius's voice echoes through the cave.

When I look over my shoulder and spot him hurrying up the path toward us, I quickly place my mother's hand on the crystal ball. "You know where Gemma's old house is, right?"

She nods, and then she's sucked into the crystal.

"I ordered you to stop!" Dyvinius cries out, his silver cape swishing behind him as he picks up the pace.

Laylen hurries and dives through the crystal. Then I reach for it, but Nicholas moves it behind his back.

"I should just leave you here, let them tie you up to the crystal again."

"That's fine," I say. "Enjoy your death."

He glares at me and I glare right back.

"I hate you," he says, moving the crystal back in front of him.

"Trust me, the feeling's mutual." I place my hand on the crystal ball right as Dyvinius reaches us.

"FINALLY," NICHOLAS SAYS as he drops down into the living room. He puts the crystal away in his pocket then dusts off his hands. "My work is done."

My mother collapses onto the sofa, her head bobbing back. "Would someone please get me a glass of water?"

I head for the kitchen, but Laylen cuts me off. "I got it. You should stay here with her."

Nodding, I flop down on the sofa and try to think of what to say to her. I've spent so many years thinking she was dead that it seems like I should have a lot to say, yet not a damn word comes to mind.

"Alex, relax." My mom places a hand on my knee to stop me from bouncing my leg up and down. "Everything's okay now."

"Why were you down there?" I ask, leaning back.

"It was part of the plan." She massages her arms and

wipes dried blood from her skin. "It was the safest place for me to wait until the time was right for me to take Gemma to the Afterlife."

"You keep saying it's what you were supposed to do, like it was pre-planned."

"That's because it was pre-planned, from a vision."

I yank my fingers through my hair, making the strands go askew. "Why does it always come back to the visions? Seriously, they're becoming the bane of my existence."

"Visions are our guidance through life," she says, her eyelids drifting shut. "There had to be one told in order for us to all end up here, at this very moment."

"It still doesn't make sense. At first, we're told a vision was fucked up, and Gemma had to fix it. Then she did, and mad chaos happened. And now you're saying a vision got us to this exact point."

"Each instance you mention happened because a vision was told. If there hadn't been multiple visions, then Gemma would've never changed Julian's mistake. Plus, the world is always changing, Alex. Each time something changes, so does a vision. And when things like the apocalypse happen, sometimes it takes seeing multiple visions in order for things to be made right again." She pulls her legs onto the cushion, tucks her feet under her, and yawns. "I know it's confusing, but life in general is."

I study her face as she rubs her eyes.

"You said you were part of death now. Are you . . . Are you a Banshee?" It's so weird sitting her with her, asking such an insane question. But anyone who's heard of my mother has said she is a Banshee now.

"I'm sorry, but yes, I am." She swallows hard, rubbing her hands up and down her arms as if she's cold. "I know that's not what you want to hear, but it has a positive side, like the fact that I'll get to be the one to take Gemma to the Afterlife."

I grab a knitted blanket that's on the back of the sofa and hand it to her. "It's not going to be Gemma." I don't mean for my voice to sound as cold as it does, but I can't help it. "It's going to be me."

She covers herself with the blanket. "I'm sorry, honey, but it has to be her. It's part of the vision. She's the one whose soul was detached. She has the gift of foreseeing and changing visions. All of this centers around her and plays a part in a much larger picture. She's going to be the one to free the souls, and then you two will go to the lake and destroy the star, just like the vision has foretold. The portal will remain sealed, and with some effort, Stephan, Demetrius, and all the Death Walkers die. Then life will go on as it should." She slips an arm out from under the blanket to clasp my hand. "Your part is to protect her, to carry the other half of the star, and to be there for her when she needs you the most."

"But it's not just her I'm worried about." I slide my hand out from under hers and scoot away, grinding my teeth. My mind is racing with ideas on what I can do to change all this destiny shit, because I can't let Gemma take all these risks, especially when . . ."She's pregnant."

"I know." My mother draws the blanket up to her neck, shivering. "The baby will be fine. I promise you, Alex. That spell Gemma had done will make it so your daughter lives a happy, healthy life."

"How did you know about the spell?" I shake my head, bitterness creeping into my voice. "Never mind. I think I already know—a vision."

"Don't blame the visions, Alex," she says. "It's people's choices and decisions that map destiny, too, like your father's."

That's the last straw that pushes me over the edge. "And this is such bull!" I slam my fist against the armrest, causing her to flinch. "You sit there and say all this like it is her destiny to die. Like it's fair. It's *not* fair. It's my father's fault all of this shit started."

"Life sometimes isn't fair, sweetie. I'm sorry, but that's just how it is."

"This isn't fair." I grind my teeth, restless and angry, on the verge of exploding. "There's got to be a way around her dying."

"There's no way around it," she says. "The portal's opening unless the star's power is destroyed." She tosses the blanket off her and stands, gripping onto the armrest for support. "Have you ever wondered why Stephan is so focused on you two, but not Aislin, Laylen, and Aleesa, even though they play a part in the ritual of opening the portal? Because Malefiscus has the power of the star in him, too."

I look down at my hands where I can see the faint lines of my veins that carry blood through my body and the same power that's apparently inside Malefiscus. It makes me hate myself for being connected to him.

Sucking in a deep breath, she lets go of the armrest and stands straight. "There are three ways this could go. Either Stephan can bleed you two out, mix your blood with Laylen, Aislin, and Aleesa's, and free everything inside that portal. Or you can run and hide, let the portal open, Malefiscus will be trapped inside it because the star's energy still exists, but all the Death Walkers inside the portal will be freed to enter the human world. Or you can destroy the star, destroy Malefiscus, and stop the portal from opening."

"But you already know which way it goes, don't you?" I ask quietly.

She presses her lips tighter and nods her head once.

"This isn't fucking fair," I say again, adrenaline coursing through my body as my anger nearly hits the roof. "You sit here and talk about life and how it's hard and how some people just have it tough, but Gemma hasn't even had a chance to have a life. She's spent most of her time walking around half dead and out of it, with no memories, no emotions, no nothing. That's not just a hard life; that's no life."

Not wanting to hear any more of what she has to say, I storm out of the room and up the stairs. When I reach the top, I rest my head against the wall and take a few measured breaths, trying to settle the fuck down. But then I hear someone crying from Marco and Sophia's room.

Worried, I rush toward the open door to find Gemma curled up in a ball with her wings wrapped around herself. My heart splits in two as I kneel down beside her and touch her shoulder.

"What happened?"

Her body tenses under my hand, and she wipes the tears away before she turns her head and looks at me. "Nothing happened. Everything's fine."

"Nothing's ever fine." I look around the room. "Where's Aislin?"

"Stealing some witch's power." She sits up, tucking her wings back behind her. "Did you find your mom?"

I nod, still sensing something's wrong. "She's downstairs."

She perks up. "Is she okay?"

I nod again, examining her from head to toe, trying to figure out what's wrong. "She's tired, but yeah, I think she's okay."

"Does she know how to help us?"

"Yeah, she's got a plan and everything."

"Why do you sound so mad about that?"

"Because I hate the fucking plan."

"Alex, I know you don't want me to do this, but—"

I cover her mouth with my hand. "Let's talk about something else for a bit, okay?"

She nods and then I remove my hand, not ready to accept this vision destiny crap just yet

My mom told me my job is to be there for Gemma, to protect her. And that's exactly what I'm going to do until I take my last breath.

CHAPTER
THIRTY

Gemma

FTER ALEX FINDS me crying, we go downstairs
so I can meet his mother. Alana doesn't seem that
shocked by my wings, like she already knew I was
going to end up with them.

We chat a little bit about what's going to happen, and
then Alana takes a moment to touch my stomach. The
whole belly-touching thing seems to be happening more
and more, but I'll admit, it still makes me uncomfortable,
mostly because I'm not used to people touching me.

The longer the four of us sit together talking, the
more exhausted I become. I don't know why, but the energy buzzing around inside me has dulled to a low hum. It
has me nervous.

"Where's Aislin?" Laylen eventually asks, looking
concerned as he glances at the wall clock. "I know you
said she went to get a witch's power, but hasn't she been
gone for a while?"

"She has." I look down at my watch. "Nine minutes

left."

"Nine minutes?" he questions, slouching back in the chair. "That's pretty specific."

I absentmindedly rest my head against Alex's shoulder, feeling incredibly tired. "I gave her a timeframe, and if she's not back by then, I go looking for her."

Alex's muscles tense underneath my head, and I start to move away, realizing I shouldn't be doing this. But he quickly wraps an arm around me and places a hand on my cheek, securing me there.

"Why didn't she just steal a witch's power from one of the ones hanging out outside?" Laylen kicks his feet up on the coffee table

"She said something about needing to do it with a witch that won't know where she's hiding out," I explain. "I guess they're going to get pissed off and chase her down."

Laylen chews on his lip ring. "That worries me."

"It worries me, too." I check the time again. "In seven minutes, we'll go looking for her." I don't bother to mention we'll have to look for her in Vegas, because I don't want to worry him more.

Silence encases us as the clock ticks, and Alana starts to doze off.

"I hate to interrupt such a good time," Nicholas's voice flows through the living room, "but you owe me one life."

My gaze skims the walls, the furniture, and the mantle, but without the ring, I have no clue where he is. "No one owes you a life."

"How can we suddenly hear him?" Laylen asks, planting his feet on the floor.

"It's one of the many talents of a Banshee," Alana says without opening her eyes. "We have connections through the ghost world, and I'm channeling it to all of you."

"Where is he?" I whisper to Alex.

He pulls me against him and brushes my hair out of my eyes. "Too close to you."

Nicholas clears his throat, startling me. "We have a bargain to attend to, and you can thank Alex for that."

I angle my head up to look at Alex. "What's he talking about?"

Alex shrugs. "It was the only way I could get him to tell me where my mom was. I told him, if he helped me find her, I'd make sure his soul was freed with the other lost souls."

"Give me the ring back," I say, ducking my head out from underneath Alex's arm. "I want to talk to him."

Alex promptly shakes his head. "No fucking way."

I shove my hand at him. "I'm going to need it back for the Afterlife, anyway, so you might as well give it back now." When he shakes his head again, I reach over and wiggle the ring off his finger.

He grumbles, pissed off as hell as he slumps back on the sofa, pouting. "I wish you never had to wear that ring again."

"Me, too, but the fact is I do." I slide the ring onto my finger right in time to see Nicholas wink. Then he spins around, leaps over the coffee table, and waves a hand in front of Laylen's face.

"I'll kind of miss this part about death. Getting to mess with everyone without them knowing is absolutely fantastic."

"That's sad if it's true," I tell him. "Maybe you should reconsider how you treat people. Take your second chance and do something good with it."

He rolls his eyes then flicks Laylen's hair. "No way."

Laylen leans to the side. "Why do I have the feeling he's messing with me right now?"

"Because he is," I tell him. "But don't worry; he's going to stop."

"I am?" Nicholas questions with a crook of his brow.

"You are if you want to live again." I flash him an arrogant grin.

He glowers at me, but then his gaze darts to the clock, and he smirks. "Bzzzz. Times up."

I look at the time then spring to my feet. The blood rushes from my head, so I reach out for something to hold onto as a spout of dizziness overcomes me. Alex leaps to his feet and catches me right before I fall.

"Are you okay?" he asks, holding me in his arms.

I nod, still a little woozy. "I just moved too fast. That's all."

"You look a little pale," he notes. "Maybe you should rest."

"I'll rest when this is all over."

He traces his fingers along the sliver of skin peeking out from the bottom of my shirt. "Gemma, you need to take care over yourself better."

"I know I do," I tell him, "but after I go find Aislin. I promised her I'd look for her if she wasn't back by now."

"I'll go look for her." He helps me stand but keeps a grip on my arm. "You go rest."

"Alex, I—"

Poof.

Smoke swiftly fills the room, and in the center of the mist, Aislin appears. She looks fine except for a scratch on her cheek, and her hair is a mess.

"You made it." I recline against Alex as the stress and tension evaporate from my body.

"Of course I did." She wiggles her fingers in front of her. "And I got the power." She pops her hip out and puts her hand on it. "So let's get those wings off you . . ." Her jaw drops as her eyes land on Alana who's now wide awake and standing, looking more coherent. "Mom?"

Alana tears up as she wraps an arm around Aislin. Then she grabs Alex with her free hand and pulls him in, too. I back away with the painful realization that I'll never have this kind of moment with my mother. Even if I do see her again, she's a ghost now, and I can't even touch her.

I slowly turn to Nicholas. "You and I have a little problem."

"Don't we have more than one of those?" he asks cheerfully.

I jab a finger at him. "Where's my mom?"

His silence sends a cold chill up my spine

"I'm not going to see her again, am I?" I can barely get air into my lungs.

He nods once. "I'm sorry."

I don't say a word—can't—otherwise, I'll lose it.

I leave the room, go up to my bedroom, and flop down on the bed. Rolling onto my side, I hug a pillow to my chest and let the tears pour out.

A minute or two later, someone knocks on my door. Before I can get up to answer, the door opens, and Laylen tentatively walks in.

"Are you okay?" he asks as he sits down on the edge of my bed.

"Yeah, I'm just being overemotional." I laugh hollowly. "It's kind of funny, isn't it? All those years of being unemotional, and now I'm too emotional."

"There's no such thing as being too emotional when

you lose someone you love." He reaches out and rubs my back. "I remember when my parents died. It hurt so badly, and I didn't know how to deal with the pain. I kept wishing for time to stop so I didn't have to go through life without them. But life kept going, and after a while, all that hurt gnawing inside me became a little easier to bear. I won't lie to you, though; it won't ever fully go away."

Tears bubble in my eyes again. "When does it get easier? How much time will it take?"

"As much as you need," he says. Then he pulls me into his arms, and I cry against his shoulder.

I'll never see my mother again. I'll never get to know her. I'll never have memories of her other than the horrible ones I have now.

She's gone.

And I have to move on somehow.

But not yet.

SOMEHOW, I FALL asleep, and even though I can feel the weight of my mom's death crushing my chest, my body actually feels ten times lighter.

I push up and glance over my shoulder to see the wings are no longer there.

"They're gone."

"Yeah, Aislin took them off while you were asleep," Alex says, scaring the bejesus out of me. He's lounging in my computer chair with his arms tucked behind his head. "Aislin thought it might cheer you up a little if you woke up and they were gone," he explains, swiveling in the chair. "How are you doing?"

"Not great," I admit, tucking my feet under me. "But I don't think I'm supposed to be great."

He shifts forward in the chair. "No, I don't think you are." He scoots forward more. "Gemma, I know you don't want to hear this, but I think we need to find another way to fix this. I know everyone says it has to be you, but there has to be another way. You've already given up so much of your life. You don't need to give up more."

"Alex, we've been over this. There's not another way, so you need to stop searching for something that doesn't exist. It just wastes time that we don't have." I climb out of bed, stretching my arms and legs. "In fact, I think we should get going now. We've already wasted too much time."

"Gemma—" he starts, pushing to his feet.

"Is your mom ready to do this or what?" I talk over him, ready to get it over with. Alex may want to find another way, but there isn't one, and looking only wastes time and puts more stress on everyone. "And what even happens? Because no one has explained that part."

His Adam's apple bobs up and down as he swallows hard. "The Banshee in Iceland wasn't lying. You have to fake your own death so you really look dead, or Helena won't let you in."

"With poison?"

"My mom said that's the easiest way." He restlessly starts clicking the mouse. "Please don't do this. If not for me, for our daughter."

"Our daughter's going to be fine. The spell won't let anything happen to her."

In three long strides, he's stolen the space between us. Electricity surges as his fingers fold around my hips, and he pulls me to him.

"We could leave," he says in desperation. "Just you and me. Run away and never look back."

"And then what? Just let the world end? Could you really do that?"

He presses his lips together. "Could you?"

I shake my head, my hands trembling as I loop my arms around his neck. "It's time to end this, Alex. We can't run away anymore." I brush my lips across his mouth before stepping out of his arms and turning for the door. "You don't have to be there for this if you don't want to, but I-I really want you to be."

Even though I can tell he's not happy about it, he still takes my hand. That's when I feel the softest prickle against the back of my neck. I think I know what emotion is coming, and it scares me to death, so I bury it down and focus on my death, instead.

CHAPTER
THIRTY-ONE

Alex

IT ACHED LIKE hell to see Gemma hurting over losing her mother. I started to go after her, but Laylen said he'd go see if she was okay. Even though it nearly killed me, I let him go, knowing he can relate to Gemma's situation better.

After he helps her deal with the death of her mother, I'm left helping her fake her own death, which again, is just about killing me.

We gather in the living room to get everything going. Aislin mixes the poison in a glass vile then gives it to Gemma, looking as anxious as I feel.

"Be careful with it," Aislin tells her. "If you get any on your skin, it'll kill the cells."

Gemma gulps then carefully takes the vile of clear liquid. "So I just drink this, and then it'll make me look like I'm dead?"

"It will once I seal it with the essence of death," Aislin

says, twisting a lid back on a bottle.

"It sounds like something straight out of Shakespeare." Her violet eyes sparkle as she studies the vile with her head slanted to the side.

"Like Romeo and Juliet," Nicholas remarks from somewhere in the room. "Let's just hope this one over here doesn't pull a Romeo and take his own life. Then you'll both be dead."

I figure he's talking to me, and usually, I'd be all over getting him to shut the hell up, but I'm too stuck in my own head, racking my brain for another way.

There has to be another way.

"Nicholas, I'm glad you're still around." My mother takes sip of water before setting the glass down on the coffee table. "I need your help with something."

"Oh, I'm intrigued," he says with a wicked laugh. "I hope it has something to do with hauling Gemma to the other side. Gives me a chance to be alone with her."

My jaw clamps down as I bite my tongue. "How is Gemma even supposed to convince Helena to give up the lost souls? Because from experience, queens aren't too thrilled to just hand over things that belong to them."

My mom leans over and taps the ring on Gemma's hand. "With that. It belongs to the queen."

"The last time we tried to make a bargain with a jewel, it didn't work out so well," Gemma says, a deep frown setting in. "We ended up trapped in The Underworld."

"That won't happen," my mom assures us. "As long as you're still tied to the human world, the queen can't trap you there or hurt you. And she'll want that ring more than anything since it carries her soul."

Gemma blinks at her then stares wide-eyed at the ring. "This is the Queen of the Afterlife's *soul?*"

My mom nods. "That's why you can see the dead when you wear it."

"There's something really bugging me," I interrupt. "How does the poison even work? I mean, when and how does it bring her back to life?"

My mother pats my shoulder. "That's your part in all of this. You'll help keep her connected to the real world because you're part of her in every way: through the promise, through the star, through your connected souls."

"Connected souls?" Gemma gives me a confounded look. "Did I miss something?"

"Yours and Alex's souls are connected, dear. When he decided to break the spell Sophia put on you, he gave you a piece of his soul."

Gemma gives me an indecipherable look that makes me feel very exposed, as if I'm wearing all my emotions on my sleeve for everyone to see.

"And to answer your question, all you have to do is revive her when it's time," my mom says with an encouraging smile. "And Nicholas is going to inform you when it's time."

I frown, deflated. "You actually want to leave someone like him in charge of something as important as that?"

"He's the one who can see into the Afterlife," she says. "And, Alex, I assure you he's not going to mess this up, or there will be consequences."

Nicholas is surprisingly quiet, but his silence still does nothing for my nerves. This isn't just anyone's life we're discussing. It's Gemma's, the woman who owns part of my soul, who made me feel things I never thought were possible, the mother of my unborn child, and the person I'd die for in a heartbeat.

"Why can't you just come back and tell us?" I ask my

---

mom. "It seems less risky that way."

She averts her gaze to the floor. "Once I cross over into the Afterlife, I can't come back, sweetie."

"What!" I shout and Gemma gasps, almost dropping the vile.

"I've been avoiding my duties as a Banshee," she explains quietly. "Once I turned into one, I got myself sentenced to the Foreseer's crystal to keep my whereabouts hidden. But now . . . When I go to the Afterlife, Helena will make me stay and pay my debt. But afterward, I'll come back. This isn't the last time you'll see me." She smiles at me. "Besides, I'm going to need to come back to see my granddaughter."

"Maybe we should find another Banshee to take me there, then," Gemma says, her fingers tightening around the vile.

"No other Banshee will bring your soul back," I tell her sadly. I wish there was another way, too, but I can't risk you getting stuck in the Afterlife, too.

With nothing left to discuss, we go up to her room to get started. I'm still racking my brain, trying to think of a better way. I even consider stealing the vile and drinking it myself, but what if my mom's right? What if it does have to be Gemma? What if I go and ruin it, and Gemma's left here dealing with the guilt of what she's done?

There's one thing that makes it easier to deal with—knowing that, as long as I'm breathing, Gemma is, too.

Gemma lies down on her bed and overlaps her arms on her stomach. "In the dream I kept having, Nicholas was the one who showed up to take me to the Afterlife."

"That's because you secretly have the hots for me," Nicholas says, his voice filling the room as the computer chair rolls around on its own

"Or maybe it's because for three straight weeks you wouldn't leave me alone," Gemma snaps. "You were watching me day and night, even when you shouldn't have been."

"Would you all get your head in the game?" Aislin asks, gently shaking the vile to mix up the liquid. "I don't want to mess this up."

Sealing my lips, I sink down on the foot of the bed beside Gemma's feet. "Are you doing okay?"

She bobs her head up and down, her gaze fixed on the ceiling. "I just can't wait until this is all over."

"Me, either." I rub my hand up and down her leg, which seems to relax her.

"I need complete silence." Aislin waits until everyone has shut the hell up before she starts chanting, "Signa hoc venenum cum osculum vitae," she whispers, swishing the liquid. "Servare quicumque bibit spirans. Sed signa voluntas osculum mortem et eorum cor mittimus." Once the liquid in the vile bubbles and darkens to a deep grey, Aislin lifts it to her face and squints at it. "Now, that's death."

"I guess it's time," my mom says quietly.

Aislin runs over and throws her arms around my mom. "I can't believe you're leaving already."

"This isn't good-bye," my mother whispers, embracing her tightly. "I'll be back one day."

Tears flow from Aislin's eyes as she pulls back and nods.

After my mom gives me a hug, too, she turns to Gemma. "And I'll see you even sooner. Remember, don't fight death. If you fight it, it'll look suspicious." Then, quicker than she arrived, my mother vanishes into thin air.

A rush of sadness crashes down on me and makes me really fucking uncomfortable, so I clear my throat, trying to pull my shit together.

"Are you ready?" Aislin asks Gemma as she sinks down on the edge of the bed.

Gemma takes the vile from Aislin. "As ready as I'll ever be," she says, forcing a stiff smile.

Aislin glances over her shoulder at me. "You need to go downstairs. You can't be near her at all. She needs to be calm, and you make her the opposite of calm."

"I can't be away from her," I say with my gaze locked on Gemma.

"Alex, please go," Gemma begs. "The spell might get messed up if I'm not totally relaxed."

Brushing my finger across my palm, I think of the promise we made. Two kids who were trying to hold on to something that might never be. Gemma must read my mind because she also touches the scar on her hand.

Forever, she mouths.

Forever, I mouth back.

Walking out of the room is one of the hardest things I've ever had to do, but I somehow manage. When I enter the kitchen, I find Laylen messing around with the pipes under the sink.

"What are you doing, man?" I ask.

He focuses on twisting a bolt. "Distracting myself . . . It's easier this way."

I bob my head up and down then roll up my sleeves. "Need any help?"

He shrugs. "Sure."

I reach for the wrench, trying to ignore the feeling of Gemma's life slipping away.

CHAPTER
THIRTY-TWO

Gemma

A S I WATCH Alex leave, I swear I feel him taking a part of me with him as the electricity dissipates from inside my body. I'm so terrified right now over what I'm about to do that I almost call him back, but deep down, I know I can't. This is something I have to do on my own.

I hold the vile of poison in my hand, my heart slamming deafeningly inside my chest. "I'm nervous," I admit to Aislin.

"You don't need to be nervous," Aislin reassures me as she side braids her hair and secures it with an elastic. "I promise nothing's going to go wrong. I can't let it this time, not with this."

I inhale then exhale, trying to calm down. "I feel so silly. I mean, I know I'm going to come back, and I know I'm not going to die, yet I'm still terrified out of my mind."

"Gemma, you're about to drink death. Of course you're scared." She pauses, eyeing the vile in my hand.

"You don't have to do this. You know that, right?"

"A vision said I did it."

"Fuck the visions. They don't always have to map the future for us."

I can't help smiling. "You sound just like Alex."

"I do, don't I?" A thoughtful look crosses her face. "You know what? A few months ago, I would've been insulted, but now it's not so bad—he's not so bad—and that's because of you. You changed him, brought him back to the loving, caring brother I used to know when we were kids, before my father tried to mess him up." Her smile grows. "You two together are going to be great parents. I can feel it."

I force down the lump lodged in my throat. "Aislin, will you promise me something?"

She wavers. "That all really depends on what it is."

"Will you . . . ?" I lay my arm over my stomach. "If something happens to me, will you take care of her? You're such a good person, and I just want . . . I want her to grow up and have a better life than I did with a good mother figure."

"Gemma, you're going to be okay," she says, choking back the sobs. "But if you need me to promise that, then I will."

"Thank you." I clear my throat as tears burn my eyes. "Now let's get this over with." I bring the vile to my lips, tip my head back, and gag as I force the liquid down my throat. "It tastes just like . . . death."

As the poison swims through my veins, my limbs numb, and then my eyelids shut as I fall into the darkness.

MY EYES SNAP open, and I trip back, gasping for air. I quickly run my hands all over my body, making sure everything's intact, then take in my surroundings.

I'm in a grassy field just outside of a forest. A light breeze kisses the grass, and crows circle above my head.

"This is just like my nightmare," I mutter to myself then quickly duck as the crows dive for my head. "Stop!" I shout at the top of my lungs, and they scatter like mice.

I stand back up and look around the field for Alana. I can't see her anywhere but notice one crow hovering above my head like it is dancing.

It circles around and flies off toward the trees. Like in my nightmare, I chase after it until it takes off upward, disappearing into the sky and leaving me all alone. Then I trample through the grass, walking for what seems like forever until I finally stumble across a rundown house that looks like it once caught fire.

Trembling from nerves, I carefully walk up the porch stairs and open the front door. When I step inside, I'm standing in a house with charred walls.

"This is the house that was in Iceland," I whisper to myself as I inch inside.

The floorboards groan underneath me, and the door slams shut.

"No." I spin and yank on the doorknob, but it won't budge. "Please, please open. Don't lock me in here."

"Calm down, Gemma. You're all right," Alana says from behind me.

I turn to face her, still tense. "I wasn't sure if I was in the right place or not. Then I realized I've been in this house before and I panicked."

"Everything's going to be okay." She offers me her hand. "But we still have a ways to go."

I take her hand, and then she guides me up the

creaking stairs. With each step, the weight I have been carrying in my chest becomes lighter. I don't know if it's the place or the fact that I'm technically dead, but I can see reality clearer and accept it.

"I'm going to die and so is Alex," I say to Alana. "We have to, don't we? Otherwise, there's no way of killing the star and Stephan. I mean, I always kind of knew it was going to happen, but now I know it . . . can actually feel it."

"Death is like that," she says, resting her hand on the banister as we reach the top of the stairway. "It makes accepting things—even death itself—less difficult because you don't have the complication of life."

"Are you sure there's not another way?" But as soon as I ask it, I can feel the answer, understand there's not another way. I'm going to die for real and very soon. "Maybe a way to at least save Alex."

"You'd do that? Choose his life over yours?" As we stop in front of a solid door, she looks at me, appearing astonished.

I nod, wholly aware at that moment just how much I care about Alex. "I care about him . . . And I want out daughter to have her father around while she's growing up."

The door makes a grumbling sound and Alana stiffens.

"Hold that thought for a while, okay?" Alana extends her hand for the doorknob. "Right now, we need to focus on getting you to the queen."

"I have a feeling this isn't going to be as easy as you said."

"Nothing's ever easy, even in death."

She swings the door open, and we step into the darkness. The air is so thick and suffocating I nearly pass out. Then the most rancid smell burns my nostrils, and suddenly I'm kneeling down and throwing up on the dirt floor.

Once I've emptied my stomach, Alana helps me to my feet.

"Keep your head down and try not to look at anything," she whispers as we head down a narrow tunnel.

I slant my chin down and let my hair curtain my face. I hold my breath and quickly realize I no longer need air. I grow fascinated with the idea, trying to suck air in and out of my lungs until I get a glimpse of a bony foot in my peripheral vision. My muscles wind tight as I turn my head.

Bodies cover the wall, wrapped in aged and torn fabric like mummies. Some of their limbs and faces are hanging out, their bodies' pale and frail, their eyes hollow.

"These are some of the souls you're here to save," Alana utters quietly over her shoulder. "Try not to look at them, though. It upsets the queen." She slows down to walk beside me, matching my steps as she leans in and lowers her voice. "And, Gemma, whatever you do, don't give her the ring until you've sealed the promise for the freedom of the lost souls, the ones who ended up here because of the apocalypse."

I jolt as one of the lost souls cries out. "Does she know why I'm here?" I whisper.

"She's the Queen of the Afterlife, not the Ruler of the City of Crystal, so you're going to have to explain it to her."

I dare another look at the souls, worried that somehow one of them might be my mother. Is this where she ended up? If so, does that mean she'll be freed when I release them?

"Your mother's not there, and be grateful she's not," Alana whispers like she read my mind.

Maybe she's right. Maybe I should be grateful my

mom isn't in this god-awful place. Still, for some reason, I just feel more heartbroken because that means she won't be part of the souls I free.

When we reach the end of the tunnel and step into a large room, I start to get why Alana told me to be grateful. The souls down here aren't just lost; they're tortured.

In the room, the mummy-like bodies are being forced to drag large trailers of coffins up a dirt path as men dressed in armor beat them. Cries haunt the air, and blood stains the ground.

It reminds me a lot of The Underworld, but the difference is that these souls aren't evil.

They're just lost.

CHAPTER
THIRTY-THREE

Alex

"NOW WHAT DO we do?" Laylen asks as he leans back against the counter and folds his arms. "I mean, there's only so much crap we can attempt to fix before we have to admit we're not handymen." He looks down at the pool of water on the floor, proving his point.

I sit down in a chair, trying to think of an idea, but my thoughts keep drifting to Gemma and what's going on upstairs.

"I honestly have no fucking clue." I pause. "Maybe we should just go upstairs and check on things."

"You know you'll go crazy if you see her like that."

"I know."

The room grows quiet.

"Okay, so who wants to help me?" Aislin enters the room, looking as cheerful and happy as a cheerleader on crack.

"If you're going to be cheerful, then leave," I grumble. "And where's Gemma?"

"She's upstairs in her bed, completely fine. I even checked her vitals and did a spell to make sure the baby is doing okay." She nudges me in the foot with her shoe. "So stop being a downer and come help me."

"With what?" Laylen asks, mildly curious.

Aislin claps her hands together. "With removing your Mark of Immortality."

"You've finally figured out that spell?" I sound way too surprised, causing her to glare at me.

"For your information, it's a completely unknown spell, and most witches can't even do unknown spells," she says, "so the fact that I've gotten far enough to test it says how much of a badass I am."

Laylen's eyebrows shoot up when Aislin looks at him. "You want to try it on *me?*"

She nods almost too energetically. "It'd be much easier to try it out on you than anyone else." She chews on her fingernail. "You don't have to, though. I get it if you don't want the mark gone."

He looks down at the mark branding his forearm. "You can try it on me."

"Are you sure?" she checks.

"I'm sure," he says confidently.

"Awesome." She scratches at her arm. "Then, after I've perfected that spell, it's on to the shield removing spell. Although I'm not sure how I'm going to figure out if that one works without being right next to Stephan."

"That's not happening. No one's ever going to be around him again," I say and Laylen nods in agreement. "It's a good thing you guys never told him where we were when you went all crazy."

"That's because I put an Interpres Incantatores on all of us, which keeps any of us from divulging our location to any person who means us harm," Aislin says, getting a bottle of water from the fridge. "When you went on that I-need-to-get-away-from-Gemma journey of yours, you missed out on a lot of amazing spells I learned." She unscrews the cap off the bottle and takes a swig.

"But you didn't do the spell on me," I remind her. "Maybe you should."

She sets the bottle down on the table and elevates her hands in the air. "Non proferre verbum ad hostis." Sparks of silver shoot from her hands and land all over me, singeing my skin and clothes.

"Dammit, Aislin!" I jump to my feet, brushing off the sparks on my arms and shirt.

Laylen chokes on a laugh, and Aislin grins at him. "Don't get too giggly; you're next."

She sits down at the table and opens up her spell book to a marked page titled "Bonum et Malum Cantus."

"The Good and Evil Spell," Aislin reads the title as I sit back down. "It separates good from evil when it coexists inside one entity."

Laylen joins as us the table "But how is that supposed to work on Stephan when he doesn't have any good inside him?"

She traces her fingers along the page. "I know, but for now, it's all I have. Maybe, deep down inside him, he has some form of good in him." She shrugs. "He's a father, so there's that."

"But he was a shitty father," I mutter.

"I know." She tips her head down.

We grow quiet, and my thoughts instantly drift to Gemma again. Is she okay? Is she in the Afterlife yet?

When will we know if she's freed the souls?

"There's just one tiny, little problem with the spell," Aislin says, breaking the silence. "There's this thing about blood." She flips the page. "The spell requires the blood of a person who's both good and bad."

"I have an idea on where you can get that." Laylen says then points at himself. "Me."

"Oh, I don't think that's what it means," Aislin skims the spell. "It couldn't be . . ."

I decide to put my two cents in, even though Aislin's more than likely going to get pissed off at me.

"He's a vampire and a Keeper, and that's bad and good."

"Alex, be nice," Aislin hisses, glaring at me.

"I'm not trying to be mean," I say. "And I'm not saying he's bad, just that he carries vampire blood inside, and vampires are usually bad."

Laylen places a hand over Aislin. "It doesn't hurt to try it."

She mulls it over, running her finger along the page. "We can try it, but I still need a few more ingredients." She scoots back from the table. "Let me go check my supplies and see what I have."

She skips off toward the stairs, swinging her arms.

"Sometimes, she can be so crazy," I say, shaking my head.

"She's your sister"—Laylen crosses his arms on the table—"so wouldn't that make you crazy, too?"

"I never claimed to be completely sane, but what I really want to know is what Aislin is to you."

He shifts in the chair, seeming uneasy. "Where the hell did that come from?"

I shrug. "You guys just seem really close lately, yet at

the same time, you're close to Gemma, too." I recline in the chair. "I just want to make sure no one gets hurt."

"Gemma and I are just friends."

"Okay, but what about you and my sister?"

"I care about Aislin. You know that." He pats the table then scoots the chair back and stands up. "I think I'll go help Aislin."

The second he walks out, the silence sets in, and my head crams with worry. I hate not knowing what's going on. I want go upstairs and check, but worry I might mess something up.

But all I can do is wait and hope everything will be okay.

CHAPTER
THIRTY-FOUR

Gemma

"THIS IS WAY worse than I thought it would be," I tell Alana as we hurry out of the torture chamber and down another long, narrow tunnel that, fortunately, doesn't have any lost souls bound to the wall. "They look so . . . so broken. I don't get it. Why does she have to torture them?"

The glow from the red lanterns hanging on the walls lights up her face as she looks at me. "When people die before their time, their soul is considered lost. There's no real place for those souls to go, so they end up here. Queen Helena collects them and turns them into those mummy figures you saw. She has them work for her in order to keep her world thriving."

I swallow hard. "You know for sure my mom's not one of them, right?"

"When she died, it was her time," she tells me as the tunnel makes a dip downward.

"But she took her own life; how can that be her time?"

I hunker down as the space between the ceiling and my head shortens.

"Just like when you sacrifice your life to save the world, you mother's life ended when she took her own life to save you."

"But how did it save me? She didn't know if she'd lead Stephan to me. She just feared she would."

"No, she knew." She stops in front of an archway. "Just like I knew you needed to come here."

"So you've seen how all of this is going to turn out?" I question.

She nods then inches through the archway and vanishes into the darkness. I follow after her, trying to keep track of her silhouette, but darkness suffocates me, bearing down heavily. I feel so heavy.

When I can finally see clearly again, I'm standing in front of a throne made of twisted, thorny branches. The legs are perched on a blood-red platform that grows out from the charcoal floor.

"She's not here," I say to Alana, turning in a circle, taking in the rippling sheet of silver metal above my head.

"Oh, she's here." Alana points upward.

The sheet warps, and a shimmering spiral of metal twists down and connects to the seat of a throne, forming an eyeless woman with glittering, sliver skin.

"Quomodo audent intra hic sponte. Ubi non est libertas," her voice ripples through the room.

"I've come to turn myself in," Alana calls out, moving in front of me. "And she would like to make a bargain with you."

"I do not make bargains!" the queen bellows, thankfully in a language I can understand. "There are no bargains to be made here, only souls to collect."

"Feel her soul, Helena," Alana speaks passionately as she stands tall in front of the throne. "Feel it and you'll see."

I don't understand what's going on. I just hope Alana does, hope I can trust her. Hope. All of this is riding on hope.

"She's broken." He mouth moves fluidly, liquid steel flowing. "Why do you bring her to me? Your first time in the Afterlife after escaping your debt for years, and this is what you bring me? A broken and tortured soul that belongs to another?" She flicks her wrist, shooing us away. "Take her away." She unexpectedly freezes then leans forward in her throne with eagerness written all over her face. "No, better yet, stay now that you're here."

"She's come to make an exchange for the lost souls' freedom." Alana moves in front of me, blocking the queen from my view. "She's the one responsible for the heavy amount of traffic you've had lately."

"How dare you!" Helena shouts, slamming her fist against the armrest, liquid splashing from her body and pooling around the throne. "There's nothing you can do or give me that would ever, ever make me want to free any of my souls!"

Alana spins toward me, her hair whipping around. "Show her the ring. Show her now."

Stepping around Alana, I lift my hand and show the queen her ring.

Helena gasps, jerking back in her throne while covering her mouth with her hand. "Where did you get that?"

Before I can respond, she dives off her throne. With a swish, her liquid body pools in front of me, and she rises, taking form. Then she dips her nose toward me and smells me like a dog.

"Who are you?" she growls "And why does your soul feel unnatural, like venom in my lungs?"

I look to Alana for help because I have no idea what to say. Alana opens her mouth to say something, but the queen cuts her off.

"It's invigorating," she purrs, sniffing me again. "I want it." She swoops up and dives down with her mouth open.

I can feel my limbs being pulled inside her body as her liquid seeps through my skin like hot, polluted water.

"Let me out!" I scream, but my voice gets trapped in her body.

She slinks back to the throne and sits back down. "There we go. Much better."

I dry heave as I feel what she's feeling, feel how much she wants to keep me.

"Let me out." I start to cry.

"Oh, sweetie, you're not going anywhere," she says. "Ever again."

"YOU CAN'T HOLD onto her forever," Alana tells the queen after hours have gone by. She's been pacing in front of the throne ever since the queen . . . well, ate me, I guess. "You know you can't. She's not one of your lost souls; therefore, you can't keep her."

"I can keep her if she offers herself to me. And you know the souls that offer themselves to me are the best kind." She slams her fists against the armrests, throwing a tantrum, but I can feel her weakening around me as she struggles to keep me trapped inside her body. "She can offer herself up! She can offer herself up! And then I can keep her forever and ever and ever!"

"Helena," Alana says, sounding exhausted but patient. "You can't keep her, and you know it, so let her go and hear what she has to say about the bargain."

She rumbles, and the walls vibrate around us. Then liquid swells inside her lungs as she unhinges her jaw and, with a yack, spits me out onto the floor.

I slide out and roll over onto my back, wiping away her silvery spit and God knows what else that now coats my skin.

"Well, that was lovely," I say, pushing myself to my feet.

"You're lucky I let you go," she snaps, wiping her lips with the back of her hand. "Now tell me more of this bargain before I lose my temper again. You want me to free souls in exchange for my own ring back? Because I'd really like to know how you ended up with the ring to begin with."

I touch the ring, remembering when my father gave it to me. There's no way I'll ever out him, however he ended up with the ring.

"You know as well as I do that those souls are supposed to be free." I square my shoulders. "You were never supposed to have them, and I think you know that."

She leans forward on her thrown. "How dare you talk to me like that? This is the Afterlife—my Afterlife—and I'll rule it however I want."

"Not even for this?" I raise my hand, giving her a glimpse of the ring again.

She licks her lips, eyeballing the ring. "Give me my ring back."

I shake my head, tucking my arm behind my back.

"Not until you free the souls."

"I could just take it from you," she warns in a low tone.

"I really don't think that's true." I struggle to stay composed. "Otherwise, you would've already."

She curls her fingers around the armrests. "Maybe I will, then."

I shrug, even though anxiety and worry bounce around inside me like an out-of-control bouncy ball.

She fixes her attention on me and I stand firm, refusing to cave or show weakness. When she finally reclines back on her throne, hope sparks inside me that maybe this will work.

"If I free these souls, then you'll give me the ring back?" she asks. "Without any stipulations?"

I nod. "All I'm asking is for you to free the souls that were taken during the apocalypse . . . And to give the life back to a half-faerie named Nicholas."

"Give back a life." She erupts with laughter. "I have no control over such things."

"Yes, you do." Alana dares to step up onto the podium. "Through your sister, Annabella."

"I don't have any connection with Annabella or her decisions," the queen snaps. "And how dare you suggest otherwise!"

"Oh, I'm pretty sure you do, even if you won't admit it," Alana says confidently. "I know you want your soul back. You've been stuck in that hideous body ever since you lost your own, melting away into a pathetic excuse for a queen. And you can't take that ring from Gemma's hand. Whoever holds that ring owns your soul and can only choose to give it back to you. That's how the curse works."

Helena snarls, her growl ripping through the air. But

when neither of us budge, she settles down.

"If I was to speak with Annabella and free this faerie's essence, I'd want to talk to Gemma alone before giving her the lost souls she requests and then letting her back into the mortal world."

"I . . ." I glance at Alana in a panic. The idea of being alone with the queen is horrifying.

"That's my final offer," Helena says, relaxing back on her throne and crossing her legs.

"Fine, I'll do it," I say in a shockingly confident voice.

Alana bows her head and curtsies to the queen. "I'll go, then."

"Don't go too far. You owe me your debt by collecting my souls for me, just like all humans who make the choice to cross over into the Banshee world. Immortality doesn't come without a price, and you've been hiding from your debt for a very long time, ever since I agreed to give you the gift of Banshee blood and preserve your body's state."

"I know what I owe." She backs away and out into the tunnel, leaving me alone with the queen.

Even though I can't see her eyes, I can sense her watching me like a hawk, and I try not to squirm.

"I know you," she finally says. "You're important, filled with an essence I've never tasted before. Annabella would be thrilled to get a taste of you."

"As much as I'm flattered about that, I really don't think I want to be tasted ever again."

Her laughter reverberates throughout the room. "You're clever, but I wonder just how far that cleverness could take you."

"I'm not sure I'm following you."

"You're freeing these lost souls for the purpose that they aren't supposed to be here, but tell me, why not free your own soul?"

I pause as her question really sinks in.

"I didn't realize it needed to be freed."

"Everyone's soul needs to be freed in some way or another," she says. "But yours is different. Yours needs to be freed from the pain you've always carried around."

I place my hand over my heart, but I lack a pulse. "My soul's fine." With everything that's happened to it, though, I'm not so sure.

"It might be okay for now, but not after you die, and you will die very soon."

"How do you know about that?"

"All humans die," she replies. "Your life just ends sooner. But you won't be alone. You'll die with someone important to you, someone you desperately wish you could save."

I swallow the pain down as I think of how Alex will die with me. "Maybe."

"But you can't save others from death," she says, "not without a price."

"What kind of price?" I inch toward the throne. "Are you saying there's a way to save Alex and me?"

"Not both of you; only one of you." She smiles, seemingly pleased. "Only one of you can survive, with a sacrifice. One life in exchange for the other. But the question is, who will live and who will die?"

CHAPTER
THIRTY-FIVE

Alex

IT'S BEEN TOO long. I can feel it in my bones, in my heart, in my soul. I want to run upstairs and wake her up, but Aislin's watching me like a hawk.

"Quit fidgeting," Aislin says to me as she sorts through a box of herbs. "You're driving me crazy."

I flip through the television channels, and each station talks about the same thing: all the madness, chaos, and death happening. It's too depressing to watch and think about, so I turn off the TV and pick up my knife and sharpener.

"You're driving me crazy, too," I say as I drag the edge of the blade along the sharpener. "You've been looking through that box of herbs for, like, an hour. It's taking forever, and we don't have forever."

"I know, but I didn't mark any of them." She opens a bag and sniffs the green flakes of leaves inside it. "Or, well, I did, but the crazy me pulled off all the labels."

"You know, you're kind of crazy and self-destructing when you're evil," I point out. "You tear the labels off all your herbs. Then you go free a Black Angel and risk getting trapped yourself, all so you can seek revenge on Gemma, and for what?"

She shrugs. "Jealous rage. For some reason, I had it in my head that Gemma was trying to steal Laylen from me, which is crazy."

Jealously twists in my gut. I don't really believe Gemma was trying to steal Laylen from Aislin, but there's definitely a connection between Gemma and Laylen that I hate.

I glance around the living room. "Where is Laylen, anyway? I thought he went to check on Gemma, but he's been gone forever. Maybe something's wrong."

"He's been gone for, like, two minutes, Alex." She seals the bag shut and drops it into the box. "Just chill out, okay? You're making a stressful situation worse."

I point at the stairway. "Gemma's lying dead in her bed, her spirit's in the Afterlife, and you want me to chill out?"

"Everything's going to be okay, Alex. I won't let anything happen to her." She picks up another bag, this time filled with dry, red petals. "What is that?"

I shrug. "Why are you asking me? I don't know anything about herbs."

"No, not this." She sets the bag down and twists around. "That banging noise . . . It sounds like it's coming from the basement."

A ripple of tension waves through me, and my Keeper senses kick into full gear. "This place doesn't have a basement, Aislin."

She leans to the side, listening. "Well, then it's coming

from under the house."

When I strain my ears and hear the faintest bang, I'm on my feet in an instant, carrying the knife as I head for the kitchen. The noise grows even louder, and I push my weight down on each tile, searching for a loose one, thinking maybe Marco and Sophia have a trap door.

After checking each one, I drag the table to the side and check the tiles that were underneath it. One feels loose, so I bend down, and with my knife, I chip away at the grout. The tile shifts to the side, and I pull it out along with a few others then discover a trapdoor tucked underneath them.

I contemplate what to do. I'm not sure what could be down there making that noise. Anything's possible, really.

"Hello," someone says from below.

I take a step back, aiming my knife at the trapdoor. "Aislin, get in here."

"Coming!" she calls from the living room.

The trapdoor opens, and a hand appears out of the dark hole.

"Hello? Is anyone there?" someone says from below.

The voice sounds familiar, but I can't exactly place it.

A woman with auburn hair suddenly pops out of the hole and heaves herself onto the floor. Panting, she rolls over on her back and looks up at me.

"Alex, is that you?"

I know who she looks like, but I'm not buying her appearance just yet.

I bend over and grip her throat. "Who are you?"

Her body shakes, scared to death. "It's me . . ." She struggles to breathe. "Sophia, Gemma's grandmother. You know me, Alex Avery."

"Sophia's dead, so you may look like her, but I'm not

buying it." My grip tightens. "Tell me what you are? A Banshee? A witch?"

"I swear I'm Sophia," she says, trying to pry my hands away from her throat as tears slip from her eyes. "I don't know how to prove it to you, but I'm really her."

Suddenly, a pan comes flying through the air and hits the woman square in the forehead. She gasps one final breath of air before she passes out. Then I let her go and jump to my feet, only to find a wide-eyed Aislin gaping at the woman on the floor.

"What is that? Like a zombie?"

"Zombies don't exist." I lean down to examine the woman, trying to figure out who she really is. There's now a gash on her forehead and a trail of blood running down her cheek. "No, she's alive." I check her pulse to make sure then look over my shoulder at Aislin. "Did you really have to throw a pan at her?"

She shrugs. "I thought it was a zombie, and I panicked." She moves up beside me. "What is it, do you think?"

"I'm not sure, but there's one way to find out if it's really Sophia." I slide the collar of her shirt over, and sure enough, a ring of flames tattoos her skin.

"It's her? How the hell is that possible?" Aislin asks in shock. "I did a Tracker Spell on her, and it said she didn't exist. And Marco, too."

"Well, something went wrong, obviously."

"How? I never mess spells up."

I lift my brows, giving her a *really* look, and she smacks me in the back of the head.

"So if it is her," Aislin says, glancing at the trapdoor, "then where's Marco? And why was Sophia down there?"

I turn around and lie flat on my stomach, looking

down into the area the trapdoor leads to. "There's only one way to find out."

With a deep breath, I lower myself into the hole. It reeks like someone has been down there for a long-ass time. Other than some food supplies and the stench, there's not really anything else down there, so I climb back up into the kitchen and fill a cup with water.

"Go tell Laylen who we just found," I order Aislin. "And make sure everything's going okay with Gemma."

Nodding, Aislin heads for the doorway, calling over her shoulder, "Be careful."

Once Aislin's gone, I crouch down beside Sophia and sprinkle some water onto her face. "Wake up." When she doesn't move, I give her face a pat and sprinkle some more water on her.

Her eyelids flutter open. "Alex," she croaks, touching her head. "What happened?"

"You jumped out of a hole in the floor," I tell her. "Then Aislin threw a pan at your head because she thought you're a zombie."

She winces, blinking dazedly. "A zombie? Why on earth would she think I'm a zombie?"

"Because apparently you're supposed to be dead, and clearly you're not."

As she glances at the knife in my hand, I can see her mentally calculating whether to steal it from me or not.

"Choose your next move really carefully," I warn. "I won't hesitate to kill you if I have to."

She shakes her head, sitting up. "You're just like your father," she bites out as she wipes some dirt away from her cheeks.

My eyelids narrow to slits. "See, now that's the kind of thing to say if you want to get killed."

She shakes her head, glancing around her kitchen, looking disoriented. "Sorry. I'm so confused. I can barely remember anything except"—her brows knit—"Aislin and that vampire showing up."

"What are you talking about? When were they here?"

"I don't know." She massages her temples. "My brain feels so foggy . . . I can remember Gemma disappearing and Stephan yelling at me for letting it happen. Then he went on this rampage and started murdering Keepers. Marco and I were going to run, but Aislin and that vampire showed up then threw me through that trapdoor and used magic to seal it. They said they needed my gift of unus quisnam aufero animus to detach Gemma's soul again. When Stephan found us, I was stuck behind that door, but I could hear him . . . killing . . ." Tears flood her eyes as a sob rips from her throat. "He killed Marco."

"Okay." I try to be compassionate, but I've never really been that good at it. "Why didn't you just bang on the trapdoor to begin with, though? We could have freed you weeks ago when we first showed up here."

"Because of this." She jerks up her sleeves, revealing the triangular mark on her arm. "It's begging me not to keep quiet any longer."

She lunges for me, bearing her teeth, and I clock her in the face, knocking her out again. Her body slumps to the floor as Aislin and Laylen come rushing in.

She catches sight of the unconscious Sophia and stops dead in her tracks. "She's still passed out? I thought I heard her talking."

"She was, but I had to knock her out again because of the mark," I say then quickly add, "And I think you two have some explaining to do, because she says you two are the reason she was stuck down there."

Aislin scratches her head, glancing confusedly at Laylen. "She's lying. She has to be."

"What happened during that time you two disappeared?" I cross my arms. "And not just recently. I mean a month ago in Colorado. When Aislin transported Gemma and I to the cabin then went back for you"—I point my knife at Laylen—"you guys just disappeared."

"We already told you we were running from the Death Walkers in Nevada." Laylen leans against the doorway, his face laced with confusion. "That's where we were." He looks at Aislin. "Weren't we?"

Aislin's face contorts in perplexity. "I really don't know."

"You two seemed pretty confident when you showed up in Colorado to save us, and now you're saying you have no clue what you were doing? Seems a little bit odd if you ask me."

"Well, you seemed pretty confident when you told us the Death Walkers just picked up your dad and left," Laylen counters. "Seems just as suspicious."

"Why are we even arguing about this?" Aislin asks. "It's in the past, and we should focus on the future. You know, the one we're supposed to save."

"It's important," I say, "because we might have a traitor in our midst."

CHAPTER
THIRTY-SIX

Gemma

T HE QUEEN'S LIQUID body slides like a blob down the tunnel as she leads me to her sister Annabella. White wisps of ribbon dangle from the ceiling around us and brush against my head as we duck into an open area lined with blooming tulips and roses. Petals float through the air as a light breeze sweeps across the garden.

"She's going to want something from you," Helena explains to me, running her fingers along the flowers as she passes them. The petals instantly wilt from the contact and crumble to the ground. "An essence would work well if you have one on your hands to give."

I flick a dead rose petal off my arm. "Okay, but what exactly is an essence?"

She twirls around on the path, making the petals dance with her. She laughs as she stops, and all the petals drop to the ground.

"An essence is a spirit or a ghostly form of a once living

being. The person is still themselves in the sense that they possess a soul, can move, and can communicate. An essence is what humans turn into after they die. They're not like my lost souls who have disconnected their minds from their bodies due to dying before they were supposed to."

I think of Nicholas and how he walked the world. He has to be an essence. "But why do you torture your lost souls?"

"Why does anyone torture?" Her silvery lips curve into a grin as she crushes a tulip with her fingers. "For power."

"But you lost your own soul," I point out. "Doesn't that make you want to be . . . I don't know . . . more sympathetic toward those who've lost their souls?"

"Sympathy is weakness, something you should keep in mind before you make your decision." She dances around again, her silvery body shimmering in the light peeking through the tree branches canopying above us. "You're a powerful girl, Gemma—I can sense that from you—but your compassion for others makes you weak."

"I don't agree with you," I say, touching my stomach and thinking of how I would throw down my life in a heartbeat to protect my daughter. "Compassion makes me strong."

Her lips twitch as she spins around and snarls at me, "You're a stupid girl, then."

I don't reply, not because I agree with her, but because I know there's no point in arguing.

As we near the end of the garden, the queen glides to the side where the path dead ends at a willow tree. Below the drooping branches is a woman with hair like cotton and silvery eyes that sparkle.

"Annabella," Helena says coldly to the woman.

Annabella smoothes her hand over her floor length dress and bows her head. "Helena, I sensed you crossing here."

"Of course you did." Helena stretches her body to rise taller than her sister. "You always do."

Annabella's eyes land on me. "And you've brought someone with you who seeks something from me."

"I have." The queen's voice is like an arctic breeze.

I warily step below the branches of the willow tree and join the two of them.

"I've come to ask you for a favor."

"I know why you're here," she says, her tone lacking emotion. "You want me to free an essence." She moves around her sister and steps in front of me. "But I don't understand why you ask for their freedom. I can feel your dislike for this person immensely."

"I feel guilty over his death," I admit.

"But Nicholas isn't a lost soul," she says. "Therefore, no one is responsible for his death."

The willowy branches brush against me as the wind picks up. "I still feel guilty for what happened to him."

She tilts her head to the side, her hands resting in front of her. "Why do you feel responsible for things that are out of your hands?"

"He died because I exist." Guilt twists in my stomach. "Many people have."

"It's not your fault," she insists. "Everyone has a path in life, even the lost souls. They're there because they're lost, but that's still where their path led them." Her silver eyes carry my gaze. "You're a better person than you think you are. Your soul is so pure." She holds out her hand, and her skin begins to shimmer gold as an orb forms in her palm. "Nicholas's essence."

I hesitate. "You're just giving it to me?"

She smiles kindly. "Not everything is complicated. Sometimes the answers are right in front of us."

I graze my thumb across the scar on my palm. "Yes, but not everything is uncomplicated, either."

She urges the orb at me. "But sometimes our questioning the answers makes things even more complicated."

"Maybe." I pick up the essence, noting its warmth against my skin, like sunshine.

"Remember, not everything is as hard as you think, Gemma," Annabella says, lowering her hand. "Sometimes the answers are right in front of us."

I nod as she fades away into the tree, her words echoing in my head. Once she's gone, I follow Helena back through the garden and to the world of lost souls.

"My sister makes things too easy sometimes," Helena complains as she slips back onto her throne.

"It's hard to believe she's your sister." I cup the orb in my hands. "You two are nothing alike."

"That's because she believes in good, which makes her weak."

"And what do you believe in?"

She sneers. "Myself."

I can't help thinking of the story of Malefiscus and his brother Hektor—one selfish, the other good. In the story, good triumphed for the time being. But I wonder how the story would have gone if Hektor had to sacrifice his life to trap Malefiscus in the portal. Would bad have triumphed, instead? Or would he have thrown down his life to save the people he cared about?

"I have the answer to the question you asked me earlier," I say to the queen, approaching the throne, not steady and sure, but trembling and terrified because that's who I am. I'm not fearless. I feel almost everything now. I'll never be able to be someone who fearlessly lays down their life to save others.

I'll always just be a girl doing what I have to in order to make things right.

CHAPTER
THIRTY-SEVEN

Alex

"A TRAITOR?" LAYLEN says, appalled. "Okay, I think you've finally lost your damn mind. Seriously, man."

"That sounds like something a traitor would say." I aim my knife at him.

He stares me down. "You're fucking insane."

"Aren't we all?" I question, eyeing the two of them, wondering if they're really Aislin and Laylen.

"Laylen's not a traitor!" Aislin shouts as she finishes removing the Mark of Malefiscus from Sophia's arm. "And neither am I."

"Then why was I trapped in that floor?" Sophia wakes up, blinking. "I don't understand how any of this happened."

"Are you sure about that?" I inch toward her, still armed with my knife. "Or could your confusion be an act to make us turn on each other?" I lean down, getting in her face. "Is this a desperate attempt by my father? Did he put you in the floor to get to us? That way, you'd have time to detach Gemma's soul again?"

"I never wanted to detach Gemma's soul in the first place," she mutters, sitting up. "I thought what I was doing was right. I thought I was protecting the world."

"No, you were ending it," I say, pointing the tip of my knife into her throat.

"I know that now, but before . . . What I was trying to do made sense." Blinking, she desperately clutches onto my arm "It's your father. He must've brainwashed me."

"Trust me," I say, shaking her hand off my arm, "we've all been there."

Glass suddenly shatters across the floor.

I spin around, ready to fight, only to find Aislin standing there with half of a ceramic cow in her hand and glass scattered around her feet.

"I can't deal with this anymore," she says, her hands trembling. "I can't stand that our father's a horrible man who messes with minds and murders innocent people. I just can't take it." She smashes the rest of the ceramic cow against the floor. "What are we going to do to fix this?" she asks, breathing heavily as she looks from Laylen to me

"We're going to take care of the problem." I reel around and grab Sophia's arm. "Sorry, but until we know who's in control of their own actions, I can't trust you."

I push her back through the trapdoor, and she falls into the hole.

"Alex, please!" she begs as she trips to her feet and tries to climb back up. "You can't do this! I've run out of food; I'll starve!"

Aislin grabs some snacks and bottled water, tossing them into the trapdoor. "That should hold you until we work this out."

"Alex, please don't leave me down here. I—"

I shut the door and slide the tiles back over it. "Seal that up," I order Aislin, feeling the slightest twinge of guilt, but drastic times call for drastic measures.

Aislin traces her finger along the cracks between the tiles. "Signa eius intus et clauditis hoc usque." The floor shimmers as the cracks fade away. When Aislin stands back up, her eyes are nearly popping out of her head.

"Oh, my God. No." She turns to me. "Alex, I've done that before."

I'm about to take her down and tie her up until I can figure out what the hell is going on, but Nicholas suddenly appears in the room, looking very human and very alive.

He stares at his arms and hands incredulously. "It's time to wake her up."

I shove past him, charge up the stairs, and barge into her room. Gemma is lying motionless on her bed, her skin is pale, and her arms are resting on her stomach. I can't feel the electricity until I get right next to the bed, and when I touch her cheek, her skin is ice cold. I wait for her to open her eyes, but she remains still.

"Gemma, can you hear me?" I cup her face between my hands. "Gemma, please wake up."

She remains completely still.

"Aislin!" I yell, panicking. "No. No. No. Please, please, please wake up," I beg.

When she still doesn't move, I do the only thing I can think of that might spark life back inside her.

I lean down to kiss her, hoping she'll feel it, that it'll bring her back.

CHAPTER
THIRTY-EIGHT

Gemma

WHEN THE QUEEN frees the souls, they whisk away back to the world, back to their bodies. Once the last of them has gone, she holds out her hand to me, and I drop the ring into her palm.

She slips the ring onto her finger, and her body begins to transform and take shape. Her skin is mummified like the lost souls, her grey hair veils down her back, her lips are thin, and her eyes are still hollow.

She lets out a sigh as she examines her body. "That's much better." She stretches her arms above her head, grinning. "You can go now. I have what I need."

I nod then run as fast as I can down the tunnel, ready to get back home.

Alana is waiting for me in the archway. "You did it," she says. "I'm so proud of you, Gemma."

I tuck Nicholas's essence under my arm. "Are you going to be okay? I could go back and try to get her to free you, too."

She swiftly shakes her head. "No, I don't want you to do that. I need to pay my dues."

"What's going to happen to you?"

She doesn't answer my question, just draws me in for a hug. "You're an amazing girl, Gemma Lucas. You really are." She steps back, dabbing her eyes. "Take care of him for me."

I nod. "I still think—" Before I can say anything else, I'm engulfed in light.

WHEN I OPEN my eyes, I'm back in the grassy field I first entered the Afterlife in, but this time, there aren't any crows. They sky is clear, the wind still, and for a moment, I feel so at peace.

"It's about time you showed up," Nicholas says from behind me, stealing away my moment of peace. "I thought the queen decided to kill you or something."

I turn to face him, holding onto his essence. "Nope, everything went well." I hand him the orb. "Your essence."

He looks very human as he takes the orb from me, tears staining the corners of his eyes. "Thank you," he says softly.

Two simple words, but coming from him, it means a lot.

"You're welcome." I glance around the field before my gaze lands back on him. "Now can you go tell Alex to revive me?"

He shoves the orb into his chest, nods, and then vanishes into thin air.

I sit down in the field and pick at the grass, listening

to the wind. I feel different, my mind less burdened, and it feels like my eyes are suddenly open and seeing life for the very first time.

Annabella said humans made easy answers complicated by questioning them, and she was right. The answer of what is going to happen to me has always been right in front of me. There is no loophole, no magic trick. Either I can go to the lake and end everything, or I can run away and let the world die.

It's that simple, yet I couldn't fully accept it.

As I shut my eyes and let reality sink in, the wind quickens and sucks me away.

When my eyelids open again, Alex's lips are on mine. My body is on fire, and I want to close my eyes and let him continue kissing me forever. But electricity surges through me, and he shudders, stumbling back from the zap of static.

His gaze sweeps me over in a mad frenzy. "Tell me you're okay."

I run my hands over my arms and legs then sit up. Everything looks right, and I can hear our daughter's heart beating. "I think I'm good."

He releases a loud exhale. "I thought you were dead."

"I *was* dead." I rub my eyes then let my hands fall to my lap.

A beat or two skips by as reality catches up with me. I'm here, alive, breathing, and my heart is beating.

"I made it back," I declare, my muscles relaxing.

"Did you . . . ?" He rakes his fingers through his messy, brown hair. "Did you free the lost souls?"

A soft smile touches my lips. "Go look out the window and see for yourself."

He strides toward the window and pries the board off,

allowing the sunlight to filter through the room.

"You really are amazing," he says.

I climb off the bed and walk up behind him, my smile growing at the sight outside. The streets are clear of fey, vampire, and witches, and the neighboring yards have families in them. Laughter fills the air as people have picnics, water their lawn, and bask out in the sun.

"You're amazing," Alex says again, turning toward me with a look of awe on his face.

"Thanks, I guess. But it wasn't just me who did this," I say. "It was all of us, really."

"It was a little more you than all of us."

"Alex," I start to argue, not wanting to take all the credit for fixing this, especially when I was the reason behind the apocalypse.

"Gemma, just enjoy the moment, okay?"

I nod then sit back down on the bed, feeling a dizzy. "How long was I out?"

"A few hours."

"It felt like longer."

"Yeah, it really did."

As silence stretches between us, I get the feeling he might be keeping something from me.

"I have to tell you something." He fidgets with a leather band on his wrists. "And I'm a little worried about how you're going to react."

"Okay." I scoot to the edge of the bed. "I'll try to stay calm if that helps."

He offers me a sad smile, like he doesn't believe I'll be able to do such a thing. "While you were gone, we found . . . Sophia."

A gasp slips from my lips. "*What?* Where?"

"Underneath a trapdoor in the kitchen."

"How did she . . . ?" I massage my temples with my fingertips. "I don't even know how to process this."

"Maybe you don't have to process it just yet." He takes a seat on the bed beside me and smooths his hand up and down my back, his fingers carrying the slightest quiver. "You're safe. I promise. She's behind the trapdoor right now, and she can't get out."

"But how did she even get in there to begin with?" I shake my head, shock setting in. "Is that where's she's been the entire time?"

He sighs and then explains to me what happened at the house while I was in the Afterlife.

"So you think Aislin and Laylen are the ones who put her there?" I ask, astounded and doubtful.

"That's what I think, but I'm not positive." He absentmindedly coils a strand of my hair around his finger. "When Aislin and Laylen showed up at the Hartfield cabin that day, they seemed so confused about where they'd been all that time. What I'm thinking is that my dad brainwashed them temporarily somehow. And maybe, when the memoria extracto backfired on him, they were freed from his power, because that's when they showed up as if nothing had really happened."

"But they're okay now, right? I mean, we'd know if Stephan still had control over their minds?"

Sighing, he unravels his finger from my hair. "Honestly, I don't know. I mean, think of your mom and how suddenly her possession manifested. It completely blindsided us."

"How do we find out, then? There has to be something we can do that will help us trust them again."

"Usually, for this particular kind of situation, I'd ask Aislin to do a spell, but that requires trusting her." His chest puffs as he inhales. "I think we might just have to keep an eye on them, and if they show any signs of going crazy, we bail out and run."

"And what about Sophia?" My emotions over my grandmother being locked away are conflicted. On one hand, I feel sorry for her, but on the other, part of me feels like she might deserve what's happened. "Are you just going to keep her locked behind the trapdoor?"

He combs his fingers though my hair, gently pulling at the roots, and looks me dead in the eye. "That's for you to decide. Whatever you want to do with her, you tell me, and I'll handle it."

I believe him. Anything I requested at that moment, he'd do for me in a heartbeat, and it makes my pulse beat wildly.

"I don't want her to suffer." If I did, I feel like I'd be just as bad as her. "Where's Marco?"

His fingers spread across my cheek. "My father killed him. I think he spared Sophia's life because she's the only one who can . . . detach your soul."

I nod, letting everything sink in. My grandfather's dead, my grandmother is trapped under the floor, and Aislin and Laylen could still be brainwashed. It's like we fixed one problem just for another to arise.

"I think we should leave Sophia where she is until we make the sacrifice and die. Once I'm gone, Aislin can free her," I say quietly to Alex, staring down at the floor.

His breathing turns ragged as he growls, "What the hell is wrong with you? It sounds like you're fucking giving up."

"I'm not giving up." I lift my gaze to his and instantly shrink back from the rage in his eyes. "I'm doing what we have to, Alex, to make it so that damn portal doesn't open."

"It sounds to me like you're just giving up," he snaps. "And what about our daughter? Are you just going to give up on her, too?"

"Our daughter will be fine." My voice quivers, but I press on, making sure I say what I need to. "The spell will protect her. As soon as I die, she'll be born healthy and happy. And Aislin promised me she'd take care of her."

"So, you're just going to leave our daughter to be raised without a mother and father?"

"No, she'll have a mother." *And a father, too,* but I can't tell him that just yet. "Please, don't be mad at me, Alex." Tears bubble in my eyes as I wish I could tell him everything. I know, however, if I do, he won't allow it to happen. "I need you right now."

His expression softens as he catches sight of my tears. "There has to be another way," he whispers, sounding like he is in pain.

I put my hand on his cheek, wanting nothing more than to take his pain away.

There's so much more it feels like I need to say, but with the little time I have left, I decide I don't want to spend it arguing with him. So I lean in and press my lips to his, kissing him with everything I have in me. He kisses me back with an equal amount of passion, slipping his fingers through my hair and tipping my head back.

"I don't ever want to stop kissing you," he says, breathing heavily against my mouth.

"I know," I whisper back.

He rests his forehead against mine, trying to catch his breath. "I just wish . . . you knew . . . how I really feel."

The moment the words leave him, my energy level plummets. My limbs become heavy, my lungs feel tight, and my pulse dulls to a faint lull.

"I think I might already know," I whisper, my entire body shaking with fear, with excitement, with something I can't describe.

Then, with a deep breath, I push to my feet, cross the room, and pick up the rainbow candle I got from the black magic store.

"What is that?" He looks confused and tired, his skin suddenly a lot paler, and bags have formed under his eyes.

I bite back a smile. "It's a candle."

He rolls his eyes, but the corners of his mouth quirk up. "Thanks for the obvious answer," he teases then reaches out and takes the candle from my hands. "But I'm guessing by the excited look on your face that it does something."

"A witch gave it to me." I don't bother mentioning what I gave up to get the candle, even if, without my locket, my neck feels bare and exposed, just like my emotions do now. "It's a Power of Entrapment candle." Millions of images flood my mind, some real, some made up of what's going to happen the moment I light the candle. "It's supposed to trap the power of a witch in their body, at least while the wick is burning, but Aislin and I thought that maybe . . . It could trap the star's power in ours for a little while so we could have a break and just be . . . well, us."

Some of the exhaustion diminishes in his eyes, and desire and desperation take over. He rotates the candle in his hand, staring at it. "How do we know it'll work for sure?"

I grab a lighter from my desk drawer. "There's only one way to find out."

I fumble to light it, and then we hold our breaths as the wick burns. There's no magical sparks, no chanting sound effects. There's only silence and the beat of our hearts.

Then, just like when Alex and I met in my dreams, the electricity of the star sizzles out inside my body.

"I can't feel the buzzing anymore," I say, staring at him in awe.

"Me, either," he whispers, unable to take his eyes off me.

"As soon as the wick's gone, it's going to come back," I say.

"I know."

We carry each other's gazes as the flame burns, casting a glow across our faces.

He abruptly stands up, sets the candle aside on the nightstand, and places his hands on my cheeks. Looking deeply into my eyes, his lips part. "I love you, Gemma Lucas. Always have. Always will."

My heart slams to a stop inside my chest, but instantly recovers, beating more steady and even than it ever has.

I open my mouth to say something, but the words are thick in my throat. I struggle to say something—do anything—but I don't have the prickle to guide me, and it leaves me so confused.

But I'm quickly distracted as Alex kisses me with such passion I swear to God I'm going to pass out.

"Come here," he says, pulling me onto his lap.

I put a leg on each side of him and grind my hips against his, groaning as his hardness presses against my legs. God, I want him more than I can even comprehend. His hands wander up and down my back then grip my ass, pressing me closer, but it's not enough. Nothing feels like it'll ever be enough when it comes to him.

Groaning, he bites my bottom lip, his fingers delving

downward as he struggles to keep himself in control.

"I feel like, at any moment, I'm going to go too far," he whispers, digging into my flesh as he trails kisses down my jawline and neck.

"Alex," I gasp as his hand glides up my shirt, and his fingers graze across my nipple. "I'm . . . pretty sure the candle's . . . working. You don't have to . . . hold back."

He pauses, gently stroking my nipple. Then something snaps inside him, and with one swift motion, he has me flipped over onto my back. His body covers mine, his arms bearing his weight as he grinds against me. I open my legs and let him fall between them then move my hips with his. We stay like that for a few minutes, our hips moving rhythmically as our tongues tangle, until we become breathless. Then Alex moves back, but only to remove my jeans and shirt before returning his lips to mine.

The longer he kisses me, the more I feel like my body's going to explode. I want more—need more.

I gently push him back, and he bites back a smile as I nearly rip his shirt off. My hand promptly skates down his rock solid chest to the top of his jeans. I undo the button and pull down his jeans.

He leans back to kick them off before returning his body to mine. Instead of kissing me, he stares down at me, stroking his fingers across my cheekbone.

"God, you're beautiful," he says then lowers his lips to mine. "I'm never going to let anything happen to you. I promise."

Before I can argue, he seals his mouth to mine again and kisses me so slowly, so deliberately I swear I'm going to burst into flames. The longer the kiss goes on, the more I tumble into a world that doesn't really exist, where he and I can be together, where the world doesn't end, where we don't die. I'm playing with fire—I know this—because when it all comes down to it, the flame will eventually burn out and so will this world.

But I'm not ready to let go just yet.

I slip my fingers through his and pull him closer, needing him more than I ever have.

Minutes drift by, maybe hours, where we simply kiss, our lips exploring every inch of each other. When he finally pulls back again, he strips off the rest my clothes. Then he kicks off his boxers and lowers his lips to my leg

"I love you," he keeps whispering as he kisses a path up my thigh to my stomach. "I love you so much."

My toes curl as I slip my fingers through his hair, my back arching off the mattress. His kisses are driving me mad, but not as much as his words. I want to say it back— the words are on the tip of my tongue—but I'm so afraid, if I do, the candle might stop working. I'm afraid it might make dying harder, afraid of saying something so emotionally meaningful.

When his lips find mine again, he slips his fingers deep inside me, and I can scarcely breathe. His fingers and lips feel me thoroughly, and the longer it goes on, the more I forget where I am, who I am, what I have to do. When he slips inside me, it's just Alex and I lying on my bed. Nothing else matters except this moment.

"I love you," I whisper as my head falls back, and I clutch on to him.

"I love you, too," he whispers into my ear as he rocks into me. "And, Gemma, I'm never letting anything happen to you."

From the way his voice sounds at the moment, I know he means it. He's going to do everything he can to make sure nothing happens to me. I want to tell him that he's too late, that I've already sealed my fate, but his hips slam down on mine, and every worry in my head dissipates as I climb higher and higher until I completely get lost in everything that is him. The way he feels inside me, how his lips taste, how incredible he smells, how safe I feel in his arms—I clutch on to every detail, knowing this will probably be the last time we'll be together like this. And he holds onto me equally as tight while we come apart together.

Alex stays inside me for a few minutes before he slips out and rolls onto his back. He keeps his arm around me, pulling me with him, and I rest my head on his chest.

"It's almost burned out," he says, his heart racing.

I look over at the candle burning on the nightstand, and my heart plummets at how little wax is left. "We probably only have a few more minutes."

"I know." His arm tightens around me. "I love you."

"I love you, too." And then, just because I know I won't be able to say it soon, I add, "I really do love you."

His fingers stroke the side of my arm then travel to my collarbone. As he traces a path across my neck, his fingers abruptly stop moving. Then rolls on his side, forcing me on my back, and looks down at me.

"Where's your necklace?"

I touch the hollow of my neck. "I lost it." I don't bother telling him where. If I do, knowing Alex, he might go looking for it.

"I'm sorry," he says then steals another kiss, savoring the taste of my mouth. By the time he pulls away, we're both breathless and dazed, and the candle is nearly gone.

My heart aches inside my chest, and I feel sick to my stomach from knowing I'm about to lose this moment. Part of me wishes I could go back and never experience love, because the loss of it is so terrifying. Then I realize that, no matter what happens, no matter how bad it hurts, I'll never regret a single moment of being with Alex.

The room grows quiet as Alex plays with my hair, staring off into empty space while I stare at the stars just outside the window.

"Care to share your thoughts?" he asks when he notices I'm staring at the night sky

"I was thinking about death," I say and he frowns. "And about life . . . and where the star will go after this is all over." It's strange looking at the stars because I don't feel that pull like I used to. Instead, I feel a push, like the star is holding me down. "Do you think it'll just go up to the sky again?"

He doesn't speak for a while, and with each second that goes by, the candlewick shortens. "Did you know Gemma is an actual star, also known as Alphecca? It's part of the constellation Corona Borealis." He traces a finger across my lips

"Really? How did I not know this?"

"Because there are a ton of constellations and an endless amount of stars."

"Then how did you know about it?"

He winks at me, but his face carries tension. "Haven't you figured out I know everything?"

I can't help thinking how very wrong he is. There's something he doesn't know about life, about the star, about us.

And he'll never figure it out, because I'll never tell him.

CHAPTER
THIRTY-NINE

Alex

WE LIE THERE stealing kisses and talking about simple things until Gemma falls asleep in my arms. Watching her sleep with her hand resting on her stomach, looking so peaceful, might be the most perfect moment of my life next to hearing her say she loves me.

All my life, I grew up in a hateful world, carrying so much anger. Love's different. Love's calming. Love's . . . well, perfect.

I can't seem to take my eyes off her, even when the candle flickers, getting ready to fade.

How can I just let her die with me? How can this moment be her only real, peaceful moment? There has to be more for her.

There has to be a way for me to save her. I'd give up everything just so that that she'll get to live and raise our daughter. There has to be a way through all this madness for me to make this happen. It can't be impossible, not after everything we've managed to make happen.

Anything seems possible.

I think about what my mother said—that everything happens for a reason. And just like that, an epiphany slaps me across the face.

Slipping out from underneath Gemma, I roll over and stand to my feet. I pull on my jeans and shirt then lean down and kiss Gemma.

"I love you," I whisper right as the last of the candle-light dies then bury my emotions down, despite how it kills me as my skin erupts with heat.

I hate leaving her like this, but then again, it's going to be hard to ignore my feelings for her now that I've been able to feel them. It might be better if I'm gone.

With one final look in her direction, I whisper good-bye then head downstairs.

"I need your help," I say to Aislin as I walk into the living room.

"Can it wait?" She has her spell book open, bags of herbs are scattered everywhere, and she looks really stressed out. "I think I've almost got the shield spell all figured out." She perks up, suddenly looking very awake. "Oh, yeah! I totally almost forgot." She rolls back her shoulders, looking proud. "I removed Laylen's Mark of Immortality."

My head whips in Laylen's direction. "It's gone?"

Looking happier than I've seen him in years, he lifts his arm and shows me the spot where the mark used to be. "Yep, I can officially die now."

I blink at Aislin. "Why didn't you come tell us?"

Aislin shrugs, focusing on her bags of herbs again. "I could feel the power of the candle burning, so I thought it'd be better if I just waited until you guys were . . . done."

As huge as the removal of the mark is, I'm actually glad she didn't come disrupt Gemma and I while we were making . . .

I shake the thought from my head as my heart begins to quiet, and my lungs forget to breathe. *I can't go back to that memory yet, not unless I want to kill us both.*

"So all that's left is the shield spell?" I ask Aislin.

Aislin nods but doesn't seem too upbeat. "Yeah, but I still have to get close enough to Stephan in order to remove his mark and take down the spell, which is going to be a huge pain in the ass."

"We'll figure out a way to do it safely," I say then pull her to her feet, "but I really need to talk to you about something important." I glance over at Laylen who's watching us intently from the sofa. The last thing I need is for him to hear what I'm about to do. He's close enough to Gemma that he just might tell her. "Can I talk to you for a second? Alone."

"Fine." Sighing, she follows me into the kitchen and sinks down into a chair. "I'm listening."

"I need you to take me somewhere." My heart is beating so loudly I can barely hear anything over it. I'm nervous, which is a strange and very uncomfortable feeling. "To Iceland, actually."

Her eyes pop wide as she blinks up at me. "Why the hell do you need to go to Iceland? Especially when we're supposed to be stopping the portal from opening, like, really soon."

"I know what we need to do, Aislin, but it's really, really important that I go there," I say, trying to keep my composure.

She mulls over my request. "I'll take you, but only if

you tell me why."

I shake my head. "I'd rather not. You'll just freak out."

She crosses her arms and gives me a stubborn look. "Then I'm not going to take you."

I rub my hand across my face. "I figured out a way to save Gemma."

"Just Gemma?" The color drains from her face. "Please tell me you figured out a way to save yourself, too."

My silence says all she needs to hear.

She rapidly shakes her head and rises to her feet. "You can't do this, Alex."

"I have to. Saving her is what I'm supposed to do."

"No, you're just trying to be a hero," she snaps, getting in my face, "a stupid hero."

"This isn't about me being a hero," I argue. "This is about how much Gemma means to me, even though I can't say it aloud. This about me not being able to live without her. This is about my daughter and how she should have her mother. And this is about Gemma getting to watch her daughter grow up."

"You should get to watch her grow up, too," she says, tears flooding her eyes.

"I know, but if it only gets to be one of us, it should be—needs to be—Gemma. She's the one who spent most of her life unemotional. She has no memories of her childhood, no really happy memories that don't have some kind of burden attached to them. She's been tormented by the Death Walkers, by our father. Her life's never been fair. And now she's pregnant with our daughter, and we just spent the most amazing few hours together, only for it to get taken away from her the moment that fucking candle burned out. She deserves this, and I want nothing more than to give it to her."

She blinks fiercely, trying to fight back the tears, but like always, her emotions get the best of her.

Not knowing what else to do, I give her a hug.

"Your life hasn't been that fair, either," she whispers. "None of our lives have."

"That's why we need to stop all this—so no one has to suffer anymore."

"Are you sure there's not another way?" Her voice carries such hope that I feel bad knowing I'll have to ruin it. "Where no one has to die except the bad guys?"

"Mom told me the portal's going to open up no matter what we do, and the only way to seal it back is for the star to die . . . is for Gemma and I to die."

She shakes her head as we break the hug. Then she covers her mouth and continues to shake her head as she soundlessly sobs.

"If you die, then that's it," she whispers. "I won't have any family left."

"Mom will be back, eventually," I tell her and force a small smile. "And you'll have your niece to take care."

She continues to cry until her eyes run dry. Then she stares at me with her swollen eyes, her cheeks raw from the tears. "You're sure this is what you want to do?" she asks, her voice hoarse.

I nod. "More than anything."

She bobs her head up and down unsteadily. "Then I'll take you." She reaches for my hand but then hastily withdraws. "You're coming back, though. I'm not taking you to your death, right?"

"Yeah, I'm coming back until the sacrifice." I clear my throat as my voice cracks, thinking about how this is it. This is one of the last times I'll talk to my sister.

"You're a good sister," I feel the urge to say.

"I know." She smiles, but I can tell she's fighting not to cry. "You've been a great brother, even though I've had to put up with a lot of temper tantrums."

I can't help laughing, and she laughs along with me. But the laughter dies quickly as reality crashes down on us. I can tell Aislin's scared, and I'd be lying if I said I wasn't fucking scared, too.

But my mom wasn't right when she said it always had to be Gemma, because if I can make this work, Gemma's the one who is going to live.

"I NEED YOU to do me favor," I tell Laylen as I walk into living room.

He looks up from Aislin's herb box with his brows furrowed. "The last time you asked me for a favor, you left."

"I'm leaving, but I'll be back." I lean against the doorway. "I need you to keep an eye on Gemma for a bit, and I need you to make a Blood Promise with me that you'll always keep an eye on her, no matter what happens to me."

"Why?" he asks.

I rub the back of my neck. "It's just important, okay?"

He momentarily assesses me then nods, sets the box down, and stands. I straighten my stance, grab my knife from my pocket, and flip open the blade. With zero hesitancy, I drag the blade down my unscarred palm. Then I chuck the knife to Laylen, and he cuts his own hand.

His lips twitch as he looks at the blood in his hand then at mine. I can see the blood thirst in his eyes, and his muscles tense as he fights the urge to devour it.

"You okay, man?" I ask, cupping my hand so the blood

pools in my palm.

"Yeah, I think so." He takes a few measured inhales and exhales then tosses the knife on the table and sticks out his palm. "I'm just going to point out that this is kind of awkward. I never thought you and I would be doing something like this."

"I know," I reply and then we press our hands together. He's right; it's super fucking awkward.

"So what's the magic words?" he asks.

"Ego spondeo vos ut haud res quis Gemma curam et custodiam eam iniuriam," I say, wishing I was on the other side of this promise.

He nods, his eyes wide with understanding. "Ego spondeo vos ut haud res quis Gemma curam et custodiam eam iniuriam."

We lower our hands, and I wipe my bloody palm on the side of my jeans.

"Am I walking in on something I'm not supposed to?" Nicholas appears in the living room with us, leaning against the wall, a mocking expression on his face.

"Get the fuck out of here." In three long strides, I cross the living room and get in his face.

He sputters a protest as I grab the collar of his shirt and drag him toward the door

"This isn't your house," he whines, digging his heels into the floor. "Maybe you should ask Gemma if you should be kicking me out."

"Gemma would tell me to throw your ass out." I open the front door. "I'm eliminating all risk factors right now, and you're one of them."

"You don't trust me?" He tries to wiggle out of my grasp. "Wow, I feel so . . ." He snorts a laugh. "Honestly, I don't fucking care what you think."

"And honestly, I don't fucking care what happens to you." I shove open the screen door and give him a push. "Now get the fuck out."

He trips over the threshold onto the porch. "You know, she might let me in if I ask," he says. "She has a soft spot for me."

"That's because she's a nice and forgiving person, too forgiving sometimes." I give him another shove then slam the door in his face.

Aislin moves up beside me with tears in her eyes and a reluctant expression. "Are you sure you want to do this?"

"Yep," I say firmly. For the first time in my life, I feel like I'm doing something good. "Now take me to Iceland."

CHAPTER
FORTY

Gemma

"IT WILL BE all right," he promises me as we stand in front of the still lake. The sky is cloudy above us, grey like ashes, and the air has a deadly chill to it. "I'll always save you, Gemma."

"But I want to save you this time." I plead for him to understand, to let me go, to make saying goodbye easier.

His lips part, but ice crackles and steals his voice away.

"It has to be me." I grab on to his arms, holding on to him, ready to tell him what I've done and then say goodbye forever. "I need to say goodbye."

"Not this time." He leans in, his warm breath caressing my skin as he delicately kisses my cheek. "It never has to be you again. I'm saving you, just like I promised."

Shaking my head, I loop my arms around the back of his neck and grasp on to him.

Death Walkers descend from the trees, their eyes burning yellow as they trample the icy bushes and grass.

Stephan walks amongst them, dressed in his cloak with a knife in his hand and wearing an evil smile on his scarred face.

"You're not getting away this time!" he shouts.

The wind howls, and the Death Walkers cry out, sending icicles raining through the air

I whirl back toward Alex and clasp my arms around him. I don't know how, but I can feel that he's about to fade away from me.

"Please don't leave me, Alex. Let me save you."

"This time, it has to be me." He places his palm to my cheek and looks deeply into my eyes. "This is how it is supposed to be."

"No. This isn't how our story goes," I say as Stephan shouts to attack. "This isn't how I saw it happen."

"Everything happens for a reason, even this." He yanks me against him, our chests crashing together, and his body heat warms my soul. "I love you," he whispers. "Always have, always will."

The electricity scorches, freeing itself from my body and uniting with the earth. But, just as I feel myself slipping away, I'm yanked back to earth and sink to my knees, shivering from the shock. The ground is a sheet of ice and the air is bone chillingly cold. The Death Walkers have surrounded me, their yellow eyes gleaming with hunger as they tip their head back and shriek to the darkening sky.

"Alex!" I shout, stumbling to my feet, frantically searching for him.

"He's right here."

I jolt from the sound of Stephan's voice right to the side of me then spin on my heels, fully prepared to fight. But my will to survive dies in an instant as Stephan steps back and gestures at the ground where Alex lays in a pool of his own blood.

"No!" I scream, dropping to my knees. "No . . . This can't be happening. He can't die. Not without me."

Stephan steps forward and draws the hood from his head. "Haven't you learned yet, Gemma? There are always loopholes, and this one's mine." He raises a jagged blade stained with silver and red. "It's sealed with the blood of a witch. And not just any witch, one powerful enough to undo the binding of a blood promise." His grin expands as I struggle to figure out what's going on, why Alex isn't waking up. "You still don't get it? Well, let me explain it to you, then." He leans in, getting right in my face.

I want to cry, but I know that will only make the situation worse.

"The reason you two have been able to survive for so long isn't because of the star or because your souls are attached to one another. It's also because of that stupid blood promise you two made. You two are so tightly wound together that it's been a pain in the ass trying to figure out how to end you, but I finally found a way to destroy it." He moves back so I can get a good look at the man I love lying in the snowy grass that's now stained with blood. "And to destroy my son."

WHEN I OPEN my eyes, I let out a scream as I shoot upright in my bed. My room is dark, my skin damp with sweat, and my bed is empty.

Alex is gone, and the candle has burned out. I almost

start to cry, wanting him so badly, but then I remember that, if I allow myself to feel so powerfully for him, I could end up killing us.

Where did he go?

Rolling out of bed, I stumble through the dark, turn on the light, and pull on a T-shirt and a pair of jeans. I comb my hair into a ponytail then crack the bedroom door open. The house is alarmingly silent except for the sound of the TV downstairs.

I inch into the hall, tiptoe down the stairs, and chill out a little when I see Laylen lounging around on the sofa, channel surfing.

His long legs are kicked up on the table, his blond hair in his eyes, and he's munching on a bowl of ice cream.

As if he senses me standing there, he turns his head, and his eyes find me. "I was wondering when you were going to wake up."

"What time is it?" I glance at the clock, yawning. "Wow, it's late. Where's everyone?"

"Aislin and Alex had to run some errands and pick up some stuff for the spell." He sets the bowl of ice cream down then twists around on the sofa to look at me. "I think they wanted to go together so they could say . . . goodbye."

"But they're coming back, right?" I know it's a stupid question, but the dream I had makes me nervous.

What if it's not a dream?

What if something has changed?

"Yeah, they're coming back. I promise." He turns around and faces the television as I join him on the sofa.

"Laylen, do you know if witch's blood can undo a blood promise?"

"I don't know . . ." He gives me a strange look as he clenches his fist. "Why are you asking?"

I trace the scar on my palm. "I'm just wondering."

"I'm not sure if it's possible. I've never heard of anything like it, but then again, a lot of stuff has happened that I've never heard of." He gathers his bowl of ice cream and rests back on the sofa. "Are you thinking about trying to break a promise you made?"

I shake my head. "No, it's not that. I just . . ." The dream I had of Alex dying haunts my thoughts.

I've been so stupid to just accept that everything's going to work out in our favor, that we will make it to the lake and do the sacrifice without running into any hitches.

"You're thinking about doing something you're not supposed to," Laylen says, shoveling a spoonful of ice cream into his mouth. "I can tell."

I drum my fingers on my knee. I hate what I'm deliberating, but I can't get past that dream.

"I think I need to see a vision."

He frowns, nearly dropping the bowl. "I thought you weren't into that anymore?"

"I'm not"—I chew on my thumbnail—"but there's something I need to see. And I promise I'm not going to change it . . . I just need to *see* it."

I need to know if I save him or not. I thought I had, that the deal I made with Helena was going to save Alex, but now I'm worried there might be more to it than what I thought. Besides, I haven't actually foreseen a different outcome yet than Alex and I dying except for the dream I just had where I was the one who survived.

It doesn't make any sense.

"Are you sure you want to do this?" Laylen asks, extremely nervous.

"I think I have to." I lie down on the sofa, propping my feet onto his lap. "Just stay here while I go, okay? And keep an eye on me."

"I'll always be here for you, Gemma," he assures me, balancing the bowl on the armrest, "no matter what happens."

Something in his eyes makes me pause.

"Are you sure Alex is coming back?" I ask, worried he might be lying to me.

He looks me straight in the eye. "I promise he is." He scratches at his arm, and that's when I notice . . .

"Your mark's gone?" I ask, sitting up. "Holy shit, Laylen. Why didn't you say anything?"

"I was going to tell you," he says, "but decided to wait, because you looked so stressed out."

"This is way more important than me being stressed." I throw my arms around him. "I'm so happy for you."

His hand finds the small of my back, and he holds me against him. "I feel so different, you know? I mean, I know I'm still a vampire and everything, but I just . . . I feel a little bit more connected to my old self."

I pull back to look at him. "You're happy, then?"

"The happiest I've been since I got bitten."

"I'm so glad. You look happier." I smile. "And this means Aislin can use the spell to remove Stephan's mark."

He nods. "Just as soon as she gets the shield spell perfected."

I feel somewhat better than when I first came down-stairs. *Maybe this is going to work.*

But then I remember my dream and how I still don't know for sure if the future has changed.

"I'm going to see this vision real quick, and then we're going to celebrate," I tell Laylen then lie back down.

Feeling uneasy, I close my eyes and picture the lake with Alex and me standing there as Stephan and the

Death Walkers show up. But my head starts to ring, and the image blurs away. I can't see anything, like I'm being blocked. I start to open my eyes when I'm yanked down into darkness, tumbling into the unknown.

MY FEET SLAM against the stone floor, and my hand shoots out, grabbing a banister. It takes me a second to get my bearings and figure out I am in the Keepers' Castle, standing in front of the winding stairway. Ice glazes the domed ceiling and creeps up the walls. The floor is covered in a layer of snow, and footprints are imprinted everywhere, as if there's been heavy traffic.

I don't know why I'm here. Is this is part of the vision I wanted to see? Or did I manage to enter another one?

My head throbs like my skull has been cracked, and I have a hunch that somehow I messed up and went into the wrong vision. Seeing no other way to get out of here, I trample through the snow, searching for whatever I'm supposed to see.

Voices flow from the back of the castle, and I follow the footprints and head toward the noise. When I enter the room, my heart leaps up my throat.

Stephan and the Death Walkers are crammed inside the space, and the temperature is so cold my skin tints blue, making me begin to uncontrollably chatter.

"Today is the day," Stephan says, pacing the floor in front of at least fifty Death Walkers. He's wearing his cloak with the hood drawn over his head, and he's holding the knife he stabbed Alex with. "This is the day when we all reunite."

The Death Walkers' eyes flare brightly as they tip

their rotting heads back and cry out in unison.

"Don't get too excited," Stephan growls, swinging the knife upward until the blade is aimed at the closest Death Walker. "You've done nothing but fail me. You haven't given me the star, and now all I have left is a useless portal. I can't free Malefiscus without the star."

"But we'll have an army of Death Walkers." Someone else walks into the room, and I shudder, slowly turning around.

Demetrius strolls up to Stephan with a grin on his face. He has on the same black cloak, but the hood is off, so I get a better glimpse of the evil in his eyes.

"We don't need Malefiscus," Demetrius says to Stephan. "You can create marks. We'll have countless Death Walkers. You and I can rule the world with that."

Stephan traces his finger along his scar, his eyes darkening. "Are you forgetting where we came from?"

Demetrius winces but swiftly composes himself. "I'm not forgetting anything, but we don't have the star, and we can't free him without it. And we're running out of time. Our chance at opening the portal is coming, and we can either focus on getting the Death Walkers out or waste more time trying to chase down a star we might never catch." He glances at the Death Walkers then lowers his voice. "We can still do this. We can still control everything, just as long as you'll let this one thing go."

Stephan bashes his fist against the mantel, sending a candlestick toppling to the floor "He's our flesh and blood, the one who started this all. Don't tell me just to let this go."

"I'm not telling you just to let it go. I'm telling you that we have to be the ones to end this," Demetrius says. "For years and years, you've sacrificed your life to protect a world that does nothing but cause more problems. There needs to be order, structure, control. If we do this, we can control the faeries, the witches, the vampires—everyone—forever, along with the rest of the world."

Stephan clenches his jaw, his hand balling into a fist. "We are supposed to free him. It's what we were born to do," he growls, sketching the scar on his face with his finger. "It's why we have these."

I back up against the wall as more Death Walkers file into the room, choking the oxygen from the air.

"It's not time yet!" Stephan shouts at the Death Walkers, a vein in his neck bulging. "Stop asking me the same stupid question." He picks up the Sword of Immortality that's propped against the wall in the corner of the room and sets his knife down. "Breathe on this," he instructs, sticking out the sword in front of a Death Walker.

The Death Walker puffs a faint grey mist onto the sword, and frost webs across the blade. With a glint in his eyes, Stephan smashes it against the fireplace, shattering it into pieces.

"No more threats," he mutters to himself then looks up at Demetrius. "I'm not giving up yet." He picks up the other sword and runs his finger along the blade. "I'm seeing this to the end."

An orb suddenly appears in the center of the room, bright blue and the light nearly blinding. The orb begins to grow, stealing the space from the room.

"No," Stephan whispers in shock as the orb chases him down. He trips back, bumping his arm against the bricks of the fireplace.

"What is that!" Demetrius roars, skittering out of the way from the orb.

"That would be me." Aislin materializes in the center of the orb with Laylen beside her, holding her hand.

Stephan narrows his eyes at Aislin as he grips the banister and drags himself to his feet. "Has my daughter finally come to reunite with me? Or are you really just this stupid, showing up here so close to the ritual?"

She elevates her hands in front of her. "Oh, Father, I hate to break it to you, but you're the one who's stupid." Grinning, she throws her hands forward, and the orb explodes, sweeping across the room and sealing Stephan inside the light with Laylen and herself.

The Death Walkers charge, but their bodies bounce against the orb. Some trip back, shrieking out, while others fall to the floor.

Demetrius fearfully glances between the orb and the doorway, and I can tell he's contemplating bailing.

"You can't kill me," Stephan growls as he stands to his feet. "No one can."

"That's where you're wrong." Aislin leans forward and cups her hand around her mouth. "You want to know a secret, Father?" She gives a dramatic pause. "You're going to die today."

He barks a laugh and the shield ripples. "No one can kill me, especially you, my weak and overly emotional daughter."

"I know I can't, but I didn't say I was going to kill you, did I?" Her hands sparkle as she wiggles her fingers, and then shimmering swirls of light rise toward the ceiling. "Scutum aufero recipiam."

Suddenly understanding why I'm here, I inch closer to the orb and quickly try to memorize every word she says.

When nothing happens, Stephan throws his head

back and laughs.

"I have to say, I'm a little disappointed. I would hope my own daughter could do better than this, especially since I gave you the gift of Wicca. Guess I set my expectations too high for you."

"Or your arrogance is too high," Laylen says then leans over and rams his head into Stephan's stomach.

As they crash to the floor, their bodies crack against the ice. Then Laylen pushes back and takes a swing at Stephan; however, Stephan blocks the punch with his arm, reaches for his boot, and draws out a knife.

I run for them but slam to a stop when I realize I can't go through the shield.

Aislin rushes for Laylen and stabs a knife into Stephan's wrist, right in the center of his Mark of Immortality. "Accipe bonum industria a!" Aislin shouts as she retrieves a vile from her pocket. Then she dumps a thick liquid onto Stephan's arm, straight into the open wound.

Stephan jabs Laylen in the face with his elbow and then strikes Aislin across her cheek. She flies backward and hits the back of the orb.

Laylen growls and sinks his teeth into Stephan's arm, biting hard. Stephan struggles to get free and kicks Laylen in the stomach as the sphere sparks and begins to fade in and out.

"Laylen!" Aislin shouts, crawling for him. "It's time to go! Now!"

She extends her hand, and Laylen runs toward her, but Stephan catches ahold of his leg and yanks Laylen down. Laylen kicks Stephan in the head with his heel over and over again as the orb bursts like a massive ocean wave rolling for land.

The floor dusts with light and sparkles as Laylen bashes Stephan in the nose with his foot. Stephan jerks back, clutching his bleeding nose, and Laylen races over to Aislin.

"Get us out of here," he says breathlessly as the Death Walkers close in on them.

Stephan grabs a nearby knife and throws it at them. "I won't let you ruin this."

The knife lands close to Aislin, nicking her leg, but she quickly says her spell, and just like that, they're gone.

"Dammit!" Stephan shouts, slamming his fist against the floor, blood still trickling from his nose. "It's gone!"

"What is?" Demetrius asks, leaning motionless against the doorway. Not surprisingly, he did nothing to help Stephan through the attack, and part of me wonders if he wanted Stephan hurt.

Stephan's eyes scorch in rage as he glares at Demetrius. "My shield and my Mark of Immortality!"

"You can put it back on, so relax. Besides, it's almost time," Demetrius says.

A deafening ring echoes through the room, and Stephan retrieves his phone from his cloak. He stares at the screen for a moment or two before wiping the blood from his face and answering it.

"What the fuck do you want?" he snarls into the receiver.

Silence fills the room as someone talks on the other end of the line. When Stephan hangs up, he chucks the phone against the floor and shatters it into pieces like he did with the sword.

"What the hell did you do that for?" Demetrius asks, gaping at the pieces of the phone.

"Our stars are waiting for us," he says with a swish of

a cape, and then he marches for the door.

Demetrius hurries after him and so do the Death Walkers, their yellow eyes glinting with eagerness.

If it's time, then that means he's headed to . . . kill Alex and me.

Needing to know how this all turns out, I chase after them, but the second I step foot out of the room, I'm jerked back into the darkness.

I TRY AT least ten more times to drop myself back into the vision before I finally open my eyes.

"Did you see what you needed to?" Laylen asks the moment our gazes meet.

"Not exactly." My heart bottoms into my stomach as I painfully realize that, no matter how much I want to see how this is going to turn out, I might not be able to. I'm not sure why other than maybe it's considered cheating since I'm trying to skip to the end and see all the answers for myself.

My father told me once I can't cheat my way to the end, that sometimes I just have to figure stuff out on my own. It makes me sick, though, knowing there's a possibility Alex may somehow still die, that with all the sacrifices I made, he still doesn't live.

But I think I know where Stephan got the powerful witch's blood to put on the sword. From cutting Aislin. So I can at least stop that from happening, which should change what I dreamed.

"I did see something that'll help us, though." I sit up and plant my feet on the floor. "I saw how Aislin got

Stephan's shield off him and the Mark of Immortality.
You help her, too. Like, majorly."

"Really?" He scoots to the edge of the sofa, not looking as excited as I expected him to be.

"Is everything okay?" I ask

He nods. "Yeah, everything's fine."

I'm not buying it. "You know you can talk to me about
anything, right?"

He places a hand on my knee. "I know, but I'm really
not ready to talk about what's bothering me just yet."

I decide to let it go for now, but I make a mental note
to talk to him later.

If I have a later. The thought sends a terrifying chill
up my spine and I shiver.

"Laylen, I know you really don't want to talk to
me about it now, but . . . I might not have much more
time . . . And I really want to make sure you're okay . . . before I go." Tears sting my eyes.

God, this is more difficult than I thought.

He fiddles with his lip ring, sucking the metal between his teeth. "I just don't get why you guys have to die
if we remove Stephan's mark. Can't we just kill him and
end it?"

I want to throw my arms around him again, try to
erase the pain in his expression, but I know a hug's not
going to do it, not with this. This is something he'll just
have to work through.

"Alana told me something while I was in the Afterlife,"
I tell him. "She told me Malefiscus is part of the star, and
therefore, it connects the portal to Alex and me. He can't
walk free without the blood of the ritual Stephan is planning on performing with you guys, but the portal will still
open up on its own as long as the star exists. And it can do

a lot of damage to the world by just opening up. She said the only way to stop it all is for the star to be destroyed."

"So that's it, then?" He shakes his head, his jaw set tight as he battles back the tears.

"I'm sorry." I can't think of anything else to say.

"I wish things could have been different for you." He places a hand on my cheek and traces his finger underneath my eye. "You deserve so much more. You deserve a life full of happiness and freedom, where you get to do crazy things that make you laugh and smile."

"Do me a favor?" I ask and he nods. "Can you live that life for me?"

His fingers tense on my face, and I cover my hand with his.

"I promise," he says softly.

I start to smile when a bang shakes the entire house.

"Now what?" I jump to my feet and pat my pockets for a knife.

"It's just Sophia," Laylen says, guiding me back down to the sofa.

I relax as I plant my ass back on the cushion. "I forgot she's here. It's so strange she's been trapped down there all this time." I pause. "Can you make sure she's let go after I'm gone? I want to make sure she doesn't rot away down there."

His head slants to the side as he gives me a puzzled look. "You don't hate her for what she did to you?"

"I don't hate her, but I don't really like her, either. It's kind of hard to figure out how I feel because I know all those years her mind wasn't really her own. But all the pain she caused is still fresh in my mind, you know? She's my grandmother, though, and I don't want her locked underneath the house forever. I don't want anyone else to have to spend their life like that; otherwise, it feels like my sacrifice is for nothing."

He combs his fingers through his hair, brushing his hair out of his eyes. "You keep saying all of this like it's a done deal, like you're for sure going to die, but sometimes visions change—stuff can still change—so how can you know you and Alex are going to die for sure?"

"Alex isn't going to die," I say without really meaning to.

He jerks back, shocked. "What do you mean?"

I lean in, keeping my voice low. "Can you keep a secret?"

CHAPTER
FORTY-ONE

Alex

ISLIN MATERIALIZES US in front of the house in Iceland then lets go of my hand.

"Are you sure you want to do this?" she asks again, wrapping her arms around herself as the cold air hits her. "Maybe there's another way. We still have a little time left, you know. We can fix this."

I shake my head, opening the front gate. "Time's up, Aislin. This is what I'm going to do, what I want to do."

"Well, I'm waiting here." She refuses to step onto the pathway that leads to the house. "I can't watch what's about to happen."

"I understand." I hike up the snowy path to the front steps and bang on the door. "Open up! I know you're in there."

An old woman that lives in the house next door steps out onto her porch. "Keep it down. We don't want any nonsense around here."

I bang on the door again, this time harder. "I'm just trying to talk to the person who lives here."

"No one lives there," she snaps. "Now leave or I'll call the police."

I give the door a good hard kick before I stomp down the stairs and back to Aislin. I grab her arm and tow her along with me as I hurry down the sidewalk.

"Where are we going?" Aislin rushes to keep up with me.

"Just keep walking."

I glance over my shoulder at the old woman who's still watching us then turn back around. I walk to the end the sidewalk then round the corner and stop in front of the fence. I hop over it, diving into the back yard.

"Wait here," I tell Aislin then jog up the back porch.

I check the back door and the window; both are locked. In a desperate move, I punch my fist through the window of the door, and the glass gashes my knuckles.

"Alex!" Aislin hisses through the chain link fence, but I am already reaching through the window and unlocking the door.

As soon as I shove it open, the Banshee's wail rings against my eardrums. I don't bother taking out my knife since I'm here to give her what she wants.

I run up the stairs, tracking her cries to a locked door. Stepping back, I run forward and kick it down.

"Way to make an entrance," the Banshee says from the windowsill as I stumble into the room. Her blond hair is pale against the moonlight as she tilts her head toward me. "What do you want?"

I take a deep breath, ready to make my offer, ready to lay down my fucking life in an instant because it means Gemma can live, but the Banshee holds up her hands before I can speak.

"Let me guess," she says, whisking away from the window. "You found your mother, but now she's trapped in the Afterlife, paying her debt until Helena will allow her to walk the world again, and you want me to free her."

I start to nod, but then shake my head. "That's not why I'm here."

She smiles maliciously. "You want something else"— she circles me, tracing her finger across my shoulder—"but I'll have to forgive you first." She leans over my shoulder, sniffing my neck. "I can be very giving if asked the right question."

I clench my fists, knowing I have to keep my temper under control.

"I'm ready to make a bargain with you, and trust me, what I'm going to offer, you're not going to want to refuse."

A FEW MINUTES later, I return outside to Aislin who's waiting for me on the step with a fire burning in front of her feet.

"What?" she asks when she notices me staring at the flames. "I got cold."

"You should have worn a jacket." I slip mine off and give it to her.

"I didn't even think about it." She puts on the jacket and zips it up. "All I could think about is why we're here."

I rub my hands across my face and really let what I just did sink in. I feel different, scared but less burdened somehow, like knowing Gemma will be okay has erased some of my sins.

"It'll be okay," I tell Aislin. "You'll be okay."

"Maybe." She stares at the clear, night sky. "I know you think this is how this is supposed to work, but why can't someone save you, too?"

"Even if I could think of a way to make that happen, which I can't, my life isn't worth someone else risking theirs." I sink down on the step and lower my head. "I've done a lot of shitty things throughout my life, and now it's time for me to make up for it."

She sniffles as she sits down beside me. "You're not as bad as you think you are, and I think Gemma would agree with me."

"I'm sure she would, but that's not what this is about. This is about me saving her." Knowing this may be the last time I see her, I pull her in for a hug "Take care of yourself, okay? Make sure you live a good life."

Her tears soak the shoulder of my shirt. "I promise I will."

"Can we make one last stop before we go back to the house?" I ask her. "There's something I need to get . . . from the Keepers' Castle."

"Are you insane?" She jerks back. "There's no way in hell I'm taking you there."

"We're just going to sneak into my room and get something. That's all." When she still looks unconvinced, I add, "Please, this is important, and it'll help with the shield spell."

Her intrigue piques. "How so?"

"You remember how Gemma and I used to steal stuff from Stephan all the time, just to piss him off?"

"Yeah, I always thought you guys were stupid."

"Not stupid," I stress. "I have quite the collection of

very powerful objects hidden in my room, and I'm not sure, but I'm guessing you might be able to use some of them to channel more energy to help you with the spell."

"Are you sure you want to do this?" she checks. "Because I can figure out another way to get extra power."

"I'm sure," I say. "Now let's go."

She nods then begins to chant under her breath as the snow speeds away with us.

WHEN WE LAND in my bedroom and our feet slip out from under us, I brace myself against the bedpost, but Aislin falls to the floor and cracks her elbow against the ice.

"Are you okay?" I ask and she nods.

"But what's with all the ice?" she wonders, standing.

I do a quick scan of the room. Ice covers the bed, the dresser, the walls, and the floor, and icicles dangle from the ceiling.

"The Death Walkers must be living here or something," I say, shaking my head in disgust.

Aislin winces, cupping her elbow. "He really has lost his damn mind, hasn't he?"

"He really has." Getting my balance, I head for a trap-door in my closet. When I try to open it, it won't budge because of the ice. "Do you have your knife on you?" I ask Aislin.

She slides over to me, takes out her knife, and kneels down. She begins chipping away at the ice until I can get the door open.

I lower myself into the hole and feel around until I

find the bag. Grabbing it, I then roll over and heave myself back up onto my feet.

Aislin takes the bag from me, unties the ribbon around it, and her jaw nearly hits the floor.

"Holy shit." She digs around, pulling out the Flower of Malina, the Box of Aurora, and the Dust of the Burning Bridge. "Alex, this is amazing."

"Dad's always been power crazy," I say, sitting down on the floor beside her. "I just hope they'll work for you."

"So do I," she says, grinning enthusiastically as she holds a bright red jewel in her hand. "There's only one way to find out for sure."

OUR SUDDEN APPEARANCE in the middle of the living room scares the shit out of Gemma and Laylen.

Gemma springs to her feet when she realizes it's me, her violet eyes flooding with nerves.

"Where the hell were you?" She shoves me back. "Seriously, Alex, I was worried sick."

Her feistiness makes me smile and fucking turns me on. I'm going to miss that a lot—the way she looks at me with so much passion. What I'll miss the most, though, is simply holding her and missing out on holding my daughter.

"I had something to take care of before we head to the lake." My hands long to touch her like they did last night, but I know I can't yet, not until it's time to say my final goodbye.

She chews on her lips, debating whether to stay angry or not.

"You're okay, though, right?" she asks, calming down a bit.

"More than okay." I quickly graze my knuckles across her cheek, wishing the touch could last longer.

Aislin flops down on the sofa, and her head bobs back dramatically. "This is the most depressing day ever."

Gemma stares at Aislin then at me. "So you're okay with this now?" she questions with suspicion. "With both of us going to the lake and sacrificing our lives?"

I give a firm nod. "If it means saving the world . . . then, yeah, I guess I have to be." I hate lying to her, but it has to be done.

She nods, her beautiful, violet eyes flooding with tears. "Okay, then," she says more to herself then turns to Aislin. "I need you to do something."

Aislin taps her foot against the floor, looking restless. If she keeps it up, she's going to blow everything.

"I found out how you get the shield spell to work and how you get the mark off Stephan," Gemma says, touching the Foreseer mark on the back of her neck.

"You went into another vision?" I shake my head. "Gemma, I thought we—"

"There's no point in arguing about this," she cuts me off, placing her hand over my mouth, and her touch sends my body flaming with desire.

God, I want her so, so much. It nearly kills me thinking I'm never going to have her again.

"Now let me tell Aislin what she needs to do."

She only lowers her hand after I nod. Then she hastily explains to Aislin the vision she saw and how things are going to work.

I barely listen, my thoughts stuck elsewhere. I've spent so much time not really experiencing the good things in life. I've carried my father's negative energy, and here I am finally shedding it, but only when my life's nearing an end. It's scary to think about, yet then I think of Gemma and my daughter, and it calms me.

"So we go to the castle?" Aislin asks, her eyes wide as she hugs the bag we stole from my bedroom. "And everything just works out?"

Gemma nods as I sit down on the armrest behind her, the static scorching, warning. But I don't give a shit at the moment. The end is coming, and I just want to be near her.

"I've seen it with my own eyes," Gemma tells Aislin.

Aislin leans to the side and reaches for her herb box. "Well, let's get going." She picks up the box and sets it on her lap. "God, I can't wait for this to be over."

"Don't you still need more power for the spell?" Laylen asks, tracing the spot on his arm where the Mark of Immortality used to be.

Aislin hands him the bag. "Look inside."

Laylen warily unties the bag and peers inside.

"Where did you get this?" he asks, staring at her in shock.

"Alex had it," she tells him, sorting through her herbs. "He used to steal all kinds of stuff from Stephan when he was a kid."

"When *we* were kids." I comb my fingers through Gemma's hair.

She angles her head back and looks at me perplexedly. "We did?"

I nod. "It's almost like we knew we needed all the stuff farther down the road." My fingers pause in her hair as I faintly smile. "Of course, we liked to piss my dad off, too."

"Maybe, deep down, we knew what he would turn

into," she says quietly.

"Maybe."

God, I want to kiss her so badly.

Pull it together, Alex. You just need to make it through a few more hours, and then you can kiss her until you die.

Sliding onto the floor, Aislin opens her spell book and flips through the pages. "Everybody ready for this?" she asks. The room's so quiet you can hear everyone breathing. "Okay, then." She stretches out her hands and flexes her fingers before she dumps out the contents of the bag we collected.

Gemma gasps at the strange items piled on the table. "Wow, they're all so . . . sparkly."

"Pretty amazing, huh?" Aislin smiles, but her happiness instantly vanishes as she leans over the pile of powerful objects. "Ego hanc vim solummodo bonum. Hoc opus auxilium. Da me potestatem."

A heart-shaped diamond flickers first, and then all the others harmonize, glimmering against the sunlight flowing through the window and producing a collection of vibrant colors.

The four of us can't seem to look away as we watch the light loop in a circle and make a path for Aislin. It spills across her hands and arms, making her skin illuminate. She sucks in a sharp gasp as her head rolls back, her eyelids closing.

"It feels so . . . intense," she breathes, opening her eyes and staring at her hands. "Like . . ."

"Electricity," Gemma offers.

Aislin nods her head up and down. "Is this how you guys feel all the time?"

Gemma doesn't reply, staring out the window. "Do

you think it's time?" she asks to no one in particular. "Or do you think we need to wait until later today to go down there?"

"It's December twenty-first, so yeah, I think we'd better get down there," I answer quietly, my uneven tone revealing my nerves.

I turn to Aislin, fighting to keep my composure. "Is that it? Do you have everything for your spell?"

"Yeah, I have more than enough." She wiggles her fingers, beaming over her new power.

"Then I guess we should all get going," Gemma says, the electricity picking up with her anxiousness.

We all sit there, afraid to move, afraid to go. I swear to God, the world goes absolutely still at the moment, as if time actually stops. Part of me wishes it would never move again.

Aislin stands up first, and Laylen follows her lead. "Do we go all at once?" Laylen asks, crossing his arms, seeming almost as uneasy as I am.

"Alex and I are outside right after you two leave the castle, so yeah, I think we go all at once." Gemma walks over to the corner armoire and takes a cell phone out of the drawer.

"Where did you get that?" I ask, getting to my feet.

"I think it's Sophia's," she says, holding the power button down. "I know phones haven't been working since the apocalypse, but now that it's over"—she smiles as the screen lights up, showing bars—"there you go." She gives me the phone. "It's how we bring Stephan out of the house."

"By calling him?" I cock an eyebrow at her.

She shrugs. "I know. It's pretty old school, right?"

"Yeah, it really is." I stuff the phone into my pocket,

hoping she can't see how badly I'm shaking. "You ready?"

She bobs her head up and down then squeezes her eyes, holding back the tears as she wraps her arms around Laylen. "Remember what I said, and remember, don't let Aislin get anywhere near that knife."

Laylen nods, a few tears escaping his eyes. He quickly wipes them away as the two of them break apart. Then Gemma turns to Aislin, and the two of them hug. Surprisingly, Gemma doesn't look as awkward.

When they pull away, Gemma takes my hand, our fingers intertwining, and the star goes crazy inside our bodies, scorching hot, trying to burn us up, like it knows we're about to kill it.

"What was that about the knife?" I whisper in her ear.

She shrugs. "Aislin gets nicked with a knife when they're at the castle, but don't worry, it's nothing major. And now that Laylen knows, he's going to stop it from happening." She places her hands on my side, holding onto me. "Ready for this?" Her voice is off pitch, and her eyes are filled with tears.

I slide my hand across her stomach, mentally whispering goodbye to a daughter I'll never get to know. I know what I'm doing is right, though. Like my mom said, my job has always been to be there for Gemma, and right now, I'm there to save her.

"I've been ready for this forever," I say then let her take us away.

CHAPTER
FORTY-TWO

Gemma

SAYING GOOD-BYE TO Laylen is the second hardest thing I've ever had to do. Saying goodbye to Alex, however . . . That's going to be the most painful, unbearable thing I've ever felt.

I Foresee us to the edge of the lake, landing us right on the shore with our backs to the grey-stoned Keepers' Castle.

Everything seems clear now, clearer than it has ever been for me. My head has been jam-packed with worry ever since I got my emotions back, anyway, but right now, everything seems crystal clear. No more worrying.

I turn in a circle, scratching my head as I realize the ground isn't frozen. "I don't think we're in the right spot. Hold on." I get my bearings and point at the trees. "They come from there, but they're in the castle right now." I shut my eyes and breathe in the air. "You feel that?" My eyelids open. "The Death Walkers are close."

He wraps his arms around my waist and pulls me

close, kissing my neck. "I need to tell you something before we do this."

"Alex . . ." I struggle to keep my eyes open, knowing we can't go to that place just yet. "Now's not the time. We still need to call your dad and—"

He slides his hand up my chest and hooks a finger underneath my chin, tipping my head toward him. "I have to say this first, okay?"

I nod, swallowing hard.

"I need you to promise"—he fights back tears as he struggles to remain in control over his emotions—"that if you somehow do survive this, you'll make sure you and our"—he touches my stomach, and I notice how badly his fingers are trembling—"daughter will live a beautiful, long, and happy life together."

"Alex, I'm not going to live. I—"

"Just promise me," he cuts me off, his green eyes smoldering with so much passion I can feel it in my chest.

Unable to form words, I simply nod, giving him the promise he needs at the moment.

"Thank you," he says, relaxing a smidgeon.

He stares at the other side of the lake then suddenly kicks into Keeper mode, dragging me with him as he strides for the hill.

"What are you doing?" I ask, jogging to keep up with him.

"Making this right." He dodges around a large tree and picks up his pace. "You said they came from the trees, so we need to be able to see them coming and have enough time to . . ." he trails off, his jaw tightening.

I know what he's going to say.

Time to kill the star.

We run past our hideout and violet bush, going farther

into the forest. I stamp the memory in my thoughts, wanting to take it with me—two kids pressing hands tightly, promising to be together forever. Little did they know their time would be short-lived, that their forever would merely be a glitch in time.

We walk a half circle around the lake, breaking from the forest edge and out into the open. The lake stretches in front of us, giving us a clear view in every direction.

He fishes the phone from his pocket. "What did I say when I called?"

"I don't know. I didn't hear." I hold his hand. "I guess just say whatever you feel you need to."

He dials a number then puts the phone to his ear. "Look out your window," he says, raising his hand and flipping the castle off. "If you want us, come and get us, you fucking asshole." Then he chucks the phone into the lake.

"Awesome choice of words," I say.

He smiles, but it doesn't quite reach his eyes.

Then, suddenly, everything is moving in fast forward. Stephan, Demetrius, and the Death Walkers barrel out of the front door of the castle, their cloaks blowing behind them as the grass and hill freezes over like an iceberg.

Alex's grip tightens around my hand. "Breathe, Gemma."

I suck in a breath as the ice crackles across the lake, heading straight for us. Alex says something to me, but his words get lost in the wind.

Tears flood my eyes as I stare at the trees with my hand on my stomach.

"You're going to be okay," I whisper to our daughter. "Soon, this will all be over, and your father's going to take care of you."

Alex hears me, and his head snaps in my direction. "What did you just say?"

I shake my head. "It doesn't matter."

His expression turns angry as he grips my shoulder. "Gemma, what did you do?"

"What I had to," I say softly.

His eyes widen and his lips part, but before he can say anything, the sky greys as the sunlight is stolen away.

"This is it," I whisper. "The end is coming. I can feel it."

"It'll be all right," he whispers. "No matter what you think is about to happen, it's not."

Suddenly, I worry that maybe I'm not the only one who's done something on the side.

"Alex, what did you—"

He kisses me before I can get the words out. He kisses me like I've always dreamed of being kissed—with no holding back, like we're only two people left in this world, like he can finally breathe for the very first time. Like this is it for us.

That's when I feel it—the prickle tapping wildly at the back of my neck. This time, I don't force the sensation back; I free it.

I free myself and him.

I open my mouth to say the words I've never been able to utter without magic protecting me, but my words get lodged in my throat as I spot Stephan and what's in his hand.

"No, he has the knife," I whisper. "And it's stained with blood, which means . . ." My eyes dart to the other side of the lake where Aislin and Laylen are.

Aislin is shouting something at us while waving her hands in front of her.

"Gemma, what's going on?" Alex's fingers fold around my arm as he turns me toward him. "What's happening with the sword?"

"I . . ." I trail off as Stephan approaches us with a grin on his face.

"You made this so easy on me," he says, pointing the knife at the sky. "First, you give me the witch's blood I needed without me even having to go look for it. It just landed in my hands." Then he aims the knife at my throat. "And now you walk straight into my hands."

Alex shoves me back, his arms spread to the side, protecting me. "Stay the fuck away from her."

Grinning, Stephan points the knife at Alex. "If you want to go first, fine. By all means, son, let's get this over with. It's time to bleed the star out of you two."

"No!" I shout as Stephan cranes his arm back, ready to stab Alex.

Alex still has fight left in him, though, and he smashes his knuckles into Stephan's jaw. When Stephan growls and swings the knife around, ready to stab him, Alex whips around and tackles his father to the ground. The knife flies from Stephan's hands as they roll down the hill toward the lake.

I scramble after the knife, but the Death Walkers close around me and open their mouths, letting out a cry.

"Where do you think you're going?" Demetrius says as he pushes through the wall of Death Walkers.

I eye the knife in his hand then lock gazes with him. "To save Alex."

He snorts a laugh. "You do understand who I am, right?"

"You do understand who I am, *right?*" I mock then lunge for him.

He lifts the knife to stab me, but I skitter around and kick him in the back. He trips forward, falling to the ground, but rapidly regains his balance and jumps to his feet.

"You're going to pay for that," he growls, coming at me.

When I dropkick him straight in the jaw, he curses and swings his fist around, punching me in the cheek. My ears ring as I stagger back, the Death Walkers' chill hissing at my heels. But I'm not going down, not until I save Alex and the world.

I channel every ounce of strength I have in me and run at him again. He swings the blade at my chest, but I duck down and slam my fist into his stomach. He cries out in pain, and I seize the opportunity to steal the knife from his hands. Then I jump back as he runs at me with his arms out, ready to strangle me. With one fluid movement, I bring the blade down right to his chest and stab it in deep.

He freezes, blood gurgling from his mouth as he stands there, stunned.

"This wasn't supposed to happen."

He's right; this wasn't supposed to happen, which means there still might be time to save Alex.

Whirling around, I knock Death Walkers out of the way as I break through their wall. Their icy breath grazes my skin and freezes some of my muscles, but I keep running down the hill to where Stephan and Alex are battling it out near the shoreline.

I scoop the knife up on my way then march up to Stephan who has Alex in a headlock.

"Just give up," he growls as he punches Alex in the gut.

"Never." Alex grunts and flings his head back, slamming it into Stephan's face.

Stephan stumbles back, and one of his feet crack through the ice. "Shit." He trips forward before the water pulls him in, and I race at him with the knife, ready to kill him.

"No, Gemma, don't!" Alex cries, tripping to his feet as I move to strike.

Stephan's hand shoots up and grabs the blade of the knife, stopping it from piercing him. He cuts open his hand and bleeds across the snow as he pushes it away from his chest.

"You're not going to win. You were never supposed to," he says then tightens his grasp on the blade and jerks it from my hand.

Alex runs toward me as Stephan flips the knife around in his hand.

"Don't touch her," Alex warns as he reaches my side.

"Oh, I'm not planning on it yet." Drawing the knife back, he strikes the blade at Alex.

The prickle stabs at the back of my neck, and without even thinking, I jump between the two of them. The blade sinks deep into my chest, knocking the air out of me.

"No!" Alex shouts, catching me as I fall.

Stephan's laugh echoes around us. "Don't worry, she's not going to die just yet, not until I get the star."

"No . . . No . . . No . . ." Alex stares at me in horror as I lie dying in his arms.

He has cuts on his face, his eye is swollen shut, and he looks so beaten down. "This isn't right. This isn't how it's supposed to happen. You can't die without me."

"I can," I say, gasping for air. "That's what the knife was for. It has witch's blood powerful enough to break our bond."

"You knew this and you didn't . . ." He stops himself from scolding me as his eyes overflow with tears. "I was supposed to save you."

"Nope, this time"—my breath falters as I fight to breath—"I'm saving you."

Rage flares in his eyes as he picks up a large rock and reels toward his father. Stephan grins at him, and something inside Alex snaps.

"You're dead," he says, and then he lunges at him, bashing his father on the side of the head with a rock.

The sound of his skull cracking is sickening, and takes Stephan by surprise. He drops the knife as he staggers back with blood streaming down the side of his face.

Alex scoops up the knife and, without any hesitation, stabs Stephan right in the heart.

"You killed me," Stephan says, partially shocked, partially impressed. "I didn't think you had it in you."

Alex turns his back on his father and rushes toward me. "Don't die on me, okay?" He cups my face, his hands trembling. "You need to just keep breathing. I'm going to save you."

"You can't." My lungs feel tight, like they're being crushed, yet for some odd reason, I don't feel any pain. All I feel is him. "We need to kill the star now."

"Not until I know you're okay. I made a deal . . . You were supposed to be okay."

"No matter what deal you made . . . I was always going to die . . . because that's how this is supposed to go . . . It was always supposed to be me . . ." I could tell him right there that I saved him, but I know he'll only make saying goodbye harder if knows. "I love you. I really do."

"I love you, too," he says, choking on a sob. "Always

have, always will. Forever."

Those are the magic words that free our bodies from the star—that save the world. The energy smolders across my skin one final time before the heat singes the Death Walkers into ashes and then swallows me up.

I see everything that happened and everything that will never be—my past and the future I'll never have. Every emotion I ever felt flashes through me at once: hurt, happiness, pain, love, what it would have felt like to be a mother. Then my body sinks into the earth as my life slips away. The star dies, taking my soul with it and freeing Alex's.

Still, I like to believe that a tiny piece of my soul still lives inside him, that when he saved my soul, he not only gave me a part of his, but I gave him a part of mine, as well.

That, even through death, we will be bonded together. Forever.

CHAPTER
FORTY-THREE

Gemma

DEATH ISN'T AS bad as I expected it to be. It's warm and bright and weightless like air. I feel like I soared off to the sun, where nothing matters, where pain doesn't exist. Only sunshine, so much sunshine.

I feel so at peace.

That is, until I hear a Banshee wail, obliterating the harmony.

I open my eyes, remembering the bargain I made with Helena, how I promised her my soul in exchange for Alex to live and continue with his life, free from his father and the star, raising our daughter who should have been born now that I'm gone.

My eyes burn with tears just thinking about how I'm never going to hold her, but I suck it up and stand to my feet.

"And so we meet again." Helena's tattered body is perched on her throne, and she looks more than happy to see me.

"And so we do," I say, stepping onto the red podium. I no longer feel afraid. What's done is done, and now I'm going to face my decision head on. "What will you do with me? Turn me into one of your mummies and make me work for you?"

Her lip twitches as she snarls at me blasé tone. "You'll do whatever I want you to do. In fact, I think I have the perfect place for you." She lifts her hand. "You can live inside my ring where I can always feed off your soul whenever I need a snack."

"My soul's gone," I spit. "There's nothing left inside me now."

"You sound very ungrateful." She rises and steps toward me. "Maybe I should remind you this was your choice. You asked me to do this to save your lover."

"It was never a choice," I say firmly. "I did what I had to do."

"You're a stupid, little girl"—she laughs—"and now I'm going to eat that stupidity right up." She pauses then a clever look fills out the hollowness in her eyes. "I think I have a better place for you than in my ring." She unhinges her jaw and opens her mouth wide. "You can live inside me."

I close my eyes, preparing for the end.

"Helena," a familiar voice appears out of nowhere.

My eyes snap open and dart to the throne behind Helena.

Annabella is standing there with her lips pursed and her silver eyes narrowed. "Let Gemma go," Annabella says. "She's not yours to take."

Helena whirls around toward her sister, bearing her yellow teeth. "Annabella, this doesn't concern you."

Annabella calmly steps onto the podium and towers over Helena.

"You feel that," Annabella says, and Helena swiftly shakes her head, growling. "You can't take Gemma's soul because it belongs to someone else."

"She gave it to me, "which means I can take it!" Helena roars, stomping her foot.

"You've always been too greedy," Annabella tells her. "No wonder mother liked you less."

"I hate you!" Helena lunges for Annabella's throat.

Annabella seizes her hands and shoves her back, and Helena falls at my feet, whining.

"Gemma's soul is connected to another," Annabella says, raising her voice as she steps toward Helena. "You can't have it, even if you made a bargain with her. You had no right to make the bargain with her to begin with, and if I have to, I'll bring Mother down here to fix the mess you made."

Helena kicks her feet, screaming. "We had a bargain! We had a bargain!"

Annabella shakes her head, looking utterly disappointed with Helena's behavior. "I'm going to take Gemma now. She's not staying."

Helena wails, silver tears glistening in her eyes.

Annabella disregards her and extends her hand to me. "Come with me, Gemma."

I take Annabella's hand. "Where are we going?"

She leads me up the steps and around the throne where light spills across us. "To your mother."

Before I can say anything, she carries us away in a light of essence and warmth. When I can see again, I'm standing underneath the willow tree branches. Annabella is gone, and someone else has taken her place.

"Mom." I throw my arms around her neck, and an uncontrollable sob rips from my chest. "I thought I'd never see you again."

She runs her hand over my head. "Shhh, everything's going to be okay. You're going to be okay." She gives me a moment to cry it out before she pulls me away to look at me. "Do you know why you're here?"

I try to dry my eyes, but more tears pour out. "Because Helena can't keep my soul, and now I've crossed over like you . . . I'm essence now."

She shakes her head. "You're here because of who you are—my daughter who's both brave and loving. Both are such wonderful gifts that I always wished I could have. You threw your life away to safe Alex. You gave up so much."

"Is that why I'm here?" I tuck my hair behind my ears as the wind blows strands into my face. "Because I sacrificed my life?"

She wanders toward the trunk of the tree, her blue dress trailing in the dirt behind her. "You're here because everything happens for a reason. You're here because both of you made a sacrifice, and now no one knows what to do with you."

"I'm not sure I understand you. Both of us made a sacrifice?" I remember something Alex said right before I died. "Wait, did Alex give up his soul to save me?"

"He did, but that's not the whole reason you're here," she says, facing me. "You carry the soul of another, which means Helena can't make a bargain with just you for your soul. She'd also have to make a bargain with Alex, and he didn't make one with Helena."

"Am I . . . ? Am I an essence?" I turn over my arms, wondering if my appearance is going to change.

"Is that what you want?" Her blue eyes lock with mine. "Do you want to be here with me?"

"I . . ." The truth is, if I could be anywhere, I'd be with my daughter and Alex. "Do I have another choice?"

She sits down on the grass and pats the spot beside her, signaling for me to sit down. "If you choose to stay here with me, you can, but if you choose to leave, you can go back to your life."

"My life," I whisper as my knees buckle, and I collapse to the ground. "But why is Annabella letting me go? Why doesn't she keep me?"

"She can either let you go or take you both," my mother explains. "You and Alex are bonded. Take one and they have to take you both. And right now, you're both on the brink of death."

"But why not just take us both?"

"I know this is hard for you to understand, but not everything is evil." She picks a flower from the ground and twists it in her fingers. "You need to understand that everything isn't evil in the world. There is also good, and what you did to save the lives of everyone is the very essence of good. You and Alex, your daughter—that all represents good."

"And Annabella's good?"

"Annabella is what she chooses to be, just like you can be."

I let it all sink in as the wind picks up, making petals dance around us. "I didn't expect this. I thought I would become a lost soul."

"I know. And that's why you're one of the good ones. You went into this blind." She offers me the flower. "So, what will it be? Life or death?"

I stare at the flower, not ready to take it just yet. "What

about you?"

"I'm right where I belong," she says. "It's you who needs to find your place."

"I don't think I can leave you," I say, "not when I know I'll never see you again. You took your own life to save me; why don't you get a choice?"

"We'll see each other again," she promises, urging the flower at me. "This isn't goodbye forever."

I pick up the flower, thinking about life, about the pain I've been through, and how there might be more pain waiting for me when I return. Then I remember the tiniest moments of stolen kisses, of whispered promises that carry such possibilities.

I release the flower and let the wind carry it away to the unknown. "I want to go back to my life."

She nods, rising to her feet. "One last goodbye before you go."

I stand up and hug her with all I have in me, not wanting to let go yet knowing I have to. When I back away, she's gone, and I feel a piece of my heart break.

"You choose life, then?" Annabella steps out from behind the tree.

I nod, wiping the tears from my eyes. "Yeah, I choose life."

CHAPTER
FORTY-FOUR

Alex

I'M NOT SURE if I've died, if Gemma's died. All I know is that, when I open my eyes, I'm lying on the floor of the burned house in Iceland. The cry of the Banshee is nails to my ears as I push to my feet and search for her, wanting to get this over with.

When I find her, she's curled in the corner of the room at the bottom of the stairway. She's in her hag form, her skin wrinkled and her clothes tattered.

"I've been waiting for you." She smiles at me, showing me her yellow teeth.

"Tell me she's okay," I say. "Tell me Gemma lived, or I'm not doing this."

She staggers to her feet and hunches over. "I can't believe I have you," she says, ignoring my question. "I've been waiting to get my hands on a soul like yours. Not many humans like to throw theirs away so carelessly."

"It wasn't out of carelessness. It was for a reason,

a very good reason." I get in her face. "Now tell me she survived."

She trails her fingernails along my shoulder and runs her hands through my hair, but I swat her hand away. "Stay the hell away from me. Just because you own my soul, it doesn't mean you can put your gross hands on me."

She snarls, biting my cheek. "You're mine now, and I'll do whatever I want with you." She dances around, her hair thickening and her skin smoothing out as she transforms. "There. Is that better for you?"

I shove her back. "I said, don't touch me."

"You can be bitter all you want," she snaps. "But, eventually, I'll break you." She traces her hands along the burned walls, pieces of it crumbling to the floor. "You're very ungrateful. When you came here asking me to take your soul in return for freeing the girl's, I thought I was doing you a favor, but now you act as if I'm burdening you."

"I just need to know she's still alive," I say, grinding my teeth.

She still refuses to answer me, and it takes all my strength not to force her to tell me. I'm also worried because she still hasn't collected my soul, which means she could send me back, and Gemma won't be saved.

"Free souls are hard to find," she purrs. "Even Helena herself would kill for one. The power your soul will give me can help me take her down."

"So that's your big plan—you take my soul and try to take down the Queen of the Afterlife." Unable to help myself, I snort a laugh. "

Growling she wraps her fingers around my neck, and I let her strangle me since I have no fight left in me.

"Defend yourself," she demands, "or it won't be any fun."

"Let him go," someone commands from the darkness of the stairway.

The Banshee instantly releases me, her lips trembling as she spins toward the stairs. A woman with white hair, blood red lips, and silver eyes stands at the bottom of the stairway, and when the Banshee sees her, she bows her head.

"I'm sorry, Annabella, but he gave me his soul," the Banshee says, "

"His soul isn't his to give." Annabella steps off the stairway, glancing around at the charred walls. "So this is what the entrance of the Afterlife has come to."

"I'm sorry," the Banshee says, "but perhaps soon, Helena will no longer rule, and things can return to their rightful condition."

Annabella inches closer to the Banshee. "I may not like my sister, but don't you dare talk poorly of her in my presence."

The Banshee sinks to her knees, weeping. "I'm so sorry I've angered you."

Annabella walks around her, her silvery eyes landing on me. "This is what you offered in exchange for the freedom of Gemma's soul?" She pulls a disgusted face at the room. "That's very brave of you."

"You're the Queen of the Afterlife's sister?" I ask. "So that makes you the—?"

"It makes me nothing," she cuts me off, her slivery eyes darkening to grey. "I choose to be whatever I am, but if you want to know what I reign over, it's the essences."

"Why are you here?"

"I think what you really want to ask is if she's okay, if

Gemma lived because of your sacrifice."

I nod, too emotional to speak.

Please, let her be okay.

She presses her lips together, her gaze heavy. "Tell me, why did you do it? Why did you give up everything for her?"

"Because I love her," I say simply

"Love?" She considers the idea with mild curiosity on her face. "It's a beautiful concept, to love someone more than you love yourself, and maybe that's why I'm doing this."

"What are you doing, exactly?" My eyes dart to the Banshee as she crawls toward Annabella's feet.

"Please don't take him from me," she begs, her fingernails digging into the rotting floor. "I need him."

"So you can try to take Helena's place? Because that'll never happen." She turns around and heads for the stairs, kicking the Banshee out of the way. "Make sure you live your life the way you want. Second chances are precious and don't come around often."

Before I can ask her what she means, I'm sucked away into blackness.

When I open my eyes again, I'm lying next to the lake, beneath the sunlight and surrounded by ashes.

I bolt upright at the sound of someone crying, and what I see makes me want to die all over again.

Aislin and Laylen are huddled over Gemma. Aislin is crying, her hands sparkling with a glimmering red glow as she tries to use her magic to bring Gemma back to life.

"No, please don't . . ." I shove Aislin out of the way and hug Gemma's lifeless body in my arms. "Wake up. Please wake up."

"I tried to save her." Aislin sobs against Laylen's

chest as he tries to console her. "But nothing works. And I thought . . . I thought the baby would have been here by now . . . If the spell worked, then she should have . . ." She sobs hysterically as she curls into Laylen's lap.

I focus on Gemma, trying to ignore the gaping wound in her chest. "Please, you're supposed to come back to me. I can't live without you." I lean in and brush my lips across her cold lips, but the kiss feels so foreign, so lifeless. "Please, please . . ." Tears pour from my eyes as I kiss her again. "I don't want to be here without you."

She remains lying still, her skin pale in the sunlight, and most of the blood from her body now stains the ground around her.

I lose it. Start crying. I want nothing more than to die right along with her.

I hug her tightly, refusing to ever let go.

Thump. Thump. Thump.

I hear the baby's heart beating, and I don't know what that means, but it gives me hope. I lean down and kiss Gemma again. I kiss her with everything I have in me, begging her to come back to me. I feel the kiss all the way through my body, through my soul, and I swear I feel her move.

She gasps against my mouth as her eyelids open. "Alex."

CHAPTER
FORTY-FIVE

Gemma

THE FIRST THING I see is Alex's face, and the sight of it makes me feel better, despite that I've just risen from the dead.

"Am I okay?"

He glances down at my chest, and the tension in his expression alleviates. "You're okay."

I sit up and look down at my chest where I remember the knife entering, but there's no blood, no wound.

"I can't believe I'm here," I say, resting back onto the grass with my arm on my stomach. I can hear the baby's heart beating steadily, and knowing she's okay causes my eyes to overflow with tears.

"It's going to be okay," he says, hugging me to his chest. "But what happened? I'm still so confused why I'm here. It was just supposed to be you who came back."

"The first time I went to the Afterlife," I say, breathing in his scent, "I told Helena I'd give her my soul when I died in exchange for your life."

"I made the same promise with a Banshee." He brushes my hair out of my eyes then leans down to kiss me, taking his time, savoring every second our lips remain touching without the electricity ruining the moment. "God, we really are bonded together," he breathes as he pulls away. "We even made the same self-sacrificing choice." His brows furrow. "But I don't get why we're both back here. And alive."

I smile up at him and lift my hand, showing him the scar from the promise. "Because our souls are connected. If they take one, they take us both."

He lines his hand with mine. "Then why not take us both?"

"Because, apparently, good does exist."

He smiles down at me, his eyes swollen from tears, and he looks like he's going to cry again.

"It's going to be okay," I assure him. "And you want to know why?"

He nods. "Did you see a vision about it?"

I shake my head. "No, I can feel that it's going to be okay."

"How can you feel it?"

"Because it's gone."

He catches on to what I'm saying, and a smile touches his lips as he leans down and kisses me again.

The kiss only lasts a few moments before Aislin practically jumps on top of us.

"I'm so glad you guys are alive," she cries as she hugs both of us. "I thought when the knife cut me that things . . . that things . . ." She can barely speak through the tears, and honestly, I'm so overwhelmed right now I feel like crying with her.

I hug her for a while then move to Laylen, wrapping

my arms around him.

"I'm so glad this didn't turn out the way you saw it." He chokes back a sob.

"Me, too," I agree.

We take turns hugging each other before we calm down and sit beside the water. The ground is covered with the ashes of the Death Walkers from when the star's power was freed and killed every last one, but the air is still, calm, peaceful.

But the peace crumbles the second my wrist starts to burn. At first, I don't look at it, not wanting to shatter the calm moment we're sharing, but the pain becomes too intense, and I have to I tear my eyes from the water to look down at my arm.

My head slants at the sight of the star tattooed on my wrist. I trace my fingers along the angled lines. "What is this?" I ask Alex.

"I've never seen that before . . ." he trails off, turning over his wrist.

To our surprise, he has the same mark on his wrist.

He smiles at me. "I think it might be ours."

Sliding his hand across my cheek, he leans in and kisses me as the sun slips away behind the mountains, and the stars wake up to dust the sky. Still, we keep kissing, taking our time because there's no more rush, no more worry.

We have all the time in the world.

CHAPTER
FORTY-SIX

Gemma

10 months later . . .

"OKAY, I GET why you said she's a bitch," I say as I hike through the grass toward the castle, "but I didn't expect her to be so . . . so . . ."

"Short?" Laylen finishes for me, laughing. "What did you think, that faeries have to be tall or something?"

I stick out my tongue at him. "No, but I did expect the *Empress* of the Faerie Realm to be tall." I duck underneath a branch and jump over a log. "And what were those little creatures? One of them tried to bite me."

"Those are sprites," Aislin explains, shoving vines out of her way. "And those little bastards are mean."

"Did you know you'll turn into one if they bite you?" Laylen says, but I can't tell if he is joking.

"I still can't believe Aleesa didn't want to come back with us," I say, enjoying the sunlight as it kisses my skin

"I'm not," Laylen says, urging me to the right as the

path forks. "She was always a little off, and I think she fits right in with the fey."

From behind me, I suddenly hear the pitter-patter of tiny footsteps. I whirl around just in time to see a sprite running at an impressive speed for having such tiny legs. With its teeth and wings out, it makes a beeline for my ankle. Panicking, I drop kicked it like a soccer ball, and it flies through the air and lands far back in the trees with a thud.

"Okay, now Gemma's the mean one," Aislin says, gaping at me.

"I didn't want to turn into one of them." I feel a pang of guilt for kicking the little critter.

Laylen busts up laughing. "You do realize I was kidding about that?"

I shake my head but smile and pick up the pace, leaving the two of them behind. I'm anxious to get back to the castle and my family.

As I break through the Faerie Realm, I take off in a full sprint.

When I decided to go with Laylen and Aislin to get Aleesa, I thought it would be good for me to get some fresh air. But about five minutes after I left, I was already missing Alex and our daughter.

When I reach the castle, I throw open the door. Even though the electricity doesn't connect us anymore, I can still sense where Alex is and even my daughter as I head straight for the living room.

As I enter the room, I pause in the doorway at the sight of Sophia holding my child in her arms. Even though she turned out not to be so bad once the evil was out of her blood, I struggle sometimes to be around her because it reminds me of the past.

She's rocking back and forth, trying to get my daughter to sleep while talking to Alex about something.

His eyes find mine, and he smiles in a way that makes my body burn for his touch.

"I'll be right back," Sophia says to Alex, and then she sees me and smiles. "Oh, good. You guys made it back okay?"

"Yeah, Aislin and Laylen are coming." I nod at the window as I walk toward her with my arms out.

"Good. I'm glad everything went well." She gently places my daughter in my hands then steps back. "I'm going to go make dinner for everyone," she says then rushes out the doorway.

"Why's she making dinner?" I ask Alex.

"Because we're having guests tonight," Alex says, walking over to me

I smile down at our daughter, and she looks up at me with her violet eyes, making a cooing sound as she tries to smile.

I'll never get tired of this, of being able to see her and hold her.

"Hello, my beautiful Alana," I say to her. "Did you miss me while I was gone?"

"She did. We both did." Alex cups my chin, angles my head back, and kisses me deeply, tangling his tongue with mine.

It's amazing how much my body burns on its own whenever he touches me.

"I missed you way too much," he says when our lips part.

"Me, too," I say, dazedly looking up at him, high from his kiss. "I don't think I'll be leaving again for a while."

"That's fine by me." He laces our fingers together then

leads me toward the sofa. "You look tired. You should rest." He sits down and pulls me down with him.

"I'm tired, but it was good to get out and feel like I'm helping try to fix stuff." I lean back on the sofa, cradling Alana in my arms. "So, who's coming over for dinner?"

He bites back a grin, and I suddenly realize how excited he is. "You know how we've been trying to figure out a way to free your father from the Room of Forbidden?"

I nod. "But I thought it didn't look very promising."

"It wasn't," he says, "but then I found a loophole. Since your father technically didn't change the vision of his own free will, he should've never been punished for it. I had to go above Dyvinius's head and persuade enough Foreseers to let him go, but I finally did it."

I straighten in the chair. "So my dad's . . . ?" I blink back the tears. "My dad's free."

He nods, scooting closer to me. "He'll be here tonight."

"But he's okay, right?"

He nods. "I saw him yesterday when he was freed, and he looked great. I even talked to him for a while, and he's really happy to see you"—he smiles down at our daughter—"and her."

I brush my lips across his scruffy cheek. "Thank you."

"I just want you to be happy, and I know you miss your father."

"I do miss my father, but I'm happy, Alex. I promise."

He relaxes back in the chair, wrapping an arm around my shoulder and bringing me with him. "How did things go for you guys?"

I shrug. "Well, Aleesa didn't want to come home with us, and the Empress threatened Aislin that she was going to collect on her spell soon."

"We'll figure out a way to fix it. And besides, Aislin's

so powerful now, I don't doubt she'll be able to take Luna down if she needs to, but let's not talk about that right now. There's something important I need to ask you," he says, his voice sounding a little off pitch.

"Is everything okay?" I ask.

He nods nervously, sliding to the edge of the couch. "Everything's fine." He sticks his hand into his pocket. "In fact, everything's perfect." When he pulls out his hand, his fingers are clasped around a silver object.

"What's going on?" I ask as he stands to his feet.

With an uneven breath, he opens his hand to show me what he is holding, and I gasp at the sight of the heart-shaped pendant my mom gave me. Only, it's not secured to a chain, but welded to a silver ring.

"How did you get this?"

He arches a brow at me. "You think two witches scare me?"

I shake my head, staring at the ring in awe. "But why did you put it on the ring?"

"Why do you think?" With his gaze fastened on me, he gets down on one knee. "Gemma Lucas, will you marry me?"

Tears flood my eyes, not just from his question, but because I'm here, breathing, holding our daughter, fully able to experience this beautiful moment. I'm lucky to be alive, and I cherish every moment. But this one, I'll probably cherish a little bit more than others.

"Yes," I say through my tears.

Looking almost as happy as he did when our daughter was born, he slips the ring on my finger and then presses his lips to mine.

We kiss, our souls beating as one. Always and forever.

About the Author

JESSICA SORENSEN IS a *New York Times* and *USA Today* bestselling author that lives in the snowy mountains of Wyoming. When she's not writing, she spends her time reading and hanging out with her family.

Other Books by Jessica Sorensen

The Coincidence Series:
The Coincidence of Callie and Kayden
The Redemption of Callie and Kayden
The Destiny of Violet and Luke
The Probability of Violet and Luke
The Certainty of Violet and Luke
The Resolution of Callie and Kayden
Seth & Grayson

The Secret Series:
The Prelude of Ella and Micha
The Secret of Ella and Micha
The Forever of Ella and Micha
The Temptation of Lila and Ethan
The Ever After of Ella and Micha
Lila and Ethan: Forever and Always
Ella and Micha: Infinitely and Always

The Shattered Promises Series:
Shattered Promises
Fractured Souls
Unbroken
Broken Visions
Scattered Ashes

Breaking Nova Series:
Breaking Nova
Saving Quinton
Delilah: The Making of Red
Nova and Quinton: No Regrets
Tristan: Finding Hope
Wreck Me
Ruin Me

The Fallen Star Series (YA):
The Fallen Star
The Underworld
The Vision
The Promise

**The Fallen Souls Series
(spin off from The Fallen Star):**
The Lost Soul
The Evanescence

The Darkness Falls Series:
Darkness Falls
Darkness Breaks
Darkness Fades

The Death Collectors Series (NA and YA):
Ember X and Ember
Cinder X and Cinder
Spark X and Spark

The Sins Series:
Seduction & Temptation
Sins & Secrets
Lies & Betrayal (Coming Soon)

Unbeautiful Series:
Unbeautiful
Untamed

Unraveling You Series:
Unraveling You
Raveling You
Awakening You
Inspiring You (Coming Soon)

Ultraviolet Series:
Ultraviolet

Standalones
The Forgotten Girl
The Illusion of Annabella

Coming Soon

Entranced
Steel & Bones

CONNECT WITH ME ONLINE

jessicasorensen.com
and on
Facebook and Twitter

29426943R10216

Made in the USA
San Bernardino, CA
21 January 2016